Bolan jammed [...] his enemy's ri[...]

The man's eyes were pinholes of hatred as he withdrew the broken needle. Bolan fired again, and the hardman tensed and coughed blood. His thumb pushed down, and yellow fluid sprayed from the tip of the needle. Bolan's blood ran cold as it splashed into his eyes. The man went limp, and the Executioner shoved off the corpse and rose to his feet.

Manning stood at the top of the stairwell. "Mack! Are you—"

"Stay where you are! Close the door!"

Manning's boot creaked on the top landing. "What's—"

Bolan's voice rose to a parade-ground roar. "Do it!"

The door slammed shut. Bolan wiped his eyes and put his earpiece back in place. He spoke calmly into his throat mike. "Gary, the virus is loose down here in the cellar. I've been exposed."

MACK BOLAN ®

The Executioner

DON PENDLETON'S
EXECUTIONER®
THE
PLAGUE WIND

THE
**POWER
TRILOGY**
BOOK II

A GOLD EAGLE BOOK FROM
WORLDWIDE®

TORONTO • NEW YORK • LONDON
AMSTERDAM • PARIS • SYDNEY • HAMBURG
STOCKHOLM • ATHENS • TOKYO • MILAN
MADRID • WARSAW • BUDAPEST • AUCKLAND

First edition July 1998
ISBN 0-373-64235-0

Special thanks and acknowledgment to
Chuck Rogers for his contribution to this work.

PLAGUE WIND

Printed in U.S.A.

Flinch not, neither give up nor despair...

—Marcus Aurelius Antoninus
121-180 A.D.

It is not enough to fight. It is the spirit which we bring to the fight that decides the issue. It is morale that wins the victory.

—George Catlett Marshall
Military Review, Oct. 1948

Attack the enemy with a single-mindedness. Don't be distracted by anything that will deter you from your course of action. You *will* be victorious.

—Mack Bolan

THE

LEGEND

Nothing less than a war could have fashioned the destiny of the man called Mack Bolan. Bolan earned the Executioner title in the jungle hell of Vietnam.

But this soldier also wore another name—Sergeant Mercy. He was so tagged because of the compassion he showed to wounded comrades-in-arms and Vietnamese civilians.

Mack Bolan's second tour of duty ended prematurely when he was given emergency leave to return home and bury his family, victims of the Mob. Then he declared a one-man war against the Mafia.

He confronted the Families head-on from coast to coast, and soon a hope of victory began to appear. But Bolan had broken society's every rule. That same society started gunning for this elusive warrior—to no avail.

So Bolan was offered amnesty to work within the system against terrorism. This time, as an employee of Uncle Sam, Bolan became Colonel John Phoenix. With a command center at Stony Man Farm in Virginia, he and his new allies—Able Team and Phoenix Force—waged relentless war on a new adversary: the KGB.

But when his one true love, April Rose, died at the hands of the Soviet terror machine, Bolan severed all ties with Establishment authority.

Now, after a lengthy lone-wolf struggle and much soul-searching, the Executioner has agreed to enter an "arm's-length" alliance with his government once more, reserving the right to pursue personal missions in his Everlasting War.

PROLOGUE

Uganda

Dr. Eliza Thurman scowled pensively as she swatted at her shorts a third time before pulling them up. She kicked the door in front of her open, then slammed it shut again vigorously. If there was one thing on God's green earth she hated above anything else, it was using outdoor facilities in equatorial Africa. She could deal with Uganda's hundred-degree heat and nearly one hundred percent humidity, and the less than hygienic environment of the flimsy wooden outhouse shack was simply a fact of research station life that had to be dealt with. In her work for the Atlanta Centers for Disease Control, Dr. Eliza Thurman worked with some of the deadliest bugs known to man.

The spiders in the outhouse were more than she could bear.

They were big, and they were multicolored. Spritzing them with the local antibug juice from the camp's squeaky old atomizer simply made them drop from their webs and hide in the cracks. It also made the already disgusting air in the outhouse unfit for humans to breathe, and the spiders were always back the next day.

She was genuinely tempted to steal one of the eight Sunbeam electric frying pans in the camp and seal the outhouse with plastic tape. All she had to do was put a few disinfectant crystals onto the pan and dial it to high. The crystals would dissolve, and then she would see how the eight-legged bastards liked being nuked with formaldehyde gas for twenty-four hours.

Thurman suddenly looked up and cocked her head. She paused for a moment until the sound registered above the subliminal, and then she smiled. Someone was coming, and with any luck there would be mail.

Her mother had promised to send her some real toilet paper.

Out over the blue waters of Lake Victoria, the thumping of a helicopter flying low over the water resolved itself.

Thurman frowned. The supply choppers didn't usually come over the lake from the east. The doctor shaded her eyes with one hand to cut the intense midafternoon glare coming off the water. Her father had been a pilot, and she had grown up to be something of a bird watcher herself. The helicopter coming over the water wasn't their usual weather-beaten Vietnam-era Huey. She squinted at the approaching bird, and then her eyes flared. The approaching helicopter was an Aérospatiale Super Puma.

She almost started to get giddy.

This was better than mail. It was even better than two-ply American toilet paper. The big twin-engined helicopter could mean only one thing—the new equipment from Germany that Dr. Lamb had been hinting about had arrived.

She quickly buckled her shorts as the helicopter thundered over the research station and kicked up a storm of red dust. The portly figure of Dr. Lamb walked out from among the small maze of tents toward the helicopter pad that had been tamped into the dirt, and waved. The big helicopter orbited once, then seemed to hover in the air directly in front of him. The aircraft pivoted and the side door slid open.

Lamb gaped. From her vantage point by the outhouses, Thurman gaped, as well. The men in the helicopter were encased from head to foot in bulky, hooded, plastic camouflage coveralls. Their hoods were sealed, and the men's faces were totally obscured behind mirrored bug-eyed goggles and the masks and hoses of respirators. It looked as if the camp had suddenly been invaded by men from Mars.

Thurman's eyes flared wide as the import of what was happening dawned on her. The men in the helicopter were wearing Russian chemical-biological-warfare protection suits.

In their gloved hands they carried long black automatic rifles.

One of the men raised his rifle, and yellow flame shot from the muzzle. Lamb shuddered as the bullets tore through him, and he fell to the ground. A squad of similarly suited men spilled out of the helicopter before it had even touched the ground, and began to run among the tents of the research station.

Thurman watched helplessly as her boss crawled through the dust, leaving a wet trail of blood. One of the men walked up behind him and pressed the muzzle of his rifle against the back of the doctor's head. Thurman screamed as her friend and mentor was brutally executed. Her scream was drowned out by gunfire and the noise of the helicopter's rotor wash. Even without the shooting and rotor noise, no one would be likely to hear her. The camp was full of screaming.

The invaders were killing everyone.

The scream died in Thurman's throat as three more figures emerged from the helicopter. They didn't wear Russian chemical-biological-warfare gear. The suits they wore were bright orange and were fully self-contained with their own integral battery-powered air supply. Thurman was intimately familiar with the Racal, or "orange" suit. She wore one on a daily basis in her work.

As the spacesuited men marched directly to tent number four, an icy sense of dread in Thurman's mind began to underscore the immediate terror of being shot.

She ducked back behind the outhouse and with an inhuman effort of will forced herself to think. She was unarmed. The invaders obviously knew the layout of the camp, and it only made sense that they had to have some idea of the camp's roster, as well. If they did, it would only be a matter of moments before someone realized she was missing, or someone came to check the outhouses on general principle.

Thurman glanced behind her. The forest was a one-hundred-yard sprint to the west, and seven miles into the interior, there was a missionary station administered by a British couple. The doctor's face set into a grimace of cold determination.

The missionaries had a radio.

Thurman took a deep breath, and then a second and a third. She had learned a deep-breathing exercise to center herself and keep fear under control in the highly dangerous and claustrophobic environment of the hot zone in tent number four. She used that centering technique now to conquer the terror hammering at her heart. Her choice was very simple. She could hide behind the toilet until someone came and blew her brains out, or she could make a run for it. Thurman became almost supernaturally calm. Her personal survival was secondary. Her duty was crystal clear. She had to get a message out.

Billions of lives depended on it.

She burst out from behind the outhouse and headed for the trees at a dead run.

Washington, D.C.

The face of the President of the United States was as grim as Hal Brognola had ever seen it. Next to the President sat a United States Army brigadier general whose unit designations the big Fed didn't immediately recognize. The general's face was a mask of stone. One of the President's senior cabinet members and his personal adviser looked upset and bewildered. The head of the State Department looked close to a nervous breakdown.

The President took a deep breath and gave Brognola a haggard smile. "Have a seat, Hal. We have a real problem on our hands."

Brognola took a seat in the Pentagon's secure briefing room and waited. The President inclined his head at the general. "Hal, this is Brigadier General Frank Elway, of RIID."

The Justice man blinked. RIID was short for USAMRIID, the United States Army Medical Research Institute for Infectious Diseases, and it was located in Fort Detrick, Maryland. Its main function was to study all forms of diseases in an effort to protect the United States armed forces from biological warfare. Brognola's eyes widened, and his skin started to crawl. If he had been called into a room with the President of the United States and a brigadier general from USAMRIID, something unthinkable had to have happened.

The President sighed heavily. "Well, Hal, I can see by the

look on your face you've already gotten an inkling of the situation."

The Man glanced at the general. "Frank, why don't you fill in Mr. Brognola?"

The general peered at Brognola for a moment, and was obviously wondering why he was dealing with a civilian from the Justice Department. The general kept those thoughts to himself and spoke in a clinical voice. "Mr. Brognola, one hour and forty-five minutes ago we received a communication from the military attaché in the United States Embassy in Kampala, Uganda. The military attaché received a radio message from a British missionary station near Lake Victoria. The message was from a Dr. Eliza Thurman, who was working at a U.S.-sponsored medical-research station on the western shore of the lake."

The general read from a fax sheet.

"Research Unit Two has been attacked. No other survivors. Hot suite penetrated. Hot agents stolen. Attackers unknown. Helicopter assault, attackers heavily armed and wearing Russian-made chemical-biological-warfare protection gear. Technical team among attackers observed wearing Racal hotsuits. Am assuming they have the hatbox. Am being pursued and heading west."

The general set the sheet back down on the table. "That was all."

Brognola frowned. "I'm assuming a hot agent is some sort of bacteria or virus."

The general nodded. "Indeed. A hot agent is a living bacteria or virus, and one that is lethal to human beings. It also generally means the agent is contagious."

"So someone has stolen these hot agents from a research station in Uganda?"

"So it would seem."

The Secretary of State stared at the general and spoke in a

highly agitated voice. "None of this is confirmed. All we have is one radio message from some doctor out in the African bush. We have no real idea what is going on, and we're already considering risking an international incident. I don't think this is a time to start panicking and doing dangerous things on the basis of an incomplete radio message from some hysterical woman."

The general regarded the diplomat without changing expression. "I think this is an excellent time to start panicking."

Brognola blinked. People didn't normally say things like that in front of the President of the United States. "How reliable is this Dr. Thurman?"

The general passed Brognola a United States Army personnel file. There was a file photograph of a ferociously grinning blue-eyed woman along with fitness reports and her career file.

"Dr. Eliza Thurman is a captain in the United States Army. She is a highly competent virologist, and she is on loan to the CDC research unit in Uganda and is acting as our Army liaison there." The general glared at the Secretary of State. "I know Dr. Thurman personally, and I have every confidence that she is not the kind of person to send hysterical messages. She has sent us a message saying that every member of the research staff in Uganda has been murdered, and the attackers were wearing protective suits, which means they knew what they were doing. She has told us that the hot suite has been penetrated, which means that unauthorized personnel entered the level-four containment area in the camp, where the hot agents were stored. She believes the hatbox has been stolen, which means the hot agents and their containment vessel have been taken. She says she is being pursued. If what she says is true, we have a biological worst-case scenario on our hands."

The head of the State Department shook his head. "Listen, I think you are talking—"

The tabletop shuddered under the general's fist, and his already deep voice sank an octave. "I'm talking about billions of human lives, you stupid son of a bitch."

The Secretary of State goggled and sputtered.

The President cleared his throat. "Frank, let's try to stay cool on this one."

The general looked at his Commander in Chief with icy calm. "Sir, the clock is ticking, and we're wasting time debating politics with civilians." He peered at Brognola. "No offense."

"None taken." The big Fed met the general's gaze. "What kind of agents are we talking about?"

The general sighed. "You've heard of Ebola?"

Brognola nodded. He had heard of Ebola. It was an African rain forest virus, and it was a slate wiper in humans. Depending on the exact strain, Ebola was approximately eighty to ninety percent lethal in humans and highly contagious. There was no known cure, and thankfully, up to this point, the few outbreaks of it had been isolated and the speed with which it killed had helped it to burn itself out quickly. "Yes, I've heard of it."

The general nodded. "Well, then, you know what we are talking about. In the human body, Ebola does in ten days what it can take the AIDS virus ten years to do. Research Unit Two was doing its work on strains of Ebola taken from the Sese Islands on Lake Victoria. In our line of work, they're known as the Plague Islands. Monkeys have been mysteriously turning up with all sorts of unpleasant infections in those islands, and most of the local human populations have been wiped out. Their isolation makes the islands ideal for study. Outside factors can be controlled that can't be out in the wild, so the Centers for Disease Control set up a lab on the lakeshore. We thought it was an ideal on-the-scene laboratory situation, until this happened."

Brognola grimaced. "Why would someone want to steal hot viruses?"

"I can't think of any good reasons." The general's shoulders sank. "But I can think of some very ugly ones."

"I can see the potential as a weapon, but it would be almost suicidal to let it loose in any population. It would be just as likely to spread and kill the people who were using it."

The general peered into space. "Fanatics might not have a problem with that."

The statement hung in the air for several moments. The idea of terrorists armed with a communicable biological agent that was ninety percent lethal was almost unthinkable. The President stood up from his chair. "Thank you, gentlemen. I need a moment alone."

The head of the State Department started to speak, but the President cut him off. "A moment alone, please." As the room emptied, the President motioned to Brognola. "Why don't you stay for a moment."

As the door closed, the President sat back down. "Hal, I'm already scrambling a Navy SEAL team, but it will take them at least twelve hours to get on the scene."

Brognola knew what the President was asking. "Striker is in London, along with several Stony Man Farm employees. After his last mission, where the Royal Family was attacked, there was a great deal of debriefing to be done with the British government. A woman Russian agent was wounded in assisting us, and Striker elected to stick around during her rehabilitation. Several others chose to stay and visit friends and family after being debriefed, as well."

The President nodded. "Excellent. I need to know what really happened in Uganda. If Dr. Thurman is still alive, I need her retrieved so she can give us a full report. If she is still being pursued, I would be very interested in having one or two of her pursuers taken alive for interrogation, as well. However, Uganda isn't particularly an ally of the United States. Whoever I send in must be deniable. Even if they are successful, extracting them may be very difficult, and I need all of this done an hour and forty-five minutes ago. How soon can you get Striker on-site along with whatever kind of team he can assemble?"

Brognola sat back in his chair. "Well, first off, we're going to need the fastest plane the British can loan us."

2

Uganda

The borrowed British Aerospace Nimrod jet streaked across the late-afternoon African sky at just under six hundred miles per hour. The maritime patrol plane shuddered as its four Rolls-Royce jet engines screamed toward overheating at full emergency war power. Mack Bolan sat in the main radar operator's chair and waited. Jack Grimaldi's voice finally buzzed in his headset.

"We're over Lake Victoria, heading west toward the camp." Grimaldi paused a moment. "I see smoke."

Bolan rose and peered out over the pilot's shoulder. Through the narrow windshield the Executioner could see thin plumes of white smoke rising into the sky from the west side of the lake, exactly at the coordinates of Research Unit Two. "Do a low flyby."

"Roger." Grimaldi banked the jet low over the water. According to the briefing Bolan had been given, Research Unit Two had consisted of six large military tents, as well as a few prefab outbuildings. From his vantage, he could see six blackened squares smoldering in the red lowland soil. Several smaller blackened squares burned outside the research camp's perimeter, too. The Executioner's eyes narrowed slightly. "That's white smoke, and it's still smoldering. I'm betting they used white phosphorous grenades to burn the entire camp."

Grimaldi nodded. As a member of the Stony Man Farm team, he was all too familiar with what white phosphorous could do. "I'll buy that." They left Lake Victoria behind as the jet roared past the camp and tore out over the Ugandan lowland forest.

Bolan checked his map. "The mission station should be just ahead."

Grimaldi jerked his head forward slightly. "I'd say it's right over there."

More plumes of brilliant white smoke rose up out of the forest dead west of the research unit's position. There was little to see as they approached. The mission station had been little more than an old Victorian-style house and a barn that occupied a large clearing. Incendiary grenades had eaten the old wooden structures to the ground and left nothing but smoldering ash as the remaining traces of white phosphorous elements fed upon themselves in the dust.

Bolan could only hope the old couple who ran the station had bugged out with Dr. Thurman.

Grimaldi took the jet up slightly. "Which way now, boss?"

Bolan consulted his map of Uganda. "She said she's heading west. If she hasn't been caught yet, I'd say she'll continue almost due west. Our Dr. Thurman is a soldier and a scientist, so let's assume she's smart. Due west keeps her in the lowland forest. She can make good time and still stay under cover. That'll take her straight to the Ruwenzori National Park, and beyond that is Lake Edward. There are lots of big-game and tourist safari outfits working the Lake Edward area. She might be able to find people who could help her there."

"Give me a heading."

Bolan peered at the map, then at the military file he had been faxed on Captain Thurman. The diminutive sandy-haired woman barely cracked five feet tall, but her latest fitness report stated she was thirty-two years old, her overall fitness rating was excellent and she practiced karate in her spare time. Bolan nodded to himself as he factored in the fact that she was running for her life. "The missionary station was seven miles from the research unit. It's been eight hours since that transmission. Mostly flat ground and open forest. I give her twenty miles, tops. A straight line from the camp takes her to the Ruwenzori National Park. Then things start to get mountainous. I'm betting she'll head straight up the first valley she comes to and bear north for the lake."

The Executioner stood and handed Grimaldi the map. Behind him Gary Manning and David McCarter rose, as well, and began tugging on their parachute harnesses and doing a final prejump check of their equipement. Bolan shrugged into his own jump harness. They would be doing a LALO jump, jumping from low altitude and opening their chutes even lower. Bolan glanced at Manning and McCarter and saw that they were ready.

He turned back to Grimaldi. "Take us to the foot of the mountains, due west of the missionary station. That should put us a few miles ahead of Dr. Thurman and whoever is after her." Bolan speared a point on the map with his finger. "There."

DR. ELIZA THURMAN STAGGERED into the clearing and nearly impaled herself on the shotgun as she fell. Tears welled up in her eyes against her will at the relentless burning in her lungs and the leaden ache in her rubbery arms and legs. She felt like throwing up. Despair rose up from her soul and gripped her mind. She was finished, and she knew it.

The bastards were still behind her. She could hear them shouting to one another in some foreign language that wasn't English or her high-school French. Her teeth clenched in helpless anger. They had killed the Lowenthals. Of that she was certain. The old couple had let her use their radio and given her a canteen of water. They would have given her their battered old Land Rover, but the vehicle was down and a man from the village wouldn't be out to look at it until the coming week. They had offered her a horse, but Thurman had never learned to ride.

The Lowenthals had paid a price for that kindness. They had refused to leave their missionary station. The Lowenthals had withstood everything East Africa could throw at them for forty years, from famine and disease to the terror of Idi Amin. They weren't about to be moved now. They had radioed the local constable and told the doctor that she should keep moving. They said they would tell whoever came that she had gone south.

Soon after Thurman had headed out, she had heard the distant snarl of two bursts from an automatic weapon. Soon after, the smoke of the old house burning had been visible for miles. If her hunters had been fooled about which direction she had taken, they hadn't stayed fooled long.

Thurman took a shuddering breath. She couldn't run any more. Her canteen was empty, and her legs felt like they were full of sand. She had been running for hours, and she knew that she was perilously close to heat exhaustion. Thurman's fingers tightened around the weapon in her hands and the grim alternative it represented.

The Lowenthals had given her their shotgun.

The missionaries were pacifists, but a double-barreled 12-gauge shotgun loaded with buckshot was standard leopard insurance in much of East Africa, and few homes outside of the cities were without one. Thurman would have preferred an M-16 rifle like the one the United States Army had trained her on, but the short-barreled shotgun and the twelve shells they had given her sure beat a pocketful of rocks.

Thurman took a shuddering breath and dug the butt of the shotgun into the dirt like a crutch and levered herself to her feet. To the west, the mountains of Ruwenzori National Park loomed out over the trees. They seemed very close, probably less than a few miles away. She knew with unpleasant certainty she would never make it to the mountains and Lake Edward beyond. Her hunters would quickly overtake her as she staggered, exhausted, through the trees. She had no doubt they would kill her, although there was an ugly chance they would interrogate her first to see what she had communicated over the Lowenthals' radio. Almost as if in confirmation of her thoughts, Thurman heard another shout as her pursuers probably found her muddy footprints where she had staggered through a creek less than half a mile back.

She peered about the clearing for a moment as a vague plan formed in her mind. She was through running. She dropped her empty canteen where she stood, then walked over to a fallen tree ten yards away and crouched behind it. There was a fold in the ground behind the tree, and it led a dozen yards to a thicker stand of trees farther back. She nodded tiredly to herself. It would do. Of course they would quickly flank her and overwhelm her. They were obviously professionals, and there were at least six of them, possibly more. However, they didn't know exactly where she was right now, nor did they know that she was armed. Thurman pulled back the shotgun's twin hammers and waited.

She soon heard the soft thud of footfalls of boots. Thurman peeked up over the edge of the log as the footsteps stopped.

A man stood in the clearing. He was tall and blond, and he wore a khaki fatigue shirt and matching shorts. He carried a big black automatic rifle in his hands. The rifle was much bigger than the M-16s that she was trained on, and the man carried it with practiced ease. Sweat stained the front of his shirt, but the man didn't appear tired. He was wide eyed and eager, the picture of a hunter engaged in the chase. The man shifted his rifle to his left hand as he knelt to pick up the canteen Thurman had deliberately dropped. The man smiled and nodded to himself as he shook the empty canteen. The woman's gaze narrowed. There were darker pinpoint stains that didn't run with the sweat on the man's shirt, and there were pink smears across his face, as well.

The light spattering of blood wasn't his.

It came to Thurman with utter clarity that this man had shot the Lowenthals at point-blank range with his rifle.

The man looked back over his shoulder and shouted in his guttural-sounding language. Voices from not too far away shouted back in response. A part of Thurman's mind thought the words sounded like some kind of German. The rest of her mind was concentrated with the cold clarity she used in the hot environment of a level-four viral area as she put the brass-bead front sight of the shotgun on the man's chest.

The man dropped the canteen and looked around the clearing. His head snapped back in shock and his green eyes flared as he looked around and saw Eliza Thurman and the twin muzzles of the shotgun pointing at him accusingly over the fallen tree. His rifle suddenly whipped around and was raised to his shoulder with blinding speed.

Thurman pulled both of the shotgun's triggers simultaneously.

MACK BOLAN RAN through the open Ugandan forest in long, loping strides. Gary Manning and David McCarter followed behind him in a loose wedge. In their hands the Stony warriors carried highly modified Steyr SSG sniper rifles. The bolt-action rifles' barrels had been cut down to a very short twenty inches, the last ten of which were sheathed in flat black suppressor tubes. The .308 high-powered bullets the weapons carried in their 5-round magazine had also been highly modified. The heavy 250-grain hunting bullets pushed the limits at which the barrel of a .308 rifle could stabilize. The powder charge behind the massive bullets had been reduced to propel them just under the speed of sound to eliminate the crack of a supersonic rifle bullet. The suppressor tube mounted along the shortened perforated barrel contained and diffused the rifle's muzzle-blast to little more than a short, whispering hiss.

On paper the modified Steyr rifle might almost seem feeble compared to a normal rifle. To a ballistics expert the over-heavy .308-caliber bullets would be traveling in slow motion compared to their normal supersonic speeds. In the grim reality of combat, however, the modified Steyrs were throwing a 250-grain bullet at over a thousand feet per second, and doing it in almost complete silence. Mounted well forward of the rifle's receivers were wide-relief 2.5-power telescopic sights, which would allow the shooter to keep one eye on the crosshairs and still keep his other eye open for movement outside of the scope's narrow view.

The rifles they carried were short-range assassination weapons, and as they loped through the Ruwenzori forest, the Stony team had no illusions.

They were entering the game late, and they were heavily outnumbered. A set battle with their opponents was out of the question. They had to try to locate Eliza Thurman and extract her from the East African bush while a squad of men heavily armed with automatic weapons also hunted her. They were literally engaged in a lethal game of capture the flag. Speed and surprise would be their only allies, and silence and stealth their only edge.

Bolan scanned the forest ahead. The sun would be setting in another hour and a half. He checked the compass on his wrist. If Thurman had continued due west, then she would be almost on a collision course with the Stony Man team.

The twin thumps of a shotgun split the forest in sudden confirmation.

Bolan stopped and held up his fist. Manning and McCarter halted in place behind him, and they listened to the silence following the blast. In the distance men suddenly started to yell, and moments later an automatic weapon ripped into life.

McCarter spoke quietly. "Those are FNs."

Bolan nodded. The big .30-caliber Belgian FN battle rifle had been the standard rifle of the British army for most of David McCarter's tenure. He had no doubt the Englishman could easily recognize their firing signature. More rifles joined the cacaphony. The battle was taking place just south of their postition. "Spread out, fifty-yard intervals. Be careful. It sounds like the doctor might be armed."

The Stony Man team spread out through the trees and tacked south. Bolan reached a stand of trees and crouched as he heard someone trying unsuccessfully to creep through it in silence.

He peered through his scope and scanned the interior of the thicket. A figure was moving toward him. Bolan's eye narrowed slightly as he suddenly got an unobstructed view of a woman's face. Sandy hair hung plastered down around her face and blue eyes looked about wildly. He knew the face from the file photo he had been faxed back in London.

It was Dr. Eliza Thurman.

Bolan spoke quietly into his throat mike. "I have contact. In the thicket. I'm going to make the pickup. Take flanking positions."

McCarter's and Manning's voices came back through Bolan's earpiece.

"Roger that."

"Understood."

The Executioner watched as Dr. Thurman sank to her knees ten yards from his position and broke open her shotgun. She grimaced as she burned her fingers pulling out the two spent shells, but she didn't make a sound. For a split second she would be helpless as she reloaded, and Bolan decided it was an excellent opportunity to make his presence known without getting his head blown off. He spoke softly but distinctly as the doctor dug in her shorts pocket for two fresh shells.

"Dr. Thurman."

The woman started and dropped her two reloads to the ground. Her eyes flew wide as she saw Bolan for the first time, and her hand scrabbled desperately in the dirt for her dropped shells. Bolan crouched slightly, and Thurman froze as a burst of rifle fire east of their postition raked through the thicket.

Bolan spoke again in a short and sharp manner. "Captain Thurman, we received your radio message from our Ugandan military attaché. I'm here to rescue you. Grab your ammo. We're getting out of here. Now."

Thurman blinked, but addressing her by her Army rank cut straight through to her military training. She scooped up her two shells and staggered forward. "I got one of them, but there's more. At least six or seven." She stopped and took a shuddering breath. "They killed the Lowenthals."

"I know." Bolan handed her his canteen and trained his scope through the thicket. He could see little through the dense thornbrush, but the sound of people moving came from out beyond the thicket. Thurman drank greedily from the canteen, then gasped as she had to stop for air. Bolan jerked his head at her shotgun. "Reload." The woman nodded and blew on the dusty shells. Her fingers trembled as she slipped the two buckshot rounds into the shotgun and clicked the action shut. Bolan took the canteen back and grabbed her by her free hand. "Let's do distance."

Thurman didn't ask any questions, and the Executioner broke into a jog. She gamely stayed in stride with Bolan for a few dozen yards, then stumbled. The soldier pulled the woman to her feet and took a second to examine her critically. Her eyes were glassy as she stared up at him, and her face was pale. Despite the ninety-degree heat, the skin of her arm was clammy under Bolan's hand, and he knew she was slipping into heat exhaustion. She gazed up at Bolan in utter fatigue. "I'm sorry, I just can't run any—"

Bolan cut her off and spoke into his mike. "Where are you, Gary?"

Manning's voice spoke out loud as he moved out from behind a tree to Bolan's left. "Right here, Striker."

"Take the doctor and head for the Congo border. I'm going to slow our friends a little."

Thurman made an indignant noise in protest as Manning swung her up over his shoulder in a fireman's carry and began to lope through the trees. The Executioner turned back to the thicket and flicked the safety off his rifle. He could hear the opposition much clearer now; they were shouting at one another. Bolan didn't know the language, but he had heard it spoken on more than one occasion. The enemy was speaking Afrikaans, the white South African version of Dutch. The enemy gunners were undoubtedly Boers. That didn't bode well. They were almost certainly ex–South African military, which meant they would be well versed in bushcraft and intimately familiar with their heavy .30-caliber Belgian FN automatic rifles.

There was a sudden cry of alarm from somewhere past the thicket. The enemy had found their fallen comrade. Bolan took his position behind the bole of a tree and spoke to McCarter through his throat mike. "Where are you, David?"

The Briton came through loud and clear. "About fifty meters north of you, Striker. Sounds like you have a pack of bloody Boers out there."

"I'm going to hit them, then I'll be coming back toward your postition mighty fast. Pin them down as I come."

Bolan could hear the click of McCarter's safety coming off. "Roger that. Understood."

The soldier trained his scope on the thicket. The enemy didn't know he was there. Thurman had left a trail of broken branches through the thorn thicket. They would follow it, but if they were clever, they would have two men flank the thicket, as well, to avoid another point-blank ambush.

The Executioner waited with his rifle raised.

One of Bolan's eyebrows raised slightly. They were coming, quietly and with great skill, but he could hear one of them approaching through the thicket. The flankers would be along any moment. He spoke again. "I think they may be flanking the thicket. Keep an eye out on your side of it."

"Roger."

Bolan brought the scope smoothly up to his eye. There was a man just south of the thornbrush. As he approached, the man kept one eye on the thicket as he looked for signs of Dr. Thurman possibly veering south. Bolan let him come a little

closer as he examined the man through the Steyr rifle's tele-
copic sight. The killer was dressed in a pair of khaki shorts
and a matching fatigue shirt. He wore no insignia or emblem
on his clothing, and with his bush hat and light canvas boots
he could have been a white hunting guide in almost any part
of sub-Saharan Africa. The long black FN automatic rifle in
his hands and the pair of hand grenades clipped to his belt
betrayed him as something else.

The Executioner put his crosshairs on the man's chest and
fired. The Steyr rifle barely whispered as it pushed against his
shoulder in recoil. The loudest sound it made was the muted
click of the bolt as Bolan immediately chambered a fresh
round. The South African staggered as the heavy bullet hit
him. He had heard no shot; all he felt was the blow. He went
down on one knee in confusion, then his eyes widened as he
saw the spreading stain on the front of his shirt.

Bolan grimaced as he heard a questioning voice hiss from
somewhere behind the man. The enemy was using two-man
flanking teams. As the wounded man began to open his mouth
to speak, the soldier put a second round into the man and
hammered him to the ground.

The second man yelled in alarm from somewhere out of
Bolan's line of sight, and a burst of fire raked through the
trees close by. The Executioner spoke grimly into his mike.
"One target down, and I think they're onto me."

"Roger that. Am maintaining position."

More bursts of automatic fire tore through the trees as the
enemy fired for effect. The Executioner eased backward and
took position behind a stump and searched the forest. He
swung his scope around as another burst went off somewhere
ahead of him near the thicket, then froze as he saw a puff of
red dust settling to the ground in front of some brush fifty
yards to his left. He had to wait only a few seconds.

Flame spit out of the dense bush, and red dust kicked up
off of the ground. Someone with an automatic rifle was prone
behind the bush. Another rifle opened up nearby. They were

using standard fire-and-movement tactics, leapfrogging from position to position and covering one another. A man burst from behind the bush and moved forward at a run directly down Bolan's sights.

The soldier squeezed the trigger, and the Steyr rifle banged back against his shoulder. The running man staggered and fell across his rifle as the round took him dead center.

A single, dulled rifle shot thumped from near the thicket, and Bolan instinctively threw himself flat. For half a second there was a rushing sound as something hurtled through the air at speed, then the forest was split by the thump of high explosive. Bolan grimaced as a blast wave rolled over him from uncomfortably close by.

The enemy had rifle grenades.

Bolan spoke quickly to McCarter. "I'm breaking cover."

"Roger that. I'm ready."

The Executioner rose up from the stump and began to zig-zag through the trees at a dead run. Behind him he heard shouting, and more fire raked the trees. Bolan made a beeline for a fold in the terrain and dropped behind the small embankment of a dry creek bed. Bullets tore across the top of the embankment, and dirt and dust rained on him as he moved at a rapid crouch toward McCarter.

The Briton spoke in Bolan's earpiece. "I have multiple targets. Do you want me to engage?"

More debris rained to the ground as more and more fire tore across the top of the embankment. Bolan knew that someone was about to lob a grenade on him any second. "Engage all targets of opportunity. Look out for grenadiers."

"I have one in my sights now. He's aiming at you." There was a moment's pause. "He's down."

The crescendo of automatic weapons seemed to suddenly double. "Striker, they are now aware of me. I have enemy coming around both sides of the thicket. At least six."

"I'm going to follow this creek bed to its next bend, twenty-five yards west. I'll cover you from there."

"Roger."

Bolan moved to the bend in the creek where a large rock afforded some real cover. He swept the forest with his scope. "In position."

"I'm moving."

He saw McCarter break from a fold in the ground and move toward a thick stand of trees. Someone yelled, and Bolan swung up his sights. Two men were charging forward with their guns blazing. The Executioner put his sights on the leading man's chest and fired. Red dust puffed off his shirt, and the man twisted and fell. The second gunner immediately knelt and fired. Several bullets ricocheted off the rock Bolan was using for cover as the man swept his arc of fire in the general direction of his target.

The man's rifle suddenly ran empty, and Bolan swung his rifle back over the rock. The man had thrown himself behind a tree, he didn't know exactly where his adversary was, but the Executioner could see his head and shoulders from his angle. The man had already rammed a fresh magazine into his rifle, and he was slipping a grenade over the weapon's muzzle.

The Executioner put his crosshairs between the man's eyes and pulled the trigger, swinging his scope backward as the man sagged to the ground. McCarter had dissapeared into the trees. "How are we doing?"

McCarter was breathing heavily as he responded. "A bit close, but no damage done."

Bolan paused. The forest had become eerily silent.

McCarter had noticed the same thing. "I have no movement, Striker."

The Executioner strained his senses. The enemy was lying low rather than pushing the attack.

McCarter spoke again. "You think they've had enough?"

Bolan's eyes narrowed as battle-honed senses told him something was happening. Seconds later the faint sound of rotors throbbed in the distance.

"Striker, I hear a chopper."

Bolan grimaced. "I do, too, and there are no friendlies within helicopter range. The boys on the ground will wait for it. I suggest that we don't. Let's get out of here and find Gary and the doctor."

"Roger."

He moved around the bend in the creek bed and then broke into a ground-eating lope through the trees.

3

Gary Manning had made good time with Dr. Thurman, but Bolan and McCarter caught up with them all too swiftly. Thurman had a chagrined look on her face as Bolan entered the clearing where she and Manning had temporarily stopped to rest. Being carried like a sack of potatoes wasn't the most ego-gratifying way to travel, but the respite, jostling as it had been, had obviously done her some good. The color of her face had normalized, and her eyes were no longer glassy.

Manning took a sip from his canteen and handed it to Bolan. "What's the situation?"

The soldier took the canteen and spoke to McCarter over the radio. The Briton was a hundred yards behind and acting as a rear guard. "What have you got?"

"I have no movement, Striker."

Bolan turned to Manning. "They're choppering in reinforcements. I'm betting they add men to the team behind us, then use the helicopter to leapfrog ahead and put a team in front of us, as well. If they have any brains at all, they'll use the chopper to coordinate the search from the air, and I'm betting it's armed."

Thurman looked extremely displeased with the prospect. Manning plucked a stem of long grass and stripped it between his teeth in meditation and finally nodded in agreement. "Well, that's about how I'd do it." He glanced up at Bolan with a grin. "So, what's the plan, boss?"

"Well, we can't outrun them, and we can't expect reinforcements anytime soon. We can't keep playing hide-and-seek with them, either. Sooner or later they're going to pin us down and pile on." The Executioner shrugged. "I say we borrow their helicopter and fly it to Congo."

Manning's grin widened as he rose up from his heels. "I can live with that."

Bolan spoke into his microphone to McCarter. "Go climb the tallest tree you can find. Give me the coordinates of the first likely spot you can see to land a helicopter and insert a team ahead of us."

"Roger."

He turned to Thurman. "I need one last run out of you. Are you up to another hard mile or two?"

Bolan almost raised an eyebrow at the look of utter determination that set on the woman's face. She seemed to compensate for her tiny size with a nearly limitless well-spring of willpower. She grinned at Bolan despite her fatigue. "You better believe it."

McCarter's voice spoke in Bolan's ear. "I see a break in the tree canopy about two and a half kilometers from your position, fifteen degrees north by northwest."

"Acknowledged. Get there as fast as you can." Bolan glanced at the compass on his wrist, then pointed through the trees. "That way, two and a half klicks." He grinned at Thurman as he picked up her shotgun. "I'll race you."

THE THUNDER OF heavy rotor blades beat the air overhead like a hurricane. Dust and small forest debris whipped in the hard vortices of rotor wash as the helicopter circled tightly overhead. Bolan squinted up against the harsh eddies of air. Just beyond the thicket of trees and heavy brush they were using for cover, the forest opened up into a long, leaf-shaped clearing cut by a riverbed. The riverbed was wide, shallow and dry, but by the way it fanned out flat, and the absence of trees, Bolan could tell the area was cleared by frequent flooding during the wet season. It was just big enough and flat enough to land a helicopter.

The Executioner flicked open the bolt of his rifle and reached into his belt pouch. He extracted five .308 rounds and began to stuff them into the Steyr's open breech; McCarter and Manning did the same. The tips of the bullets were painted with the U.S. Army's black designation for steel-core armor-piercing ammunition. The high-velocity steel penetrators would quickly burn out the suppressor tubes of their rifles, but that wouldn't matter.

What mattered was that the steel-core bullets would penetrate the body and shatter-proof windshield of an Aérospatiale Super Puma helicopter and their subsonic silenced bullets wouldn't.

Bolan turned to Thurman as the helicopter finished its circle and began to descend onto the flat pan of the dried riverbed. She leaned against the bole of a tree with her chest heaving and her face pinched with misery. She had staggered the last five hundred yards like a drunk with Bolan and Manning holding her up between them as they ran across the broken ground. When they had reached the edge of the clearing, she had promptly fallen to the ground and thrown up.

The Executioner flicked the bolt of his rifle closed and handed her back her shotgun. He shouted over the sound of the descending rotors. "Stay down behind that tree! When one of us gives you the signal, head to the helicopter!"

Thurman nodded weakly as she wiped her mouth with the back of her fist.

Bolan, McCarter and Manning were spread out at five-yard intervals at the edge of the trees. They had beaten the helicopter to the clearing by thirty seconds, and they had managed to avoid being spotted. Red dust flew up in sudden clouds as the aircraft descended to the riverbed. The soldier grimaced as he examined the big French-built helicopter. He had feared the chopper might be armed, and his worst suspicions were now confirmed. Along a rail mounted to the left side of the fuselage was the six-foot length and gaping muzzle of a Giat 20 mm automatic cannon. If they didn't take out the pilot and the copilot in the first few seconds, Bolan and his team would be ripped to shreds.

Bolan spoke into his throat mike. "Pilot and copilot are primary targets, on my mark."

He kept his crosshairs on the pilot's chest as the helicopter's landing gear crunched onto the gravel of the riverbed and the side door of the troop compartment began to slide open.

"Now!"

The Executioner squeezed the trigger of his rifle. The short-barreled Steyr recoiled hard from the blast of the high-velocity ammunition. The windshield of the Super Puma suddenly spiderwebbed with cracks as the steel-core bullet punched through the crash-resistant glass.

The pilot was obscured by the fracture lines radiating outward from the bullet hole, but Bolan kept his aim at the center of the cracks as he flicked his rifle's bolt and fired again. The glass in front of the copilot had gone opaque with cracks and fractures, as well. The soldier put a third round through the glass and into the pilot's personal space, then swept his muzzle to the side of the helicopter.

Heavily armed men were already deploying.

The Executioner put his crosshairs on the lead man and fired. The gunner fell, and for a moment the enemy soldiers were confused. They hadn't expected to meet resistance so quickly, and they were caught out in the open. Two more of them fell almost instantly to Manning and McCarter. The enemy didn't stay confused long. Automatic rifles began to blaze into the tree line, splinters flying as the high-powered rifle bullets tore through the trunk of the tree Bolan was using for cover. The gunner fell as McCarter took him out from his position five yards away. Another man fell to Manning's rifle, but more men kept leaping out of the helicopter. The hardmen were professional soldiers, and they knew that the best way to break an ambush was to go right down its throat.

The hunters charged forward with cold and determined fury.

Bolan dropped prone and fired again. One of the hunters staggered, and the Executioner flicked open his rifle bolt on an empty chamber. There was no time to reload the weapon. He tossed the Steyr aside and drew his 9 mm Beretta pistol.

More men kept jumping out of the helicopter as Bolan raised his weapon and flicked its selector lever to 3-round burst mode. Manning's and McCarter's rifles had run dry, and they had gone for their side arms, as well. Automatic-rifle fire tore through the trees as the enemy tried to pin down their adversaries and overwhelm them. Bolan took out one with a 3-round burst from the Beretta and had to roll back prone behind his tree to avoid being shredded by a burst from the man's comrade.

The soldier kept rolling and came around the other side of the tree with the Beretta leveled. Three men were almost on top of him. He put his front sight on the lead man's chest and fired as the other two tracked him with their rifles.

Off to his left a shotgun roared, then roared again. The two men staggered and fell across the body of the man Bolan had downed.

Bolan smiled grimly as he swung his Beretta onto a new target. Dr. Eliza Thurman had joined the fight.

Two men were charging McCarter's position. They fired their rifles on full-auto as they tried to keep the Briton pinned behind cover. One of the hunters spun about as Bolan put a 3-round burst into his side, then collapsed as a second burst hammered into his chest. The second man spun a moment too late and was caught in a deadly cross fire as first Bolan and then McCarter fired on him.

The Executioner tracked the muzzle of his pistol around the clearing. Except for the steady beat of the rotor blades, everything was suddenly still. Ten bodies lay strewed about in the gravelly pan of the riverbed. Bolan spoke into his microphone. "David?"

"Check. I'm all right."

Bolan nodded. Two of the bodies lay in front of Manning's position. "Gary?"

"Ready and able, Striker."

The soldier ejected the magazine from the Beretta and slapped in a fresh one as he rose from his position. "All right. Let's check the chopper. Keep your eyes open." He swung his glance over to Thurman. "How are you doing, Doctor?"

She took a shuddering breath and let it out slowly. "I'll be all right."

Bolan nodded. It had been an extremely long day for Dr. Eliza Thurman, and she was at the ragged edge of both physical and emotional exhaustion. He was greatly impressed. He knew men who were trained soldiers who would have given up under less. He held out his canteen. "Drink some water and stay put while we check out the helicopter."

Thurman murmured her thanks, took the canteen and began to drink.

The Executioner approached the helicopter with Manning and McCarter flanking him at five-yard intervals. Its engine whined at a steady idle, and the rotors continued to beat the air. Bolan moved to the open side door and swept the interior with the muzzle of his Beretta. Except for a pair of canvas packs and a large crate containing a spare belt of ammunition for the 20 mm cannon, the cabin was empty. He vaulted into the cabin and moved up front to the cockpit.

With their precision shooting, Bolan and his men had avoided destroying any of the flight instruments, but the pilot and the copilot were in a grim state. Blood was everywhere, and the windshield riddled with cracks to the point of being useless.

Bolan spoke into his mike. "The helicopter is clear. Let's get out of here."

McCarter jumped into the helicopter and moved forward to help Bolan remove the bodies. Thurman glanced at the battered corpses greenly as she and Manning clambered into the cabin. Bolan went back and took the pilot's chair, and McCarter settled into the copilot's seat.

The Executioner studied the instruments for a moment. He was an experienced helicopter pilot, but his hours on a French Super Puma were extremely limited. He grimaced at the cracked and bloodstained windshield for a moment, then put his right boot to it. The beleaguered glass sagged, then fell away from its frame. It was going to be a drafty flight.

McCarter relaxed back in his chair and grinned at Bolan. "Congo?"

Bolan nodded as he gave the engine more power. "That's what I'm thinking."

The Briton's smile stayed fixed. "You know, Congo isn't the most stable country in central Africa at the moment."

Bolan nodded as he lifted the helicopter up off the riverbed with a lurch. The Aérospatiale Super Puma was a powerful machine. "I know that."

"So you're going to make an unscheduled landing in Congolese airspace in an unmarked military helicopter with no windscreen, armed with a 20 mm automatic cannon."

Bolan squinted against the rush of air blowing through the smashed window as he took the helicopter out over the forest and pointed it west toward the Monts Bleus of the Congolese border. "Yup."

McCarter slouched in his seat and put his feet up. "This should be good."

4

Congo

Major George Umkose of the Congolese army sat behind his desk in the Beni airport and peered at Bolan narrowly. The major was a massive man in green fatigues with a suspiciously large number of deocrations on his uniform, and he carried an immense stainless-steel .44 Magnum Ruger revolver in a custom-made shoulder holster. Bolan knew well that in most Third World armies, handguns were status symbols.

The major seemed to be overcompensating for something.

He regarded Bolan critically, then swept his eyes over Manning, McCarter and Thurman. His gaze returned to Bolan, and he spoke with the English accent of a well-educated person. "So, Mr. Belasko. You say you were attacked by poachers?"

Bolan nodded. "We believe they were poachers. We can't be sure."

The major's eyes narrowed. "I am wondering what poachers would be doing with a helicopter armed with a 20 mm cannon."

The Executioner folded his arms across his chest and chewed his lower lip in thought. "You know, I wondered about that myself. I think perhaps they were shooting elephants from the air, then landing men to harvest the tusks. I've heard of poachers using military equipment before. In Namibia there has been a rash of poachers laying land mines on elephant paths and then harvesting the maimed animals at will."

The major leaned back in his chair slightly as he considered this. He grunted reluctantly. "That is not entirely outside the realm of possiblity." He leaned forward again, and his eyes narrowed to slits. "So, you took this heavily armed helicopter away from these men who were armed with automatic weapons?"

Bolan nodded toward McCarter. "Our guide, Mr. McCarter, is familiar with the Ruwenzori forest. We didn't take them all on. We just circled toward the helicopter and took it from the pilot. I don't think the poachers knew the territory very well. I think they were just flying sweeps over the forest and shooting elephants. We just happened to be in the wrong place at the wrong time."

The major tapped a finger on his desk. "Tell me. Why did you not go to the Ugandan authorities?"

Bolan spread his hands. "Well, as you know, the Ugandan government is extremely corrupt. If someone was using an armed helicopter to poach, someone in authority must have been in on the deal. There is a war going on in Rwanda, so Mr. McCarter figured Congo would be the safest place to land."

Umkose stared at Bolan expressionlessly. The major was aware that something was going on, but he was being lied to in such a convincing manner that he wasn't sure what exactly to do about it. What's more, his detainees were being cooperative, they were not demanding their nonexistent rights and, except for the woman, all of their passports and papers were in order.

Bolan smiled and gestured toward Umkose's pistol. "Say, that's a nice piece. Is that a Ruger Redhawk?"

Against his will, Umkose found himself smiling back in benevolent condenscension. "A Ruger *Super* Redhawk."

Bolan widened his eyes appreciatively. "Gee, that's pretty neat."

Umkose cleared his throat. His interrogation seemed to be slipping from his grasp.

The Executioner looked at him sincerely. "Oh, we found something else."

Umkose narrowed his gaze suspiciously. "Yes?"

"Yes." Bolan nodded. "We found a knapsack under the pilot's seat. There was a lot of money in it and some handguns. The money was in American dollars. I didn't count it, but it was a lot. At least fifty thousand."

Umkose's eyes flew wide. Bolan nodded. "I'm sure it was intended for something illegal. I'd feel better knowing it was in your hands."

The major cleared his throat again, and Bolan continued. "I don't know the legal status of the helicopter, but it was armed and involved in some kind of illegal activity, as well. I think it would be best if you impounded it, since you are in authority."

Major George Umkose sat up in his chair as he came to a decision. He had just become fifty thousand dollars richer, and his army unit had just aquired a new gunship free of charge. Other than making an emergency landing, he really had nothing to hold these people on. He could invent something, but Congo generally tried to stay on friendly terms with the United States.

Umkose rose up to his full height in his chair and regarded Bolan in an official manner. "Of course, these things would be done as a matter of course. However, I thank you for your cooperation and your suggestions. I suspect you wish to contact the American Embassy in Kinshasa." The major smiled at Bolan and pushed a rotary phone across his desk. "Please, feel free to use my personal telephone."

MACK BOLAN SAT in the briefing room of the United States Embassy in Kinshasa with Manning, McCarter and Thurman. Major Umkose had been extremely helpful, and extremely eager to send them on their way before they had a chance to rethink their generosity or the ownership of the helicopter. He had put Bolan and his team on a military transport to Kinshasa within twenty minutes of their interview. There had been little talk on the plane. Once it had taken off, sleep had overtaken the exhausted team. A nap and getting safely to the embassy had lifted everyone's spirits considerably.

McCarter grinned at Bolan over his coffee. "Well, you certainly charmed the major."

Bolan shrugged. "Fifty thousand dollars can make anyone charming."

Thurman stared at Bolan in wonder. "Where did you get fifty thousand dollars?"

"Well, we were dropped into Ugandan airspace with no air support, no reinforcements and with orders to pick you up and extract any way we could." Bolan nodded toward Manning. "We figured we'd have to pay someone off somewhere along the way. Gary was keeping fifty thousand in hundreds in his pack."

There was a polite knock at the door, and a well-built black man of medium height walked into the briefing room. His shaved head made it hard to guess his age, but Bolan noted the man's eyes and the way he carried himself. The man had obviously been a soldier, and Bolan was willing to bet the man was currently some sort of paramilitary operative. The man grinned as Bolan rose and extended his hand. "I'm Darryl Stanford, the United States cultural attaché around here. Glad to meet you, Mr. Belasko." The two men shook hands.

"Cultural attaché" was the euphemism for CIA agents in just about every American Embassy in the world. "It's good to meet you, too."

Stanford took a seat and tapped his finger on a file he had brought in with him. "That was a pretty smooth exit you made from Beni, Belasko. I'm impressed. We were afraid you might get detained. Suspicious white boys with guns scare the hell out of the local establishment. Things could have gotten sticky."

Bolan leaned back in his chair. "Major Umkose was very helpful."

The CIA man snorted. "Yes, he certainly was. I've met the major, and I'm not surprised you got along so famously." Stanford sighed. "The armed forces are as divided as the people. A military career in this country is made by acquiring the patronage of the wealthy and the politically powerful. Who gets new equipment and personnel is usually determined by who you know and who you've done favors for. Major Umkose is probably beside himself with glee that he got his hands on a gunship without doing anything other than being polite to some foreigners."

"I'm happy that we all were allowed to leave."

Stanford nodded. "And getting you and the doctor out of here and back to the States as quickly as possible are my standing orders."

"We'd appreciate that." Bolan held the CIA man's gaze and leaned forward slightly. "We had to ditch our side arms back in Beni. All we have now are three bolt-action rifles. You think you can do something about that?"

Stanford frowned. "Do you really expect any trouble? I was told your activities in Uganda are on a need-to-know basis, but I'm tempted to think you've left them behind you. I mean, if you think it's necessary, I can give you an armed escort to the airport, but this country's laws are very tough on the possession of firearms, particularly military ones, and particularly in the hands of suspicious foreigners. You bought your way out of Beni, but if you're caught with military weapons or handguns here in Kinshasa, they're going to think you're mercenaries. They're close to civil war around here, and you don't want the authorities thinking you're mercenaries. If they get that idea in their heads, I might not be able to help you."

Bolan nodded. "I understand the dilemma, and I'm probably just being paranoid, but it's a habit of mine." He cocked his head slightly. "We came into this country posing as a hunting party. Can you do something with that?"

"I'll see what I can do."

A MAN IN A DARK SUIT stood in a hotel room and opened an aluminum suitcase and picked up the phone extension of a satellite communications rig. He punched in a series of numbers, which went directly into space in a coded burst, where they were then bounced back to Earth's surface nearly a quarter of a planet away. The man waited for a few moments while the codes were being recognized and the communications link established.

To an observer the man would have been hard to describe. "A probable caucasian of medium height and regular features" would likely have been the best an observer could have done. The man's features were so regular as to be almost nondescript. No one of them stood out. The cut of his expensively tailored dark suit belied his powerfully built physique. His hair and eye color had changed three times in as many days. When he spoke his voice was carefully modulated and free of an accent.

"We have a problem."

Half a world away the old man's gravellike voice rang with the upper-class inflection of the old country, and he wasn't pleased. "What kind of problem? I was led to believe this phase of the operation had been a success."

The younger man paused a moment. "It has been. We have the product. The research camp has been wiped out and burned to the ground."

"Then what is our problem?"

The younger man steeled himself. "One of the researchers is still alive." There was a slight pause, and a part of the younger man's mind was bemused that he could hear the papers rustling on the old man's desk. If he closed his eyes, he could well believe that they were in the same room. Their communications gear was superb. Even better than that used by the Americans.

"The woman doctor." The old man paused again while he read his file. "Thurman. I was led to believe that a well-trained team had been dispatched to run her down and kill her."

The younger man sighed. "That is true."

The old man was incredulous. "And she has eluded your team? I had thought they were professional soldiers, veterans, and knew the terrain." The old man's voice dropped an octave. "This begins to sound dangerously like incompetence."

Even though the younger man was alone, he stood at ramrod attention. Some patterns of behavior were harder to eliminate than others. "She had help."

The old man grunted. "Yes, yes, the missionaries. I was informed of that nearly ten hours ago. I had also been informed that they had been eliminated and that the doctor had gone on toward the mountains on foot. This is not an acceptable excuse."

"Dr. Thurman received the help of some sort of paramilitary team."

There was another pause. "That is impossible."

The younger man briefly rescanned the notes he had taken from his conversation with one of his surviving operatives. "According to one of the survivors, the team had nearly run Dr. Thurman down when they encountered resistance."

"What kind of resistance?"

"Heavy resistance." The younger man looked down at his notes again. "The opposition was armed with silenced rifles. They apparently made contact with Dr. Thurman and then began a fighting retreat through the forest. I authorized reinforcements and the use of a helicopter to cut the fugitives off and surround them."

The old man cleared his throat. "And the result?"

"The team that followed on foot came across a battlefield. All of the team that had leapfrogged ahead with the helicopter were dead, including the helicopter's pilot and copilot. The helicopter itself was gone."

The silence across the satellite link was deafening. "This is impossible."

The younger man allowed himself a small sigh. "I believe

that the Thurman woman must have gotten out some kind of communication from the missionaries' radio.''

"It is still impossible. Even if her signal had reached any kind of official channels, the Americans would have spent hours wringing their hands trying to decide what to do. Even if they had the will to make the decision to send men, there is no way they could have sent any sufficient number in time.''

"My contacts inform me that a British Nimrod jet flew over Uganda within the time frame.''

The old man grunted. "A Nimrod. That is a British maritime-patrol jet.''

The younger man nodded. The old man had been a pilot himself during the war and was a confirmed bird-watcher. "It is extraordinary to think that a Nimrod jet could have been authorized, the men assembled, and then flown from London to Uganda on afterburners and deliver troops. They would have had to have parachuted out of the weapons' bay. It is most implausible.''

"But not impossible, and the situation remains as I have reported to you.''

The old man's voice grew steely. "Very well, what else do you have to tell me?''

The younger man relaxed slightly. He knew the old man's moods from long experience. The old man wasn't currently interested in assigning blame. What was to be done next was now uppermost on his mind, and the situation was salvageable. "According to my contacts, a helicopter matching the one I dispatched in Uganda landed in Beni. There were four occupants, including a woman matching Dr. Thurman's description. They were interviewed briefly by the local military and then put on a transport plane to Kinshasa. An observer tailed them from the airport. They were taken to the American Embassy, where they are currently.''

"How long have they been there?''

"Forty-five minutes.''

The old man took a long breath. "I am assuming you have assembled a team."

"That is correct, and I await your orders."

The old man's voice turned decisive. "Kill Dr. Thurman. Kill her and the men with her. She has had no real time to tell anyone anything, and I believe she will wait until she gets back to the United States to give a full debriefing. Only she knows exactly what we have. Kill her, and all that our opponents will be able to do is speculate."

"I will have to wait until they are outside of their embassy to kill them. To do it in the streets of Kinshasa could be messy."

"Do it in the airport. They will not expect it there. Besides, you are in Congo. The Americans have little influence there, and their power to investigate their operatives' murders will be extremely limited. See that it is done. Our local operatives mean nothing to me. The death of the doctor and the people with her are paramount. Oversee the operation yourself and observe, but do not actively participate. You are not expendable at this juncture. Report to me immediately when it is over."

The younger man took a deep breath. He would have preferred to do it himself, but it was a relief to know that he was not currently expendable. "I will see to it."

"Very well." The old man's voice didn't change. "But do not fail."

5

Darryl Stanford grinned and shook his head. "Okay, so it was the best I could do on short notice."

The CIA man's grin was infectious, and Bolan grinned back as he looked down at what the man had procured for him. Stanford shrugged his shoulders helplessly. "You were the one who said to try to work the hunting angle, and these weapons are technically legal for sporting purposes in this country."

Bolan looked down at the weapons again, as did McCarter, somewhat skeptically. Gary Manning beamed. He was an avid hunter, and for him, the massive, big-bore handguns on the table were a pleasure to handle. Stanford put what looked like an overstuffed garment bag on the table. "I also managed to scrounge up three sets of soft body armor. They should fit you guys." He ran a sympathetic eye up and down Thurman's petite though impressive proportions. "I'm sorry, Dr. Thurman, we just don't have anything in your size."

The woman smiled coolly. "Hardly anyone ever does."

Bolan picked up a dark blue Dan Wesson .44 Magnum pistol with an eight-inch shrouded barrel and checked the cylinder. The pistol showed signs of some holster-wear, but the action looked sound. Manning picked up an equally massive clone of Major Umkose's Ruger Super Redhawk and sighed appreciatively as he sighted down the barrel.

McCarter lifted a Smith & Wesson .44 Magnum Mountain Revolver and frowned. "This will kick like a mule."

Manning nodded gleefully. "Oh, you'd better believe it."

Bolan picked up a Ruger single-action revolver in his other hand. The weapon could almost have passed for a pistol from the Old West except for its massive frame and modern target sights. It was chambered for the .44 Magnum cartridge, as well. Two similar single-action revolvers lay on the table, except they were stainless steel and were chambered for .357 Magnum rounds. Manning and McCarter each scooped up one of the remaining pistols while Stanford pulled out several tattered cardboard boxes of ammunition.

The Executioner raised an eyebrow. All of the ammunition was heavy, hard-leaded, full-metal-jacketed hunting ammo. With their grab bag of massive revolvers and hunting cartridges, it looked for all the world as if Bolan and his team were going to the OK Corral to get in a gunfight with a gang of water buffalo.

Bolan finished checking his pistols and began to load them. "What's our carry?"

Stanford picked one of several attaché cases that he had stacked in the corner. He flipped the catches and opened it up to reveal a lining of packed foam that nearly filled the case. "Normally we have the foam inside these cases custom cut to fit whatever weapon they're supposed to be carrying. We don't have time for that, and if you really need them in a hurry, you don't want them packed away securely anyway. I'm thinking you can just jam the pistols between the uncut packing and keep just one of the latches shut. If trouble comes, you can just flip the one latch and the pistol will be right there." The CIA man shrugged as he handed the case to Bolan. "And if nothing happens, you can check the pistols onto the plane like regular carryons. Your flight is leaving in about half an hour, and I've made sure that the customs agents on duty have been given a cash incentive not to scrutinize your party too closely."

Bolan nodded and put the loaded Dan Wesson revolver into the case and shut it with one latch. The packing seemed to hold the pistol securely enough as he shook the case experimentally. He dropped the case to his side with his left hand and took a slow breath. He held the breath for a moment, then let half of it out. The Executioner suddenly blurred into motion. His right hand rose and slapped the case's one closed latch as his left brought the case in front of his body. His right hand continued its motion and slapped the lid open. His hand stopped and his thumb cocked back the hammer as the massive revolver fell from the case and into his fingers.

Stanford whistled in appreciation. There had barely been half a second between the click of the case latch and the cocking of the hammer. "Damn!"

Bolan eased the hammer back down and put the big pistol back in the case. He positioned the Ruger single-action beneath it, then flicked the one latch closed. "It'll do."

McCarter and Manning began to pack their weapons in a similar fashion. Thurman looked at the CIA man accusingly. "What about me? I'm the one they're trying to kill."

Stanford nodded and produced a small athletic bag. Inside it was an extremely ancient and battered-looking Walther .22-caliber Olympic Model target pistol. "I know, it doesn't look like much, but the action is sound, and it has ten rounds of high-speed hollowpoints in the magazine and one in the chamber. Just cock it and you're ready to go."

Thurman took the pistol and checked it herself. After a moment she grinned up at Stanford. "It'll do." She suddenly looked back up at the CIA man again as she put the pistol back in the bag. "What about you?"

"Well, the law is making your boyfriends go the Great White Hunter route. Now, me—" the CIA man raised the left side of his tropical suit with a flourish and revealed a darkly gleaming 9 mm Uzi machine pistol in a shoulder holster "—I've got what they call diplomatic immunity."

THE RIDE TO THE AIRPORT was uneventful. Stanford drove Bolan and his team in a Ford Bronco with diplomatic plates. A

Ford Escort sedan in front and in back of the Bronco formed a protective convoy, and in each sedan was a pair of armed United States Marines.

The tangled streets of Kinshasa rolled by. The city had once been named Leopoldville after the King Leopold of Belgium, back when Congo had been the Belgian Congo. The colony had gained its independence in 1960, and many things had changed. Many others hadn't. Modern buildings and paved roads quickly gave way to shacks and shanties, and goats and chickens scurried out of the way as the little caravan moved out of the urban district and headed toward the airport.

A French TransAtlantic jet flew in on the runway as they pulled into the terminal, and the embassy guards leaped out of their sedans and closed ranks around the Bronco. Stanford rolled down the window and conferred with the commanding officer. "I didn't see any sign of a tail, Sergeant, how about you?"

The Marine scanned the road approaching the terminal. "No, sir, we didn't see anything."

The CIA man turned in his seat. "How about you, Belasko? I noticed you checking the mirrors."

Bolan shook his head. "I didn't see anything unusual."

Stanford nodded. "Then let's roll. Your plane leaves in about fifteen minutes."

They entered the terminal in a loose phalanx around Dr. Thurman. Two of the Marines stayed with the vehicles, and two came in taking the lead as they walked through the sliding glass doors. Bolan glanced around. The main terminal was fairly busy. The majority of the people inside seemed to be foreign businessmen sweating in their tropical-weight wool suits, although a sizable number of natives were in the terminal, as well. The country was dominated by an almost impenetrable rain forest. Few roads could manage to make any kind of straight line across the country. The country itself was shaped by the mighty Congo River and its thousands of tributaries, and travel by boat had been the most frequent mode of travel for thousands of years. However, riverboat travel was slow, and although it was prohibitively expensive for most Congolese, travel by air was the most efficient way to get anywhere across the vast and often hostile interior.

A number of soldiers also stood about at checkpoints, carrying a mix of Belgian FN and Russian AK-47 assault rifles casually slung over their shoulders with the stocks folded. A number of others carried Uzi submachine guns.

Bolan's combat senses flared to life. There was something wrong in the terminal.

The Executioner had been in more firefights than he could count, and his senses had been honed in hundreds of battles. He wasn't psychic, but subliminal cues that even well-trained men might miss were like warning flags before his eyes.

Those flags were waving urgently.

Bolan glanced about casually from behind his shades and he noted the soldiers on guard. Soldiers on this kind of guard duty were universally bored out of their minds. Some of the guards in the terminal obviously were, and stood talking and smoking cigarettes or looking at women, but some of the guards weren't bored. Some of them appeared to be on a high state of alert and were scanning the crowd. Bolan momentarily locked his gaze with a soldier standing near the rest rooms. The soldier carried his 9 mm Uzi submachine gun slung on his hip assault style and was wearing mirrored sunglasses. As Bolan looked at him the reflective surfaces quickly jerked away from his gaze.

The Executioner walked on and kept his face forward, but his gaze slid upward under his brow as he looked up at the railing of the airport's observation deck. Another soldier armed with an Uzi stood at the railing. He looked past Bolan toward where the first soldier was standing and nodded his head. He gazed down at the big American for a moment and then raised his radio to his lips and spoke quickly.

Bolan smiled and clapped Darryl Stanford on the back in a

friendly fashion, then leaned close to him. "I think we're about to get hit."

The CIA man's shoulders tensed very slightly under Bolan's hand, but his outward demeanor didn't change. He grinned back as if Bolan had told him a joke, but his voice was low and serious. "You're sure?"

Bolan released Stanford's shoulder. "I'm not sure of anything, but we're being closely monitored by some of the soldiers, and they're acting edgy."

"What do you want to do about it?"

The Executioner considered. He'd recently had firsthand experience in how corrupt the Congolese armed forces were, but Bolan doubted that someone could bribe his soldiers to be hit men in broad daylight in an airport. He suspected that all wasn't as it seemed.

He smiled at Stanford. "I'm going to see if things check out. Stop and tie your shoe or something, alert everyone else. Keep an eye on the observation deck, and anyone in a Congolese army uniform carrying an Uzi."

The CIA man suddenly bent over to his shoe and called to the rest of their group. "Hey! Hold on a minute!"

Bolan split away from the group and walked back toward the men's room. The soldier was there, and he studiously avoided looking toward Bolan, but the Executioner could feel his eyes watching him from behind the mirrored sunglasses. He pushed open the bathroom door and walked through the doorway while the soldier pretended to ignore him.

The Executioner considered the opposition he had met in Uganda while rescuing Dr. Thurman. Bolan had been to South Africa on several occasions, and he knew that most all soldiers of the South African Defense Forces, black or white, spoke at least some Afrikaans. Bolan spoke enough words to string some phrases together, and as he wheeled about in the doorway he barked out in rapid Afrikaans.

"Soldier! Your fly is undone!"

The man jerked to attention and almost against his will shot a glance at the front of his pants. As he looked down, the mirrored sunglasses slid down his nose, and Bolan could see the man's eyes flare in shock as his hand closed around the pistol grip of his slung Uzi.

Bolan swung the briefcase carrying his heavy pistols upward in a vicious arc and clipped the man in the chin. He slapped the latch with his right hand and caught the big Ruger .44 Magnum revolver as the case flew open. He released the case and caught the second pistol with his left hand before it reached the floor.

The soldier staggered backward a step from the blow and bumped into the wall behind him. Bolan gave him no time to regain his composure. He swung the heavy eight-inch barrel of the .44 Magnum revolver and whipped the man across the temple.

The soldier collapsed to the floor as if he had been shot.

The Executioner whirled with a massive revolver filling each hand and swept the interior of the terminal. Several civilians had seen him suddenly strike the soldier down, and they gasped and stepped back in shock. Bolan ignored them as he raised the pistol in his right hand high.

The soldier on the observation deck had dropped his radio and slapped the folding stock of his Uzi submachine gun to the extended position. He brought the weapon up to his shoulder for an aimed shot and dropped the muzzle toward Dr. Thurman and the knot of Americans around her.

Bolan put the bright orange insert of the Ruger's front sight on the soldier's chest and fired.

The report of the .44 Magnum revolver was deafening inside the terminal. The assassin on the observation deck toppled backward as the Magnum hunting slug slammed into him, and a wild burst from his weapon flew high and wide into the ceiling as he fell.

The floor of the terminal erupted into bedlam as people began to scream and shout. Some started to run, while others froze or clutched one another in panic. Bolan grimaced. The terminal was full of innocent civilians, and he doubted whether the enemy cared. He shouted for everyone to get down, his voice holding the unmistakable power of command.

Almost like magic the civilians around him dropped to the floor. The iron of his voice and the weapons in his hands brooked no argument.

Darryl Stanford's Uzi machine pistol buzzed into life. He held the weapon in both hands, and his 3-round burst dropped one of the Uzi-armed soldiers to the floor in a bloody heap. In the same instant Manning and McCarter had produced massive stainless-steel handguns from their own attaché cases, and their booming reports were like thunder inside the terminal. The two Marine Corps embassy guards had shoved Thurman to the ground as they drew their .45 automatics.

Bolan's big revolver rolled and bucked in his hand as he fired. Two men with submachine guns had dropped to the ground, and they aimed their weapons at Thurman and her Marine protectors with grim determination. A burst from one of the gunmen knocked one of the Marine's legs out from under him, and he fell on top of Thurman protectively while he tried to return fire. Bolan's first round shoved one of the prone assassins sideways across the floor. He still fumbled with his weapon, and Bolan's second shot hammered him into stillness. His confederate rolled and switched his aim to the big American a second too late. The massive pistol roared in Bolan's hand, and the soldier slumped over his submachine gun with a shattered skull.

The Executioner threw himself away from the doorway at the sound of boots in the rest room behind him. As Bolan came up, a soldier exited the bathroom. He had a radio in one hand, and the small, silenced automatic pistol he held in the other condemned him for the assassin he was. The massive Magnum roared, and the man staggered backward. Bolan put a second shot into the gunner to punch him down, then whirled about as bullets stitched the linoleum floor near his feet.

Another soldier had appeared on the observation deck, and

his Uzi spit down at Bolan on full-auto. A bullet punched into the big American's shoulder, but the soft armor he had received at the embassy held. The Ruger revolver roared, and a strip of the observation deck's hand rail shrieked away from the impact. The soldier flinched, and Bolan dropped the spent revolver in his right hand and raised the one in his left.

The muzzle of the Uzi swung back in line as the assassin desperately drew a bead on Bolan. The Executioner thumbed back the hammer of the massive single-action revolver as it rose in his hand, and the two soldiers exchanged fire.

Bolan staggered backward with a grimace as a round from the Uzi hammered him in the chest. On the observation deck the Uzi suddenly cut short as the gunner spun under the blow of the .44 Magnum bullet. Bolan's armor had held; the soldier's body had not. The Executioner thumbed back the big revolver's hammer and took a two-handed hold on the weapon as he surveyed the scene.

Except for low moans and subdued sobbing, the terminal was suddenly very quiet. The battle had taken less than seven seconds. Two Congolese soldiers stood stupefied by the sudden carnage with uncertain hands hovering over their AK-47 rifles. Bolan could hear shouted orders in French and the thud of booted feet farther down the terminal. The real Congolese army was coming on the double. The two soldiers on the scene swallowed hard as they faced a ready and willing firing squad consisting of Manning, McCarter, Stanford, a United States Marine and Thurman. All of them held smoking handguns.

The two soldiers looked extremely unhappy.

Bolan spoke quietly. "Stanford, your French is better than mine, tell these men that the men we killed aren't Congolese soldiers. Tell them we have no desire to start killing any Congolese."

Stanford spoke in rapid and surprisingly friendly French. The soldiers didn't look entirely convinced, but they shot suspicious looks at the men littering the ground. Stanford spoke again, and one of the men nodded hesitantly. The CIA man peered up at a the departure board near the observation deck, then jerked his head at Bolan.

"Your plane is boarding at the gate, Belasko. I suggest you board it and get out of here if you can. Me and the Marines have diplomatic immunity, but this could get messy for you. With any luck I can delay the army." One of the wounded assassins on the floor groaned, and Stanford smiled unpleasantly. "I'll squeeze a few words of Afrikaans out of this gentleman for the troops, and they might forget about you for a few minutes."

Bolan nodded and glanced at his team as he dropped his remaining pistol to his side. "We're out of here."

He, Manning and McCarter formed a wedge around Thurman and marched down the terminal away from the gunfight while Stanford began another speech in rapid-fire French. They walked down the opposite hallway toward their gate. As they approached, Bolan casually dumped his gun through the swinging door of a trash bin, and the rest of the team did the same.

A woman at the gate glanced at their tickets and spoke in heavily accented English. "What is happening back in the terminal? We heard shots."

Bolan nodded and looked grim. "I don't know. I guess there were some bad men in the terminal. The soldiers are taking care of things."

The woman nodded and shrugged. "We live in a time of troubles." She gave Bolan a smile as she tore his ticket. "I hope you enjoyed your stay in Congo."

THE MAN ROSE SLOWLY from the floor of the lobby. All around him people were shuddering and sobbing while many others shouted and screamed in half a dozen different languages and local dialects. Soldiers were trying to fight their way through the crowd while people clasped at them and waved their arms. Other soldiers tried to ask questions over the shouts and the screams. The man suppressed a smile as he rose and dusted off his suit.

It had been the American commando, the same one who had trailed them from Libya, to Germany, to Russia and then thwarted the operation when they had been set to demolish and irradicate Buckingham Palace less than two weeks earlier in London.

Now the dark-suited man was here. The commando had snatched Dr. Thurman away from him, killed almost all of his African operatives and he had simply walked away down the terminal. He was probably boarding his plane even now. As the man had watched the firefight, he had been very tempted to try to kill the commando himself, but the old man had been right. He couldn't afford to expose himself, and the commando had been accompanied by armed allies. They had all been heavily armed and wearing armor. The commando's termination couldn't have been assured. The man grimaced. His own death or capture wasn't acceptable at this stage of the operation.

The man shook his head. Oh, but how he yearned to kill the American. A single head shot could have ended the farce. But the risk had been too great.

He glanced about the scene. The black American, Darryl Stanford, was engaged in an earnest argument with an army sergeant. The words "diplomatic immunity" and "let me talk to your superiors" kept coming up in the conversation, and the soldier was obviously unhappy. The man in the dark suit sighed as he watched the scene. Stanford was attached to the U.S. Embassy, and his technique with his machine pistol had been superb. He was obviously CIA. Beside him, a Marine knelt beside his wounded comrade and applied direct pressure to his leg wounds.

The man turned and melted into the crowd that was moving in a wide circle around the battle scene and hurrying toward the doors of the terminal. He had failed to kill Thurman and the people around her. He would have to report. The fact that the American commando had been recognized on the scene would do much to allay the blame others might try to lay on him for the failure. The odds had just gone up. The man smiled. One fact, however, remained unalterably on their side.

They had the product, and the United States was about to learn what true terror really was.

6

Washington, D.C.

The transatlantic flight from central Africa was long and blessedly uneventful. Bolan was more exhausted than he would like to admit and he, his team and Dr. Thurman spent nearly all of the fourteen hours sleeping. They had landed midmorning at Dulles International Airport, and as Mack Bolan stepped off of the plane, he wasn't surprised in the least to find that Washington, D.C., was currently both hotter and more humid than equatorial Africa. A diplomatic limousine was waiting for them on the tarmac and whisked them into the capital with an escort of two uniformed motorcycle officers.

Their debriefing was to be immediate. Eliza Thurman considered herself first and foremost a doctor. The military had been an excellent road to take her where she wanted to be in her study of virology. However, as the limousine slid through the woodlands outside of the capital, the side of her personality that was a captain in the United States Army was stunned that she was going to be reporting directly to her Commander in Chief.

The way for the limousine had been cleared, and they pulled directly up to the White House. A formation of Secret Service agents escorted them to the Oval Office. The President of the United States stood up from behind his desk. Hal Brognola and General Frank Elway stood to one side. The deputy director of the CIA sat to the left by himself. Thurman goggled at the President for a moment despite herself, and the Man smiled and extended his hand as she started to salute.

"You're not in uniform, Captain Thurman. You don't have to salute."

Thurman shook the President's hand and took the seat he waved at. Bolan shook hands with the President, as well, and took a seat. The President's smile faded as he looked long and hard at Thurman. "Dr. Thurman, I know you've had a very long forty-eight hours, but it's critical that you give us all the information that you can. What exactly did the attackers in Uganda take with them from the research station?"

The woman got over being starstruck, and her face became extremely serious. "They took a strain of Ebola Mayinga."

The President glanced at General Elway, and the face of the man from USAMRIID was like a tombstone. "Frank?"

Elway let out a sigh. "Ebola Mayinga is named after the Congolese nurse who was the first to contract the strain and die in 1976. Ebola Mayinga was the most virulent strain of Ebola currently known to science, Mr. President. It's an eighty percent killer in primates, and that includes humans."

The President's gaze narrowed slightly. "What exactly do you mean by *was* the most virulent."

Elway looked at Thurman gravely, and she cleared her throat. "Research Unit Two found a strain of Ebola Mayinga that appears to have mutated."

The room was silent for a moment, then the President spoke. "Mutated how?"

Thurman shrugged. "Sir, viruses mutate all the time, just like all other forms of life. Successful mutations live and reproduce themselves. Unsuccessful mutations fall by the wayside. It's generally how evolution works."

A faint smile ghosted across the President's face. "I'm vaguely familiar with the theory of evolution, Doctor. I mean in what way has the Mayinga strain you found mutated?"

Thurman let out a deep sigh. "To put it bluntly, it's more

lethal and more communicable than the previously known Ebola Mayinga strain.''

''How much more lethal?''

The captain chewed her lip. ''Well, it's a new strain, and we were interrupted before we had gotten much conclusive lab work done on it, but I'd estimate it would be a nine-out-of-ten killer in primates. That almost works in our favor—the Ebola Mayinga strain is so lethal that it burns itself out before the contagion can spread, and this new strain appears to be even worse.''

The deputy director spoke from the side. ''You mean the virus kills people so quickly that the victims don't have much time to spread it around.''

Thurman grimaced. ''Well, in so many words, yes.''

The President let that sink in a moment, then held Thurman's gaze. ''And?''

''Well, in viruses, communicability and lethality are the two factors you have to deal with. For example, the viruses we commonly call the flu are extremely communicable, but hardly ever lethal. On the other hand, the AIDS virus is one hundred percent lethal statistically, but by medical standards, it's a very hard virus to contract, and it can take years to develop and years longer to kill its host.''

''How communicable is your new virus?''

''Like I said, Mr. President, it's a new strain, and we had had very little lab time with it before it was stolen. But I believe we safely established that it was capable of airborne transmission.''

The President paused. ''Like the flu.''

''We can't be absolutely sure of that.''

The Man pressed her. ''What would happen if this new strain of Ebola was introduced into a human population?''

''I'd be guessing, and you'd have to give me a demographic area.''

''How about the continental United States?''

Thurman swallowed hard and spoke. ''Theoretically, if the

new strain of Ebola virus was introduced anywhere save the most-isolated rural communities in the United States, I believe we would see an explosive chain of lethal transmission, and within a matter of hours it would be almost impossible to stop the contagion. The slang term for such an event is 'burning.' This new strain of Ebola Mayinga would burn very hot in an industrialized nation, and there would be little or no chance for an effective quarantine. Given the access to international transportation that Americans have in every state, I believe it would also be a matter of hours before the burning went global.''

The President glanced out his window onto the White House lawn. ''So, we're talking about a virus with no known cure, which could conceivably kill up to ninety percent of the world's population.''

Elway nodded. ''Possibly, yes.''

The President leaned back in his chair. ''Which brings us back again to who would want to steal something so deadly to themselves and everyone else.''

The general sighed. ''Only terrorists could be that stupid and insane.''

Bolan mulled over his recent actions in Africa. ''I agree with you in principle, General, but the actions of the enemy didn't seem very stupid or insane. They seemed highly organized and extremely professional.''

The President raised an eyebrow. ''Go on.''

Bolan shrugged. ''According to Dr. Thurman, they were hit early in the morning by helicopter assault. They achieved total surprise. They knew the exact layout of the camp and exactly where the virus was being stored. They had a roster of exactly who was in the camp, and they killed everyone systematically. They had proper biological-warfare gear and seemed to have specialists on hand to deal with the transportation of the virus itself. When my team and I inserted to retrieve the doctor, we encountered heavy resistance, well trained and heavily armed. It's my personal opinion that the resistance we met in Uganda and the assassins in the airport in Congo were ex–South African Defense Force personnel.''

The President frowned. "You're saying they were mercenaries?''

The deputy director of the CIA spoke. "Our man in Congo, Stanford, confirms this. Two of the surviving assassins are now in the hands of the Congolese authorities, and the Congolese army is adamant about the fact that the individuals involved aren't their people. In fact, they inisist that they aren't even Congolese nationals.''

The President's frown deepened. "It doesn't sound like any kind of terrorist organization that I've ever heard of.''

Hal Brognola nodded. "No, Mr. President, it doesn't. Terrorists hardly ever hire mercenaries, except as military trainers or advisers. They certainly don't hire cadres of them to do their dirty work. There's too much of a chance that people who work for money will betray you. To actually carry out an action, terrorists prefer to use their own true believers. It's also interesting that once Dr. Thurman escaped, they were able to call in reinforcements, and hours after we had gotten her out of Uganda, they were able to organize an undercover hit team in another country.'' Brognola shook his head. "For a bunch of terrorists, they seem awfully well equipped, organized and connected.''

"So you're ruling out terrorists?''

Bolan spoke quietly. "I wouldn't rule out anything. Terrorists can be manipulated like anyone else. I just don't get the feeling that the PLO or the IRA are the movers and shakers behind this one.''

The President leaned forward. "You're suggesting a foreign power did this?''

Bolan frowned. "I don't know. I can't put my finger on it yet.'' An unpleasant thought intruded into his thoughts. "There's one other thing we have to consider.''

Everyone in the room looked up. The President looked like

he already had plenty to consider and didn't want to hear more. "Oh?"

Bolan nodded. "We should consider the possibility that our opponents don't know exactly what they have. They hit the research station and took the virus. They obviously knew the layout of the camp and had the roster of the people working there. That could have been acquired easily enough in a number of ways. But they slaughtered everyone in the camp except for Dr. Thurman. I get the feeling they didn't have any spies in the camp, at least not among the doctors working there."

Elway's eyes flew wide. "You're right. They probably know they have the Ebola virus, but not that it's a new strain, or that it is communicable through the air."

Bolan nodded. "I believe our opponents know they're playing with fire, but they might not know just how easily it could flare up in their faces." The Executioner's voice went cold. "It may be more than just a question of finding these people before they try to threaten governments or use the virus in blackmail. We have to find these people before they lose control of the virus and destroy themselves and take the rest of the human population with them."

THE MAN IN THE DARK SUIT stood with his arms behind his back and stared at the new and improved hatbox. It certainly didn't look like the deadliest object on Earth, but it contained one of the most lethal threats to humanity in the history of the world. It intrigued the man that the virus wasn't the product of any military experiment or labratory research. It had been developed over the millenia in the African equatorial rain forests through the process of natural selection, as if Earth herself had designed a disinfectant to deal with the problem of the billions of humans infesting her surface.

Human science couldn't have wrought a better weapon of mass destruction. Within the cylindrical biohazard container, the virus was alive and lethally infective. The man stood for long moments and contemplated the cylinder and what it contained through a thick pane of glass.

The old hatbox they had stolen from the level-four containment tent in Uganda had been woefully inefficient for their purposes; however, a more suitable container for transport had quickly been flown in. The new container looked for all the world like a coffin made for a child. It contained dozens of safeguards, and was made of shock-resistant, bulletproof stainless steel. It was the best mobile biohazard container that science could provide.

The man nodded to himself. That was just as well. It had been a long and bumpy ride across the Atlantic, and any kind of malfunction could have been catastrophic.

"How soon do we begin?" his companion asked in English.

The man allowed himself a small smile. The woman was incredibly gifted with languages. Her accent was untraceable, and her ability to pick up languages and change her appearance nearly rivaled his own. His gaze didn't leave the hatbox. "All is in place, and I see no reason to delay. Our contacts have selected a viable target. The operation will begin immediately."

The woman nodded and smiled. She had been wanting to visit the United States for some time now, and the luggage they had brought along pleased her immensely.

7

El Naipes, Arizona

Dr. Eugene Penn stood in the emergency room of the El Naipes free clinic. He was nearly covered from his chest to his shoes in blood that wasn't his own. He stared at his patient with mounting horror. Things like this just didn't happen in godforsaken little border towns in Arizona.

The driver's license in the man's wallet identified him as Robert E. Lee Leland, fifty-six years old, six feet tall, two hundred pounds, blue eyes with gray hair and a citizen of Arizona. He was dying—of that there was no doubt. Dr. Penn swallowed with great difficulty. Whatever was killing Robert E. Lee Leland was doing it in ways horrendous beyond words.

Fifteen minutes ago the man had staggered in out of the night at 2:45 a.m. and collapsed onto the tiles of the empty waiting room. There were two nurses working the nightshift with Penn, and the one behind the admitting desk had screamed at the sight of the man. Penn had begun treatment less than ten minutes ago, and he was now as white as a sheet, and a cold sweat broke across his brow and ran down his spine.

Leland wouldn't stop hemorrhaging.

He seemed to be hemorrhaging blood from every orifice in his body. When the nurse pressed down on his arm to insert an IV plasma unit, Leland's flesh broke under her finger and wouldn't stop bleeding. The bleeding was far from the worst

of it. Leland's appearance was horrifying. His face was a frozen mask, so blank as to be utterly without expression. The
flesh of his face was a jaundiced yellow, but no jaundice victim Penn had ever heard of developed brilliant scarlet speck-
ling like a sea of bloody, star-shaped freckles under the skin.
Leland's eyes were the worst. They seemed frozen and at the
same time slightly distended out of their sockets, and the
whites of his eyes were so bloodshot that it looked like he had
two number-five billiard balls in his head, with pupils where
the numbers should be. Blood leaked from his nose and
mouth; blood wept from his tear ducts; blood slowly leaked
out of his ears; blood leaked from under his fingernails. The
front of his shirt was covered with it, and Penn himself was
covered with it, as well.

The doctor turned his face away as Leland brought up more
blood. His second nurse, Jennifer, was twenty-one years old
and doing summer intern work at the clinic to earn units at
Arizona State University. Other than a broken arm from a
mining accident and one birth, she had seen little more than
hay fever in her short tenure. Nothing had ever prepared her
for the nightmare on the emergency-room table. Jennifer
cringed involuntarily against the wall and covered her mouth
with the back of her hand.

Penn blinked as a strange muffled sound came from Mr.
Leland. It was a sound almost like a towel being torn under
water. Suddenly blood was everywhere. Leland was bringing
up what seemed like an endless supply of blood, and the doctor realized his patient was voiding massive amounts of blood,
as well. Leland stopped breathing, but the blood continued to
flow out of him.

Penn was a small-town doctor in rural Arizona, but he tried
to keep abreast of things. He read medical journals for pleasure. As he looked down at his dead patient, it seemed to him
a vast door had opened behind him and a cold draft was
blowing through the emergency room. He suddenly realized

with terrible clarity what he was dealing with, and he became utterly aware of the blood he was covered with.

His mouth had gone dry, and his voice came out in a croak as he turned and spoke to his nurse. "Go lock the doors to the clinic. No one is to come in or out. Go use the phone on the admittance desk and call the sheriff. Tell him I want him and his deputies to block the roads. Tell him to turn back any traffic coming into town, and that no one currently in town is to leave. Tell him this is a medical emergency, and that I am placing the town under immediate quarantine." Penn managed to swallow, and his voice went cold. "Tell him he has to shoot anyone who tries to leave."

Jennifer stared at the doctor in shock, and his shout was deafening in the small room.

"Move!"

The nurse scrambled out of the emergency room, and Penn turned and walked slowly to his little office. He leaned over and shut the window, then picked up the phone on his desk. He dialed the operator and then spoke in a slow, clear voice. "My name is Dr. Eugene Penn. This is a medical emergency. I need the Atlanta Centers for Disease Control, immediately."

MACK BOLAN SAT in the cabin of the Army Blackhawk helicopter and watched the town of El Naipes rush toward him. The sun was rising behind them over the mesas, and as it shone down on the town it looked like the dawn of Armageddon.

It had taken two hours from the minute of Dr. Penn's phone call to the CDC to have the town of El Naipes cordoned off by the Arizona State Police. The delay had been due to El Naipes's remoteness, but that remoteness had been a blessing. The little town was well isolated by desert and rugged terrain, and the grim hope was that the contagion had been contained.

The United States Army had taken over from the Arizona Highway Patrol and the two roads out of town were blocked by a half a dozen armored Hummers armed with .50-caliber machine guns. The men manning the weapons were clad in U.S. Army chemical-biological-warfare suits. Many similarly armed soldiers stood about with their M-16 A-2 rifles cradled at port arms. A long string of soldiers formed a loose picket line that circled the town.

Several Blackhawk helicopters similar to the one Bolan rode in orbited the town. Door guns had been fitted, and soldiers hung over the weapons in chicken-strap web harnesses with their hands on the trigger paddles.

El Naipes was sown up tight. Nothing would be allowed to leave. Anyone trying to break out of quarantine would be shot without mercy. Only those with authorization were allowed to enter the town, and those who did faced the grim possibility that they might not leave alive. They were dealing with a relatively unknown, mutated strain of one of the deadliest viruses on Earth.

All bets were off.

Bolan glanced back as the orange ball of the sun rose over the hills and bathed the desert in a golden glow. He looked down at the soldiers patrolling the desert in their heavy protective suits and masks. Within several hours it would be eighty degrees. By noon it would be a hundred. He didn't envy them. The Executioner smiled grimly as several of the masked figures looked up as the helicopter swept over and flew onward toward the town of El Naipes.

He suspected the soldiers below envied him even less.

The Blackhawk's pilot craned around in his seat and shouted over the sound of the rotors. "You'd better finish suiting up. We'll be landing in about a minute."

The Executioner nodded. He was dressed in a bright orange Racal suit. The Racal was an entire level of protection up from the chemical-biological-warfare suits worn by the soldiers below. The Racal suit was pressurized from within. If there was a rip in the suit, the pressurized air would stream out of the breach and keep contaminants from getting in until the rip was taped. Bolan had wrapped about two feet of brown sticky tape around the left ankle of his suit for just such an eventuality. The Racal was literally a space suit, and it was a self-contained environment for the six hours of life the air supply's batteries held. When the end of those six hours approached, the wearer had to get out of the hot zone and be decontaminated.

Bolan pulled a surgeon's cap over his hair, then pulled the head-bubble helmet of the suit over his head and checked the seals. As he breathed in, the air inside the suit took on a canned, metallic tang.

The town of El Naipes spread out below. The main street of town was about a half a mile long and consisted of storefronts, then terminated in a town plaza made up of city hall, the jail and the town library, with a small park in the middle. Side streets branched off the main strip at regular intervals and made the tiny town look like a small, well-ordered grid. The town was actually larger than it seemed. Bolan had learned that there were a number of outlying ranches, and several nearby cotton concerns and copper-mining outfits.

The little plaza had been commandeered by USAMRIID. The trees had been cut down, and taking up nearly every foot of lawn was a series of four interconnected, mobile, level-four containment tents identical to the Research Unit Two setup in Uganda.

A tumbleweed rolled down the main street under the force of the descending helicopter's rotor wash. Except for the large olive green tents in the central plaza, El Naipes was a ghost town. The citizens had been told that staying in their homes with the doors and windows closed was their best defense, and, so far, people were obeying.

Bolan's face tightened. If people started to die, that could all change. The soldiers encircling the town had their orders, and the thought of a frightened mob trying to break the quarantine was too ugly to contemplate.

A landing area had been demarcated with orange plastic road pylons just outside town on the other side of the park plaza. The helicopter pulled a hundred yards outside of town and touched down among the cones. Bolan rose and picked up a pair of heavy black gear bags as the rotors continued to thrash.

The pilot looked around leerily. He obviously didn't want to linger. He gave Bolan a weak smile and shouted. "Good luck!"

The soldier gave the pilot the thumbs-up and jumped out of the helicopter. As he walked across the reddish dust of the desert, the sound of the helicopter faded into the distance and Bolan became aware of the deathly silence as dawn rose over the town.

The desert ended abruptly, and suddenly the soldier was walking on the pavement between the jail and the library.

He had entered the hot zone.

Suited figures came out to meet him from one of the containment tents. With the red light of dawn and the bright orange suits they wore, the figures could have been explorers on Mars. One of the space-suited figures barely cracked five feet tall, and Bolan smiled as he recognized Dr. Eliza Thurman.

She walked up and grinned as she thumped a finger against the front of his helmet. "Say, that's a pretty sexy fishbowl you're wearing there, Striker."

The Executioner smiled. A man nearly as tall as Bolan stood beside her and looked at him askance. He had a neatly trimmed beard and mustache, and his eyes lingered distastefully on the Beretta pistol Bolan carried in his shoulder holster. The shoulder rig was specially made of soft suede leather to avoid the possibility of his gear pinching or tearing his suit, and many of its carrying loops were currently empty.

Bolan suspected the man wouldn't approve of what he was carrying in his gear bags, either.

Thurman inclined her helmeted head at the man. "This is Dr. Jonathan Hawthorne of the CDC."

Bolan set down one of his bags and held out his gloved hand. Hawthorne hesitated for a moment, and then shook his hand. "Pleased to meet you...Striker, is it?"

"It'll do."

Hawthorne frowned. "I don't mean to sound rude, and I understand the need for the military to maintain a tight quarantine outside of town. But we have a very volatile situation here. I'm not exactly sure what use you're supposed to be to us here."

Thurman grinned from ear to ear. "Oh, he's very useful in volatile situations, Jon. Believe you me."

Hawthorne glanced back and forth between Bolan and Thurman and reserved comment. The soldier glanced at the containment tents. "So what's the current situation?"

Thurman's smile turned grim. "It could be worse. At the moment we have one death, and one case of current infection. Follow me."

Bolan followed her into one of the tents. It was mostly empty at the moment, but the room was dominated by a gurney, and on top of it lay a clear plastic body bag that was nearly obscured by streaks of blood. "In the bag we have Robert E. Lee Leland."

"The first victim that Dr. Penn reported?"

Thurman nodded. "That's right."

"Cause of death?"

"Ebola Sese."

"You've named the new strain after the Sese Islands in Lake Victoria."

"Yup." Thurman gazed at the body bag and its grisly contents. "We originally found the strain in some monkeys on one of the islands. It seemed appropriate. I didn't exactly feel like naming it after myself."

Bolan nodded. "You've performed an autopsy?"

"We took blood samples, if that's what you mean. The virus underwent extreme amplification in his body, to the point where it actually transformed a good portion of his internal organs into the virus itself. It wasn't pretty, and virally, he's still lethally hot even as we speak." Thurman raised a bemused eyebrow at Bolan. "I think we're pretty positive on the cause of death here, Striker."

"Yeah, but how did he get it?"

Thurman shrugged. "Well, someone exposed him to it, I guess."

Bolan folded his arms. "That's right. Now, Mr. Leland didn't report being kidnapped or assaulted, and the Ebola virus isn't something you just slip into someone's beer when he's not looking. Whoever did it was probably extremely concerned with their own safety. I'd like you to perform an autopsy, checking specifically for marks on the upper arms, buttocks and the major arteries in the neck and the thighs."

Thurman straightened in surprise. "You think someone injected him with it?"

Bolan nodded. "It would be the safest way to carry the viral sample, and the safest way to administer it, as well. I'm betting he was either injected while he was unconscious, or someone gave him the injection under false pretenses. If we can verify that, and if we can track his movements of the past ten days, we might be able to generate some kind of lead."

Thurman grinned at Hawthorne triumphantly. "I told you he was useful."

Hawthorne frowned in thought. "It might be difficult to find any kind of injection marks on the body. Mr. Leland suffered massive hemorrhagic bleeding under the skin, and his condition isn't getting any better." He suddenly looked at Bolan with grudging respect. "But, hell, at least it's a place to start. I'll get a team on it immediately."

"Good." Bolan turned. "Eliza, why don't you come with me? I want to talk to Dr. Penn while he's still lucid, and then have a talk with the sheriff."

Dr. Penn wasn't a well man. He wasn't showing any outward symptoms yet, but his blood test revealed that he was indeed infected with Ebola Sese, and the virus was replicating itself in his body with terrifying speed. He lay in one of the beds in his clinic and looked up at Bolan and Thurman, then grinned tiredly at the sheriff. "Good God, Dale, look at you." He lay back on his pillow again. "So, what's the good news?"

The sheriff itched uncomfortably at the Racal suit he had been issued. It was apparent that he and Penn were old friends. "Well, Gene, the government folks here tell me you have a good ten percent chance of surviving."

Penn's gaze narrowed slightly, and he peered up at Thurman. "Well, now, I thought Ebola only killed eight out of ten."

Thurman looked uncomfortable as she shook her head. She was a laboratory doctor and did the majority of her work with an electron microscope. When she did have patients, more often than not they were monkeys. "You've contracted a mutated strain of Ebola Mayinga, Dr. Penn, which we've named Ebola Sese. You're our first known human case, and a great deal of what we know about the virus and its interaction with humans is conjecture. However, Ebola Sese appears to be more lethal than the normal Ebola Mayinga, and it's much more contagious."

Penn rolled his eyes. "Well...just...honk my hooter."

Bolan smiled. Penn appeared to be a brave man. "Dr. Penn, I need to ask you some questions."

The doctor shrugged. "I'm not going anywhere, shoot."

"Did you know Robert E. Lee Leland before he came into your clinic?"

Penn shook his head. "Not by name. I didn't recognize him when he came into the clinic. His physical appearance had been somewhat changed by the virus. However, if I think about it, I think I've seen him around town once or twice before."

"Have you been doing any inoculations lately? Or do you know of anyone doing any kind of medical screening in the area? Possibly out at the mines?"

The doctor frowned. "No, and if anything like that had been going on, I'd have heard about it. The mining concerns have on-site first-aid stations, but they do most of their medical consultations with me."

Bolan turned to the sheriff. "What do you know about Leland?"

"Well, he has a little spread outside of the canyons, with a couple of horses. He used to be a manager at one of the copper-mining outfits. His wife died a few years ago. He comes into town about once a week to have a beer or two at the bar. He was a likable fella, but he pretty much kept to himself. He didn't believe in doctors. That's probably why Gene didn't know him."

Bolan mulled that over. Leland was starting to fit the profile of a perfect victim. "Sheriff, when was the last time you saw Leland in town?"

The sheriff shrugged. "Well, I'd say the Friday night before last. He was drinking down at the saloon."

"I'd like you to get a deputy to find out who was at the saloon that night if he can. See if there was anything unusual, or any strangers in that night."

The sheriff smiled. "I'm way ahead of you. I've already got a man on it."

There was a knock at the door, and Dr. Hawthorne entered. He looked directly at Bolan. "Bingo."

"What have you got?"

"I believe there is an injection mark right above Mr. Leland's left femoral artery in his upper thigh. It was done with a needle, and I can't tell exactly how old it is. But I believe it would have healed already except that the disease itself kept it from doing so. One of the first things the Ebola virus attacks is the connective tissues beneath the skin. It never healed, and once he started hemorrhaging he bled out of it and it stayed open." Hawthorne grimaced. "It's a lucky thing you brought the subject up. With all the other trauma on the body, I never would have noticed it without knowing exactly what I was looking for."

The Executioner suspected that had been part of the plan. "Can you do a blood workup?"

Hawthorne nodded again. "I will, but don't expect it to show too much. Mr. Leland's entire metabolism has been highly degraded by the virus, and any likely drug that might have been used to knock him unconscious to give him the injection probably won't show."

"Run it anyway. We might get lucky." Bolan turned to the sheriff. "How long on your deputy's report?"

"He should be interviewing Arliss the bartender right now." The sheriff placed his radio against the helmet bubble encasing his head. "Dean, what have you got?"

There was a momentary crackle of static across the radio. "I'm with Arliss now, Sheriff. He says the last time he saw Leland was the Friday before last."

Bolan and the sheriff glanced at each other. "Anything unusual at the bar that night?"

"Yeah, there was, Sheriff. That's why Arlis says he remembers. There was a woman in the bar that night. He thinks her name was Chrissy. She was blond, and a real looker. Built like all get-out. Arliss says she was really friendly with everyone in the bar. He thinks she might have been a pro."

"Anything else unusual, like, with Robert E. Lee?"

The radio crackled again. "Well, that's just it, Sheriff. Arliss says that of all the guys in the bar that night, this Playboy bunny ended up going home with old Leland. That's why he thinks maybe she was a working gal."

Bolan nodded. It didn't prove anything, but it was the only lead they had to work with. As a hunch, it crawled up and down the Executioner's spine with grim certainty. "Sheriff, I want you to find out exactly who was in the saloon that night. I need all of them interviewed, and all of them to give a detailed description of the woman. I can have FBI sketch artists here to start making composites within two hours."

"You've got it." The sheriff paused. "You don't think she's still lurking around?"

"No, not around here." Bolan glanced out the sealed clinic window. Outside, the desert stretched south toward Mexico. "But she's out there. I'm betting her name isn't Chrissy, and I'm betting she's going to strike again."

Mack Bolan sat in the sterile environment of the prefab habitation tent and spoke with Barbara Price. Her voice came across the satellite link from Stony Man Farm very clearly, and it was also clear she was concerned for him. "You be extracareful down there in El Naipes, Mack. I've been reading up on Ebola, and I don't like what I'm finding out."

"I'm eating an apple every day."

Bolan could sense Price's smile, but her tone of voice didn't change. "I'm not kidding. All it takes is one tiny mistake for something like this to blow up in your face."

"I know. I'm seeing firsthand what Ebola can do. Dr. Penn isn't doing very well, and it isn't pretty."

Price was silent for a moment. "Is there any chance for him at all?"

"The doctors from USAMRIID are trying every protocol they know, experimental and otherwise, but nothing they do seems to be having any effect. Frankly I think Dr. Penn is on his own. He's simply going to have to roll the dice with the estimated one-in-ten chance of survival, and unfortunately the virus is going to have its way with him before we find out for sure." Bolan changed the subject. "Have you got the information for me?"

"I can transmit it to you now. You think there's a connection?"

Bolan wasn't sure. A few weeks earlier, he had been trying to track down containers of low-grade plutonium that had been destined for use in one of the ugliest acts of terrorism ever conceived. The trail had led to Germany, and once there, they had discovered what had seemed like a totally unrelated recruiting scheme for mercenary work in East Africa. Specifically around the Lake Victoria area. Whoever had masterminded the plutonium affair had seemed bent on destabilizing Western Europe. The events of the past week had brought that seemingly unrelated event, and one of his opponents on that mission, clearly into Mack Bolan's mind. "Well, it's a shot in the dark. But at the moment it's the best we've got to go on."

"I'll go ahead and transmit. It'll take some time for the entire file on the plutonium incident to come through. When you have it all, look through it and tell me what else you need."

"I'll do that," Bolan replied.

"I'm transmitting now. You take care of yourself, Mack, and keep in touch."

"I'll do that, too." The line clicked off, and the fax machine attached to the satellite link began to hum.

Bolan glanced up as the sheriff walked into the habitation tent along with a tall, dark-haired female FBI agent. Both of them had undergone decontamination procedures, and they both looked haggard and worse for wear. They had been running around town interviewing witnesses all day, and the strain of constantly being in the hot zone of a deadly virus, as well as having to constantly suit, desuit and undergo decontamination procedures in the desert heat was taking its toll. Both of them sighed as they stepped into the cool, climate-controlled air of the habitation tent.

Bolan poured the two of them coffee without being asked. "What have you got for me?"

The FBI agent took a folder from under her arm. "We managed to track down six people who were in the saloon ten days ago, and who claimed to have seen the suspect. We also interviewed the bar owner again, as well as his cocktail server.

I did eight individual sketches from the interviews, then took them and made a composite." She flipped open the folder and spun it around to face Bolan. "This is what I came up with, as well as a physical description."

Bolan looked down into the woman's face drawn in charcoal pencil. It was an excellent likeness. The FBI agent was a highly competent sketch artist. She grinned at Bolan; she knew she was pretty good, too. "So, have you come up with anything from your end?"

Several sheets of information had come across the satellite link and been printed by the fax. Bolan pulled the photograph from the fax machine and placed it on the table next to the composite the FBI sketch artist had drawn. "Based on your interviews, what do you make of this?"

The FBI agent beamed. "Well, I'd say you've got a match!" She took a sip of coffee and she spent a long moment shifting her gaze back and forth between the sketch and the photo. At a casual glance the two women didn't seem the same, but to a trained eye there were telltale similarities in facial structure that left little doubt. The FBI agent seemed sure, and so did Bolan.

"I'm going to need copies of this photograph along with your composite in the hands of every local, state and federal law-enforcement officer along the border between the United States and Mexico. Prioritize that, then I need it out nationally.

"You've got it." The agent peered at the two photos again. "Who is she?"

Bolan peered into the face of a woman who had tried to kill him. "Her name is Heidi Hochrein."

HEIDI HOCHREIN EXAMINED her hair in the mirror critically. She wasn't fond of black, but it would certainly do. The long dark tresses flowed over her shoulders and almost came down to her midback. She pulled on a black leather jacket that matched the lace-up leather pants that seemed almost painted

onto her body. A wide leather belt with a huge steel buckle
and biker boots with built-up heels completed the ensemble.

She smiled at the effect she had created. Dark lipstick and
eye shadow changed the personality of her face, and even sub-
tler use of cosmetics emphasized different lines of her jaw,
cheekbones and nose. The black contact lenses made the effect
more dramatic. An elastic bandage smothered her ample cleavage, and a girdle narrowed her waist by inches. Her entire look
was taller, leaner, harsher and meaner. She looked like nothing
less than some Hell's Angels' darkest roadside fantasy. No
one could possibly take her for the cuddly blond ski bunny
named Chrissy who had picked up Robert E. Lee Leland in a
saloon in El Naipes.

Hochrein picked up her silenced Ruger .22-caliber automatic from the table and checked its load. The magazine was
filled with ten high-speed hollowpoints, with an eleventh
round in the chamber. The sound-suppressed pistol killed with
little more noise than a whisper, and she had dedicated many
long hours of practice with the weapon until it had become an
extension of her will. At fifteen yards she could dump all
eleven rounds into a playing card in exactly two and a half
seconds.

She set the pistol back on the vanity table. As a weapon,
the silenced pistol paled into insignificance beside the contents
of the silver metal cigarette case that lay on her vanity table.
She picked up the specially modified case and caressed the
latch. The case had four small indentations, which, when
pressed in the right sequence, allowed the case to be opened.
Inside the case, nestled into specially fitted high-impact foam,
rested two small, sealed syringes. Each syringe presently carried 40 cc's of the most virulent form of death known to man.

Hochrein clicked the cigarette case shut and looked into the
mirror again. "What do you think?"

The man sat on the bed and looked at her with unconcealed
admiration. Killing and seducing were what Heidi Hochrein
lived for. During the lulls between killing, she had taken to

practicing her seduction techniques on him. The man shook his head. The woman was amoral, and a sociopath; of that there was little doubt. However, she was incredibly gifted at her chosen crafts, and like all of the best terrorists, she was totally committed to her cause. The man grinned at the leather-clad hellion she had transformed herself into. "I think that you look like a Shauna."

"Shauna." Hochrein shook back her long black tresses and stared bemusedly at the image in the mirror. "Yes. Excellent. I do look like a Shauna."

MACK BOLAN MADE a call to Hal Brognola, and the man from Justice seemed tired.

"How are you doing, Hal?"

Brognola sighed. "This one is keeping people up at night, Mack. The idea of an Ebola epidemic sweeping across the U.S. and then going global has shaken everyone who's in the know."

"How's the manhunt going?"

"Well, we've got both the sketch and the composite out, and every officer and agent we have along the border from Tijuana to Brownsville, Texas, is on full alert. As of two o'clock this afternoon, Heidi Hochrein became public enemy number one, and is considered armed and extremely dangerous."

"What's the government saying about what she might actually be doing?"

Brognola's voice was grim. "The President isn't authorizing the higher-ups to let out what Miss Hochrein may be carrying, though they have issued a warning that she might be carrying biologically hazardous materials. *Ebola* is a word that is fairly well-known to the public, and there's a lot of fear in Washington of a nationwide panic."

Bolan grimaced. "Hal, there's nothing more I can do here in El Naipes. I'm going to head out to Nogales. It's more centrally located, and I can coordinate better with the authorities from there.''

''You think El Naipes is a done deal?''

''The attack here was surgical. They wanted to infect one person, and they chose a target who lived in the desert outside of an isolated town. The target was carefully chosen so he wouldn't spread the disease beyond himself. The only victims we've had are Mr. Leland and the doctor who saw him, and I wouldn't be surprised if the bad guys didn't have someone in town at the time acting as a control in case Leland started to vector off in a wrong direction.'' Bolan gazed at a map of the U.S.-Mexican border. ''Yes, I'd say El Naipes is a done deal.''

''So they're going to hit us again somewhere else.''

''Once more at least, maybe twice.'' Bolan continued to stare at the map, as if some intuition would tell him the next move.'' One case of Ebola could be considered some sort of fluke, but two or three, all in different locations, would throw everyone into a total panic.

''And then?''

Both men knew the answer to that question. ''Then they'll start making demands.''

The satellite link was quiet for a moment as both men considered what would happen if the United States, if not the whole world itself, was held hostage.

Bolan sat up in his chair. ''Hal, I want you to have a fast helicopter meet me in Nogales. It needs to be nonmilitary, but I need it armed. I also need a plane in the same kind of configuration.''

''I'll have Grimaldi meet you in Nogales with birds that fit the bill.''

''Good. I'll contact you once I'm there. Bolan out.'' The Executioner stood and looked at the map for a long time. Heidi Hochrein was out there. He could almost feel it in his bones. She was already choosing her next victim, and another innocent was being slated for a death horrible beyond words. Bolan turned on his heel and went to gather his weapons and gear. The situation was galling, but there was nothing to be done. They would have to wait for the enemy's next move.

Heidi Hochrein was extremely pleased with herself. Her second attack on United States soil had gone off without a hitch. She had left Vernon Richmond in the parking lot of the little roadside inn feeling more alive than he'd felt in fifteen years. Even as he drove off into the hills for his yearly trip of solo camping and fishing, his bloodstream crawled with death. Vernon Richmond was divorced and fifty-six years old. She knew that being picked up and seduced by a woman like "Shauna" at a roadside bar had been beyond his wildest dreams. The fact that she hadn't wanted money and had seemed to be genuinely interested in him probably had seemed like a miracle. The things Shauna had done with him during the night had to have boggled his mind.

The woman smiled again at the memory. There had been no need to drug him into unconsciousness. Richmond had been so exhausted when she had finished with him that his snoring hadn't missed a beat as the needle had gone into his thigh.

She pulled her white Ford Escort with stolen plates onto State Highway 86 and headed toward Mexico. Richmond had bragged that he had a fishing spot that no human had ever seen, and that admission had gotten him killed. Given his itinerary, he wouldn't see another person until he was very ill. Men in her employ were shadowing him to make sure that he didn't, and those men had orders to kill both Richmond and any unlucky fellow travelers he accidentally met. Once he was ensconced in his fishing hideaway, and well on his way toward dying, the anonymous phone call would be made. Then the little unknown neck of the Arizona wilderness would be swarming with desperate soldiers and scientists in space suits.

While the Americans were wringing their hands over the second case of Ebola within their borders, she would already be choosing her third target. Then, after the third attack, the real fun would begin.

Hochrein took off her sunglasses and grinned at herself in the rearview mirror. All traces of Shauna were gone, and all of her Shauna accessories had been disposed of. Her hair was now short and red, and her skin pale again with the skin-tanning dye washed away. Her eyes were now blue, and the girdle and elastic band that had compressed her figure had been removed to let her fill out an Arizona State University sweatshirt and a pair of tight jeans. To her mind, she looked like the "Tammi Jo Courtland" that her Arizona driver's license identified her as. Heidi Hochrein could barely contain her glee.

She loved her work, and everything was going exactly according to plan.

Hochrein held that thought as a car appeared in her rearview mirror. The car had a light bar across the roof, and as it approached, the vehicle resolved itself into an Arizona Highway Patrol cruiser. The cruiser came up speedily and began to pass her on the right. A trooper sat behind the wheel, and he gazed at her from behind mirrored sunglasses as he passed her.

The woman beamed at him, and the trooper smiled back.

She relaxed as the cruiser pulled away down Highway 86. For a second something bothered her down at an instinctive level, then it came clearly to her mind. She shouldn't have removed her sunglasses.

Hochrein's eyes narrowed as the cruiser's brake lights suddenly flashed up ahead of her. The cruiser slowed and pulled over into the right lane again. She maintained her speed, and the cruiser continued to slow until she passed it. The trooper's face was intent from behind his mirrored gaze. The woman smiled at him again and maintained her speed.

The cruiser suddenly yanked into her lane and behind her, and his lights began to flash. A single blare of his siren told her she was being pulled over. Hochrein's right hand slipped around the black plastic grips of the silenced .22-caliber Ruger automatic, which was concealed under her purse. She pulled over to the side of the road and parked, but left the engine running. The highway patrol cruiser pulled over a good twenty yards behind her, and for a moment nothing happened.

He was using his radio.

A moment later the trooper got out and walked toward her car. Hochrein's gaze narrowed farther. The trooper settled his wide-brimmed hat on his head and unbuckled the retaining strap of his holster as he approached. He didn't draw the gun, but his hand stayed on the grips.

Hochrein rolled down her window, then let both of her hands rest lightly on the bottom of the steering wheel. The trooper was a tall blond man, and he had to lean down to look inside her car. She beamed at him girlishly. "Good morning, Officer! What seems to be the problem?"

The trooper scanned the interior of the car for a long moment. His hand stayed on the butt of his pistol, and he looked at her with a long measuring stare. His voice was neutral as he spoke. "May I see some identification, please?"

"Certainly."

Her left hand moved up to the visor above her head and for a split second the trooper's gaze followed the movement. In the blink of an eye her right hand snatched the silenced Ruger automatic free and flicked off the safety.

The trooper's own pistol cleared leather with the speed of dedicated practice. It wasn't enough; the moment's distraction had been all the edge that Heidi Hochrein needed. As the trooper's service pistol came up, she was already firing. She knew well that most uniformed American police officers wore soft body armor that would defeat the soft-lead .22-caliber bullets from her weapon. That didn't matter. The range was almost point-blank, and the trooper's head was less than two feet from the window. The sound of the silenced Ruger firing was a nearly continuous hiss.

The patrolman's gun dropped from nerveless fingers, and he collapsed against the side of her car with the lenses of his mirrored sunglasses shattered.

Hochrein snarled and shoved her door open with her shoulder. The corpse slumped away and fell into the dust. She glared at her car. The driver's door was smeared with blood, and she had nothing to clean it with. Even if she did, she was almost certain that the trooper had called in her license plates, and now he wouldn't be calling back in at all. Someone would be coming to look for him very quickly.

Hochrein came to a decision. She bent and quickly removed the trooper's uniform blouse and pulled it over her sweatshirt, then put his hat on. They were both much too large for her, but they would only have to confuse someone for a few moments. She took his keys and got into the cruiser. She adjusted the seat and the mirrors, then put her sunglasses back on. She glanced at herself in the mirror for a moment. The short hair and lack of makeup helped, and with luck she would only be in the cruiser for a few minutes. When she got out of the car, she thought she should be able to pull off the charade for the few seconds she required.

She pulled out onto the road. Things had taken an unwanted turn, and now both she and the entire operation were in a great deal of danger. Her heart was still racing from the adrenaline of the encounter, and she deliberately forced her mind to slow down. Hochrein smiled despite herself. She had enjoyed killing the policeman, and now she was about to make her first traffic stop posing as an American cop. She sped up and scanned the road ahead as the radio squawked at her. She needed a new vehicle, and quickly.

Hochrein pulled a key off of the trooper's ring and unlocked the shotgun in its rack.

"WE HAVE CONTACT!"

Mack Bolan rose from his chair. He was fully armed and armored, and he had been sitting in the chair for almost six hours. There had been nearly a thousand "possible sightings" since the all-points bulletin had gone out and Heidi Hochrein's photograph and composite sketch had been distributed. All of the sightings had turned out to be single women in their cars. Bolan had sat in the chair of the Nogales Border Patrol dispatch office like a stone Buddha while the local and federal authorities had checked out every false alarm. The excitement in the dispatcher's voice told him something new had happened.

"Where?" Bolan asked.

"On State Highway 86. We had a possible sighting of the suspect fifteen minutes ago, and a patrol unit was checking it out."

Bolan nodded. "And?"

"Patrol Unit 35 hasn't checked back in since pulling over the car. A helicopter was near the scene and flew in. They report the suspect's vehicle is abandoned and a body believed to be the trooper is on the sight. He's been shot to death, and his body partially stripped. His patrol car is missing from the scene."

Bolan checked the load of his Beretta 93-R pistol. The roadside killing of a police officer wasn't an unknown occurrence in the United States. The act in itself didn't prove anything, but every hard-won instinct in Bolan's body told him Heidi Hochrein was on the move and about to kill again. He scanned the map in front of him. The emptiness of southern Arizona was an advantage. There were very few routes that Hochrein could take.

"She'll switch vehicles as soon as possible. Get men setting up roadblocks in San Miguel and Sasabe." Bolan scanned the map and frowned. There was very little south of the two border towns other than the desert. Beyond them most of the dirt roads and little villages probably weren't on any maps he currently had, and neither the Border Patrol nor any other U.S. agency had the jurisdiction to go on hot pursuit into Mexico. Bolan didn't recognize such distinctions, but if he went in, he would be going in alone. Then the fight would be on ground of the enemy's choosing.

He turned to Grimaldi. "Let's get airborne."

HEIDI HOCHREIN GRINNED at her driver. "Keep your hands on the wheel."

The young man shuddered, and his knuckles went white on the steering wheel. In Hochrein's experience, fear was one of the best ways to ensure obedience. The young man was scared out of his mind. Pulling him over had been remarkably easy. He hadn't even noticed that the Arizona Highway Patrol woman was wearing sneakers and designer jeans. The badge and her cleavage had been more than enough to keep his attention until it was much too late. The shotgun kept him in line with remarkable efficiency. She had been about to kill him and take his vehicle, but she'd decided to temporarily keep him alive. The police were currently looking for a lone female in a highway patrol cruiser, not a happy young couple going camping in a Jeep.

Pete Vanden had another advantage in his temporary survival. He was an avid four-wheeler, and he was very familiar with the desert around the border. He and his friends loved driving their Jeeps through the rugged terrain, and he was now taking her toward the border using the scenic route. Hochrein consulted the map spread across her knees. They had left State Highway 86, and they should be very near the Mexican border, somewhere in the desert east of the border town of Sasabe. The actual border between the two countries was very close. She slipped a hand into her bag and pulled out her radio.

"I am almost to the border."

A man's voice spoke. "Do you see any active pursuit?"

Hochrein scanned behind her. "No, not yet, but I have left the main roads and am proceeding cross-country."

"Where are you?"

"Somewhere east of Sasabe."

There was a momentary pause. "Head southwest. It will bring you across the border faster. According to my sources, state and federal authorities are scrambling to close the border."

"What if I encounter resistance?"

"You are nearly to the border. Stop for nothing. I believe you will make it across safely."

"What if the Americans follow in hot pursuit?"

"I have taken steps to prevent that."

"What if they pursue me anyway?"

The man's voice was coldly reassuring. "I have taken steps against that, as well."

Sonoran Desert

THE HUGHES 500 helicopter swept across the Sonoran Desert. Outwardly the nimble little helicopter looked like little more than a commercial traffic and weather helicopter. Within its compact interior the egg-shaped bird bristled with military electronics.

Grimaldi took the chopper across the mesas and red plains in a long, arcing search pattern that straddled the border of the United States and Mexico. Bolan half stood in the copilot's seat. The door on his side of the fuselage had been removed, and he kept one boot on the landing skid as he leaned out of the cockpit on his chicken straps. With one hand he swept the desert below with a pair of laser range-finding binoculars. His other hand rested on the pistol grip of a 7.62 mm M-60 light machine gun that also hung from a precarious chicken sling. The Executioner turned his gaze south, and his eyes narrowed as he saw a faint rooster tail of red dust rising up several miles away across the border.

"Contact."

"Dammit! They beat us. That's Mexican soil."

Bolan nodded and dropped the binoculars on their neck strap and spoke into his satellite com link. "The quarry has made it across the border. I'm requesting official permission now for hot pursuit."

Barbara Price sounded extremely perturbed. "Striker, be advised that permission to pursue suspect across border onto Mexican soil has been denied. The Mexican authorities say they will apprehend the suspect."

Bolan's lips skinned back from his teeth. Someone in power across the border had been paid off. "We're going in."

"Understood." Price's voice tightened slightly. "Be advised you and your actions may be denied if you are captured or killed."

The Executioner almost smiled. It was the story of his life. "Understood." He turned to Grimaldi. "All right, let's take her."

The Stony Man pilot grinned and banked the helicopter sharply to the south in reply. The Hughes's turbocharged engine roared as Grimaldi shoved the throttles forward and swiftly began to close the gap. Bolan raised his binoculars, and the dust tail resolved itself. He could make out a Jeep that was tearing across a flat patch of desert at high speed. A half a mile ahead of the speeding vehicle stood the brown-and-red rock walls of table land cut by arroyos and small canyons.

"They're running for the rocks."

Grimaldi's grin stayed fixed as he took the helicopter's Allison engine to full emergency war power. "They're not going to make it."

Bolan dropped his binoculars again and racked the bolt of the M-60. The light machine gun was loaded with a 200-round belt of alternating 7.62 mm armor-piercing and incendiary-tracer ammunition. The helicopter swooped down upon the speeding Jeep in a long shallow dive.

Grimaldi suddenly frowned. "Heads up, Striker!"

A figure leaned out of the Jeep's window, and short, fiery red hair swept around the figure's head as it twisted and

pointed a shotgun into the air. Grimaldi banked the helicopter
slightly as smoke puffed from the shotgun's muzzle and the
woman's head and shoulders jerked from the recoil.

Bolan flipped up the aerial ring sight and peered through
the crosshairs. "All right, let's put one across her bow."

Grimaldi kept the helicopter on the driver's side of the Jeep
and steadily accelerated forward as Bolan squeezed the M-60's
trigger. The light machine gun shuddered against his shoulder
as a stream of smoking lines flew toward the desert below.
Eruptions of red sand and dust suddenly fountained up and
marched diagonally across the Jeep's path. The vehicle
plunged onward without slowing.

Bolan frowned as the red rocks ahead drew steadily closer.
"Drop it right in front of them. We'll give her one more
chance to be reasonable."

Grimaldi pulled the helicopter a few hundred yards ahead
and suddenly spun the chopper on her axis. Bolan's stomach
lightened as the pilot dropped the bird like a stone and left it
hovering a few yards above the sand. Bolan leaned out fully
on his straps and raised the M-60 to his shoulder. He put the
crosshairs squarely onto the windshield of the speeding
vehicle.

Dust flew up in ragged clouds as the Jeep fishtailed to a
halt fifty yards from the helicopter.

For a moment nothing moved except for the dust devils and
debris thrown up by the helicopter's rotor wash. After a few
seconds a shotgun sailed out of the passenger's window and
fell to the sand. Grimaldi smiled. "You want to take them on
board or turn them around and— Dammit!"

The upper windshield of the helicopter suddenly spiderwebbed with cracks on the pilot's side. Grimaldi snarled and gave
the engine power. "We're taking hits! From the rocks!"

The Stony Man pilot surged the helicopter up into the air
and spun it about. Bolan tracked the muzzle of the M-60 into
the rocks. Yellow flashes of flame seemed to point straight at
him, and there was a sound like hail as bullets struck the hel-

icopter fuselage. Three men were in a crevice in the rocks firing automatic rifles. Bolan swung the crosshairs onto the position and held down the M-60's trigger in several long rattling bursts. Two of the men fell down across their weapons. The third dived down out of sight.

The helicopter continued to take hits. Bolan shouted above the rotor noise and muzzle-blast of his weapon as he swung his sights onto a lone gunman and cut him down. "Take us out of range!"

The engine roared as Grimaldi took the engine to full power. The helicopter streaked forward over the rocks as he tried to put the twisting canyon walls between them and their ambushers. Bolan leaned out and sent burst after burst behind them. "Jack," the Executioner suddenly shouted, "missile at four o'clock!"

Grimaldi yanked the joystick savagely and dived toward the jagged spires of rock. A long thin javelin of steel rose up at them trailing gray smoke from its rocket motor. The helicopter continued to fall toward the rocks. Bolan watched as the missile streaked at them with deadly determination. Grimaldi had already dropped the helicopter as low as they could get. Even as he jinked from side to side inches above the rocks, the missile corrected unerringly. Bolan swung back inside the cockpit.

"We're going to get hit."

Grimaldi didn't answer. Bolan's stomach lurched as his old friend turned the helicopter hard over. It was all a matter of angle now, and the Stony Man pilot was betting he could turn tighter than the missile could. Bolan held on to the fuselage frame as Grimaldi nearly yanked the helicopter sideways to the ground.

The missile detonated, and the helicopter shuddered and skewed through the air. Grimaldi's face was a mask of rage as alarms chimed and warning lights blinked on his instrument panel. "We're hit!"

The engine screamed as Grimaldi put his throttles all the

way forward. Smoke started to fill the cockpit, and the helicopter yawed drunkenly from side to side through the air. Even as the engine screamed louder and louder, Bolan could feel them losing power.

They were going down.

"Brace yourself!" Grimaldi throttled back and dipped the nose toward the top of a mesa ahead of them. The engine gave a final howl, and something snapped and began to bounce around in the engine compartment above their heads. Grimaldi cut power and yanked back on the joystick as they began to pass over the top of the mesa. The nose of the helicopter rose as he yanked the bird into a stall. The lip of the mesa was approaching with frightening speed. The helicopter skipped as one of its skids shrieked off the rock of the mesa, then it began to belly forward onto the rock. They skidded another fifteen yards, then ground to a halt in a cloud of smoke and dust. Bolan found himself staring out into a fifty-foot gorge that dropped away a few yards beyond the helicopter's nose.

Grimaldi smiled shakily. "I knew we should have had a gunship for this job."

Bolan shrugged out of his straps. The enemy had access to surface-to-air missiles. "What do you think it was?"

The pilot unstrapped and pulled a nylon flight bag from beneath his feet. "Had to have been something Russian. An SA-7 probably. If it had been a Stinger, we would have been toast." He peered into the dry red gorge below them. "What do you think?"

Bolan reached behind him and pulled his .378 Magnum Weatherby rifle out of its case. "I think we should expect company."

10

"The pursuing helicopter has been shot down. Listen to me. I believe the American commando was on board."

The man in the dark suit sat up in his chair and spoke into the radio. "You are sure of this?"

Heidi Hochrein's voice was smug over the receiver. "I cannot tell you with absolute certainty. He was in a helicopter, and dust flew everywhere. But I tell you, I felt it in my guts as I stared at the man behind the machine gun. I swear it was him."

"The helicopter was destroyed?"

"It was badly damaged." Hochrein's voice grew heavy with excitement. "It was seen by the missile team crash-landing about a mile and a half away on top of a mesa. I strongly suspect the commando and the pilot are still alive."

The man in the dark suit considered this piece of news for long moments. "Return to me at once."

"What of the American?"

The man allowed himself a small smile. "Listen to me. You are far too important to this operation to endanger yourself in a desert hunt for vengeance and self-gratification. However, I agree with you. This is far too valuable an opportunity to waste. The commando and his pilot are in the desert and illegally on the wrong side of the border. I know for a fact that the local Mexican authorities did not give them permission to continue across the border in hot pursuit. I believe at least temporarily they are on their own. Their only hope is to quickly try to make it back across the border. I have spent money well with the local authorities, and I have been assured that no Mexican law enforcement or military personnel will be allowed onto the scene for the next forty-eight hours.

"This is what I want you to do. Take one man as a driver and return here to me at once. Have the rest of the men go quickly to the crash site. If the Americans are injured or dead, take them prisoner. If they are on foot, have the men stay at the crash site. I will dispatch a backup team by helicopter and a qualified man to lead the hunt with them. I will have them there in fifteen minutes. Then we will hunt down these two Americans, and we will find out how they have continued to trail us. Failing capture, they will simply be killed."

MACK BOLAN STARED at the helicopter. A ragged, gaping hole had been torn in the top of the fuselage almost directly behind the engine. The left skid had crumpled on impact, and much of the helicopter's skin to the rear was riddled with holes.

Bolan turned his attention to their meager supplies. They had two half-gallon canteens of water, a couple of energy bars, a coil of rappeling rope, a flashlight, the binoculars and a first-aid kit. Bolan had the .378 Magnum Weatherby sniper rifle along with his Beretta 93-R pistol, snub-nosed revolver and fighting knife. Grimaldi had his silenced MAC-10 submachine gun in his hip holster and, with the M-60 across his shoulder and two belts of ammunition crisscrossed over his chest, he looked like some grinning, latter-day Italian Pancho Villa.

Bolan pulled a black baseball cap over his brow and glanced across the mesa. It had taken only moments to strip the helicopter of everything useful and strap it on their backs, but he knew the enemy was already well on its way. He held up the handheld radio and clicked it on, frowning as he was greeted by a burst of static.

They were being jammed locally across all frequencies.

He clicked off the radio and clipped it to his web gear. Both he and Grimaldi turned at the sound of a distant shout. About six hundred yards away a figure appeared on an outcropping. Bolan unslung his rifle. "I think it's about time to leave."

In answer a short pattern of bullets smashed into the stricken helicopter's fuselage ten yards to his right. A second later the report of the supersonic bullets rattled dimly across the landscape. Bolan knelt and brought the scope-sighted Weatherby rifle to his shoulder. His assailant suddenly leaped into crystal clarity in the crosshairs of the weapon's ten-power telescopic sight. The man appeared to be a Hispanic male in khaki outdoor wear, standing with an M-16 rifle to his shoulder. Bolan frowned as the assault rifle shuddered in the man's hands again. Six hundred yards with an M-16 wasn't a winning proposition. The man might well be a professional killer, but he wasn't a trained marksman. The Executioner corrected for the slight easterly wind blowing across the top of the mesa and fired.

The big Weatherby shoved back hard against Bolan's shoulder in recoil, and the thunder of its report rolled across the red rock walls. He brought his scope back down just in time to see the man swatted off his outcropping as if by a giant invisible fist.

Bolan scanned the rocks for a moment, but no more targets presented themselves. "Are we ready?"

Grimaldi had finished tying the rope to the helicopter's skid, and he gave the rope a hard tug. "We're ready."

The soldier slung his rifle and put a steadying hand on the rope. "Go ahead."

The pilot slung the M-60 machine gun over his shoulder and grabbed the rope in his gloved hands. He stepped off of the lip of the mesa and began to walk down the stone wall to the red sand below. Bolan glanced upward as he detected a rhythmic thumping in the air. "Jack?"

Grimaldi tilted up his head and squinted from his position on the rock face. "What can I do for you?"

"Step on it. Company's coming."

The pilot began to fling himself down the rope hand over

hand. Bolan stretched his gaze out over the rugged tableland. A pair of helicopters was coming in low and fast from the south. Their own ruined helicopter was a crumpled white heap on top of the flat mesa, and thin plumes of black smoke rose up from the blackened hole where the missile had struck it. Even from twenty miles away, it would have taken a blind man to miss them, and the two helicopters were making a beeline directly toward Bolan and Grimaldi's position.

The rope suddenly went slack in Bolan's grip and Grimaldi shouted from the arroyo floor. "Clear!"

Swinging out on the rope as the noise of the approaching helicopters went from a drone to a beating thunder, Bolan swiftly went down hand over hand. Within seconds thumping gusts of wind blew through the arroyo. The soldier squinted up even as his hands and feet kept moving. A helicopter was hovering almost directly overhead, and a man with a rifle leaned out and looked at Bolan through dark sunglasses.

The thumping of the helicopter was suddenly matched by the ripping snarl of automatic fire. Grimaldi stood wide legged in the bottom of the arroyo, and the M-60 thundered in his hands. Sparks shrieked off the helicopter's belly, and the aircraft suddenly dipped its nose and yawed out of sight back over the mesa.

Bolan's feet crunched onto the sand, and he let go of the rope. The sound of the helicopters didn't fade, but both aircraft carefully stayed out of view of the arroyo. Bolan knew they would be landing men on top of the mesa, and they would probably leapfrog men to other positions, as well.

Grimaldi grinned and stood up out of his firing stance. "Are we out of here?"

The Executioner glanced up and down the arroyo. Fifty yards north it choked into rubble and jagged cliffs. To the south it wound onward out of sight. Bolan unslung the Weatherby. "Let's do distance."

RYUCHI TAIDO PEERED at the fallen helicopter critically. The Hughes 500 was a small bird. A hit from an SA-7 shoulder-launched surface to air missile should have sent it tumbling and burning across the rocks. The little man grunted. The pilot had to have been very skilled. He scooped up a spent brass shell casing that sparkled in the sun. The empty case was over three inches long, and Taido's eyes widened slightly as he read the stamped lettering that circled the spent primer: .378 Magnum Weatherby. Taido grunted again. He was extremely familiar with firearms, and he knew the .378 Magnum cartridge was a long-range, flat-shooting round that was powerful enough to stop the biggest game in Africa. It had certainly stopped Gustavo. The Mexican gunman who had first spotted the downed Americans lay six hundred yards back in a crumpled heap at the bottom of a wash. He had been dead long before he hit the ground.

Taido squatted on his heels and squinted up at the sun. Not much over five feet tall, he had the build of an orangutan. The muscles of his arms and shoulders were out of all proportion to his diminutive size and the surprisingly full short beard and mustache made him look like some bizarre Buddha when he smiled. His skin was currently browned a beautiful dark copper by the sun, and if he wore sunglasses, he could easily pass for a Mexican. He sat on his heels and regarded the sun.

The heat was rising by the minute as it arced across the sky toward noon. His two helicopters sat back at the opposite end of the mesa with their rotors slowly threshing. One was dripping oil from where a bullet had penetrated the cabin floor and hit the engine compartment. The helicopter was still functional, but its loitering time in the heat of the desert had probably been cut by half. Taido shook his head. Two men, on foot, in the desert, it really shouldn't be difficult. But these two men seemed to be armed with a high-powered rifle and a light machine gun. It was within the realm of possibility that they could shoot down one or both of the helicopters. Taido shook his head again. He had absolute faith in his ability to hunt down these two men and kill them. Of that there was no question. That was why he had been given this assignment.

But he knew in his bones he was going to take casualties.

Taido raised his finger and spun it in a circle around his head. "All right! Gather around! *¡Juntarce! ¡Andale!*"

Armed men gathered around Taido and looked down at him expectantly. Taido's usual sphere of operations was the Pacific Rim, and he spoke his Spanish with the Filipino accent he had learned. The Mexicans understood it well enough, and the Russian, former East German and South Africans who had been chosen for local security for the Mexican end of the operation all spoke English fluently.

Taido ran his eye around the circle of killers. He had a total of twenty-four men, not including the two helicopter crews. The Americans had killed five of their ambushers from the helicopter, then taken out Gustavo at long distance. Still, they were only two men, and they were outnumbered and outgunned.

The Japanese jerked his head toward the edge of the mesa. "The Americans went south. It was the only way they could go down the arroyo. They will try for the border. But to do that, sooner or later they must leave the canyons and break out into the open desert. They will probably try to hide and do this at night."

The men nodded and Taido continued. "We have night-vision equipment, but it is a chance I do not wish to take. You will split into teams and follow their trail. I will coordinate you from the air. We will drive them from cover, and then pin them down."

A number of the men looked at one another. The men from the helicopter were all too aware that the Americans had a machine gun. They all knew about the fate of Gustavo. Taido decided it was time to instill some confidence.

He folded his arms. "We have been ordered to try to take them alive."

This was met with a good deal of grumbling and stony

grimaces. Taido shrugged uncaringly. "Our number-one order is to keep them from getting back across the border. To ensure this end, I have brought along some extra equipment."

This met with nods of approval. Many of the men had seen the crates in the helicopter. Taido glanced upward, and the men followed his gaze. "We have over eight hours of daylight left. I want the Americans in our hands by then, and I want at least one of them alive, if possible." His grin grew almost inhumanly wide. "I will pay a twenty-thousand-dollar bonus each to the men that bring me the Americans, bloody, broken and ready to talk."

11

Bolan and Grimaldi crouched beneath a shelf of rock as a helicopter hovered over the crevasse. The helicopter's rotor wash and noise was channeled down the narrow defile and turned it into a wind tunnel of flying sand and small debris. Grimaldi squinted against the flying dust and shouted over the noise. "You know that they're ahead of and behind us now!"

The Executioner cocked an eyebrow at his old friend. Grimaldi shrugged as the helicopter slowly moved away and the storm abated. "Yeah, well, I figured you did."

Bolan gazed upward. The helicopter was moving off east of their position, but he could hear the second aircraft's rotors beating the air somewhere off to the west. The helicopters were flying roughly parallel, and slowly moving north. The ground teams couldn't be far behind. The helicopters were a double problem. Not only did they give the enemy two pairs of eyes in the sky, but their noise also hid the sound made by the teams searching the ground. They were playing a deadly game of hide-and-seek, and with their movement masked by the chopper, the advancing hardmen had an edge. It was very likely that sooner or later one of the ground teams would simply blunder across them by surprise. Once a real firefight was engaged, the enemy would quickly pin them down on all sides and then pile on. Bolan let out a long slow breath.

There was really very little choice. They had to take out the helicopters.

Bolan glanced at the Stony Man pilot. "Jack."

"Yeah?"

"Want to shoot down a helicopter?"

"Sure."

The soldier turned his gaze to the wall of rock before them. It was definitely scalable, and if memory served, there was a long flat stretch of table rock on top of it. "I'm going to climb up there and attract some attention. When I have it, I want you to pop up and dump a belt from the M-60 into them. I'm figuring if we can down one of the choppers, the other one will rush in, bug out or stay out of range and, with luck, out of our way so that we can make a go out of bugging out ourselves."

Grimaldi smiled. He loved a nice simple plan. "Can do." His eyes suddenly narrowed slightly in thought. "Of course, you know if they have any kind of heavy weapons, they're probably going to blow us to hell."

Bolan nodded agreeably. "Yeah, but either way it gets us out of the desert."

THE RADIO CRACKLED in Ryuchi Taido's ear, and a voice spoke in rapid Russian-accented English. "We have contact! The enemy has split up! One has gone to the high ground! We are attacking!"

Taido swung his binoculars to the east. The other helicopter had dipped its nose and was rapidly diving toward a stretch of mesa. Taido swept the mesa top with his field glasses and saw an armed figure running at a full sprint across the rock. The figure suddenly stopped and whirled, swung a large rifle up to its shoulder and sighted at the helicopter.

The pilot was ex–Russian airborne, and he skillfully jinked the Huey from side to side as he continued to close on his quarry. Both of the Huey's doors were open, and each was filled with a door gunner armed with a Russian-made RPK light machine gun, as well as a pair of riflemen with scope-sighted rifles.

Taido shouted at his own pilot. "Close in!"

The Huey dipped its nose and began to dive toward the lopsided battle. The American was an expert shot, and Taido could see sparks fly from the other Huey. But the helicopter weaved and dived expertly as it bored in, and the American couldn't accurately put a shot into the engine compartment or the pilot, nor could he lay down fast enough fire with his hand-operated, bolt-action rifle. The American had been caught out in the open, and in a moment he would be in range of the Huey's door guns. He would be cut to pieces. Taido grimaced. The man should never have left his machine gunner. Perhaps the Americans had hoped that by splitting up one of them might stand a better chance of getting through, but even then it was a fool's gambit. In fact—

Taido bolted upright and shouted into his radio desperately. "Pull back! It is a trap! Stay out of range and keep the American in sight! Do not close!"

He snarled with wordless rage as chattering yellow fire erupted from the edge of the mesa and the other Huey flew head-on into the stream of red tracers. Sparks flew from the fuselage, and the windshield spiderwebbed and cracked from hit after hit. The pilot tried to swerve his aircraft away, but the range was too close. Machine-gun fire tore into the cockpit, then walked broadside across his helicopter's fuselage as it banked.

Taido grabbed his seat as his own helicopter swerved. A bullet hole had appeared in the windshield. He raised his field glasses, and in their view it looked like the American was pointing his scope-sighted rifle directly between his eyes. Taido roared at the top of his lungs. "Pull back! Yuri! Nikolai! Lay down suppressive fire!"

The door gunners opened fire. The range was too long for accurate shooting with the RPK machine guns, but their bullets raked the rock near their target in a storm of green tracers. The American broke from his firing stance and ran again for the lip of the mesa.

The pilot of the other Huey was screaming in Russian across

the radio. Smoke trailed from their engine compartment, and the entire left side of the fuselage was drilled with bullet holes. Taido watched helplessly as the helicopter spun out of control and piled sideways into the wall of the crevasse. The helicopter's fuselage crumpled into the red rock, and its rotor blades flew off into the air like giant scythes as the rotor hub broke. Orange fire squirted out of the dying chopper, then shot out in streamers as the fuel tank ruptured and burned. The flaming hulk fell down into the crevasse trailing fire and black smoke as it slipped from sight.

Taido was wordless with rage. He swept the top of the mesa with his binoculars. The Americans had disappeared back into the labyrinth of rock. He grasped his radio and his voice was deadly cold. "Attention. Your orders have been changed. Do not attempt to take the Americans alive. They are too dangerous. Track them down, corner them and then kill them."

BOLAN PERCHED on an outcropping and peered down the Weatherby's ten-power scope. A group of men was examining the wreckage of the downed Huey. There wasn't much left of it. Grimaldi's mixed load of armor-piercing and incendiary tracers had torn the aircraft's vitals apart and set them on fire. Bolan doubted anyone had escaped the crash alive.

"How are we doing on ammo?"

The Stony Man pilot held up his left hand, which was supporting the M-60's ammo belt. There couldn't have been more than fifty rounds left, if that. A few bursts and they would lose one of their main edges. Bolan had only twenty rounds left for the Weatherby. For a sniper, that was a lot of shots. But there were still many hours left in the day, and they remained heavily outnumbered. The Executioner considered their options.

Grimaldi watched the big guy expectantly. "What do you think?"

Bolan looked at his watch, then up into the sky. "It's not

quite three now, and we won't have true dark until after eight.''

"Five hours. You think we can hole up or keep playing tag for that long?''

Bolan nodded. "It's possible, but I wouldn't bet my life on it.''

Grimaldi raised an eyebrow. "But we are betting our lives on it.''

A ghost of a smile crossed Bolan's face. "If present trends continue.''

"So what are you thinking?''

"They know we're trying to head north. As long as we do that, sooner or later we're going to run into the opposition. Even if we manage to break out, we have to cross several miles of open desert to get to the border.''

Grimaldi shrugged. The big guy's take on the situation was about as grim as his own. "So?''

"So, we were denied hot pursuit by the local Mexican authorities, which I'm betting means someone got paid. If the bad guys are smart, which they are, they'll have people along the border, and at least some of them will have some kind of official status. That means that no one on our side can come across now without starting an international incident. I'll bet whoever they have along the border will also have orders to shoot any two Americans they see ambling out of the desert on their side of the border.''

"Sounds about right.''

Bolan glanced off to the east. "So, the bad guys got here pretty fast, don't you think?''

Grimaldi chewed his lower lip. "I'd say about fifteen minutes after we crashed.''

"Pretty fast.''

"Pretty damn fast if you ask me.''

"I'm thinking the enemy has to have a base somewhere very close by.''

"You want to go pay them a visit?"

Bolan shrugged. "You got anything better to do?"

THE MAN IN THE DARK SUIT smiled as Heidi Hochrein entered the room. Her smile was predatory, and she was practically glowing. "Is he dead yet?"

"No." The man restrained a frown and shook his head. "He is not."

The woman's face fell into a stony mask. "How is this possible? You said you were sending in helicopters."

The man peered out the window. "He shot down one of the helicopters."

Her mind flew back to Africa and how the commando had taken one of their aircraft across the Ugandan border into Congo. "He's escaped? Again?"

"No, the helicopter is a burned out wreck at the bottom of a crevasse. He and his pilot are still on foot among the rocks. I suspect they are still trying to thread their way past our ground patrols, or more likely they have holed up and are waiting for darkness to make their break for the border."

"What do you intend to do about it?"

The man's eyes continued to look out into the blue desert sky. "Ideally the helicopter will spot them, or one of the ground teams will make contact and capture or kill them."

Hochrein's face remained cold. "Or?"

"Or I have men along the border, uniformed men, with dogs and night-vision equipment. I have purchased another helicopter, and by nightfall both it and the one currently deployed will patrol the open desert between the mesas and the border. The Americans will not be able to hide out in the open ground. Either way I expect them dead or captured by morning."

The woman considered the information for several long moments. Her face remained a cold mask as she spoke. "Listen to me. I have had dealings with this American commando before. I do not trust him to do what we expect him to do."

An almost imperceptible line formed between the man's eyebrows. "I understand this, and I have faith in your instincts. But I believe in these circumstances, the Americans' options are extremely limited. We have jammed local radio. They cannot communicate to the outside. With the border sealed by uniformed Mexican authorities, their handlers do not dare try to send any kind of aid to them. They have no more food or water than they took from the wreck of their own helicopter. They must get across the border if they are to survive. Even if they realize how futile their situation is, they must still try. I do not believe that they consider surrendering an option.''

Hochrein folded her arms across her chest. ''I still do not trust him.''

12

"There." The Executioner trained his scope on the tiny cluster of dim lights a mile and a half to the west. "That looks like a town to me."

"It looks more like a village to me," he said as he lowered his binoculars. "You know, the bad guys have got to be onto this place."

"I'd bet the bad guys own the place." Bolan continued to run his scope up and down, scanning the village. It was little more than a collection of adobe buildings and wood-and-tin shacks huddling closely on either side of a narrow, badly paved road that ran through it and wound south. Other than lights in a few windows and over a few doors, the village was in darkness save for the early-evening stars. One low, rambling adobe building was slightly better lit and had a pair of Jeeps and an ancient Ford pickup truck parked outside. "That looks like a cantina."

"Want to go check it out?"

Bolan yawned and stretched. It had been a long day of running and crouching. "I could go for a beer."

The two of them stayed off of the dirt road as they moved quietly through the darkness toward the village. Miles to the north, the sound of rotor blades was a dim drone in the air as the enemy's helicopters swept the open desert along the border.

Grimaldi turned to Bolan as the village grew closer. "So, we just go in, bold as brass?"

The Executioner shrugged. "Why not?" He slung his rifle as they passed a cow's skull that sat by the side of the road into town. "Ditch the 60. It's too big to be walking around with."

Grimaldi sighed, and Bolan couldn't quite tell if it was with sadness or relief. The term "light machine gun" was somewhat relative for something that weighed twenty-three pounds, and the pilot had been carrying the belt-fed weapon all day. He unfolded the bipod and set the weapon carefully in a dry ditch. He dusted off his hands, and the two of them walked down the main street toward the cantina. Bolan drew his Beretta 93-R and pulled its suppressor tube from a pouch in his web gear. He screwed it onto the end of the barrel while Grimaldi drew his silenced MAC-10 submachine gun from his hip holster and checked the action.

A scrawny dog growled low at them as they approached the cantina, but the hound backed away as they marched straight on. The few windows were small and set high in the walls, and Bolan went silently down the tiny side alley and paused halfway. There was a radio playing Spanish music, and voices drifted out of the window. The soldier nodded to himself. Some were speaking in Spanish, but the voices nearest the window were speaking Russian. He couldn't understand all of the words, but mostly the two men speaking were complaining about working conditions. Bolan jerked his head at Grimaldi, and they moved toward the front door of the cantina. The Executioner opened the wooden door and stepped in.

The interior was lit by a few bulbs in the ceiling, which were augmented by several lanterns and candles. The ceiling was low, and cigarette smoke hung in a blue pall around the lights. Battered wooden chairs sat around a pair of ancient round tables. Bolan noted several newer tables made from sawhorses and fresh planking in the middle of the room. Apparently the establishment had seen a surge in patronage, and the Executioner could guess why. A bar dominated the back wall, where several Mexican men sat drinking beer, and another group of four sat at one of the new tables drinking and talking among themselves. The men at the table appeared to be Mexicans, but they were wearing pistols openly, and an Uzi submachine gun lay on the table among the beer bottles. At the table under the window, three Caucasian men in khaki pants and denim shirts sat drinking tequila.

Every head in the room turned to look at Bolan and Grimaldi. The Executioner gave the entire room a vague wave and strode up to the bar. "Cerveza, *por favor.*"

The bartender was an immensely fat man with thick reddish brown hair that looked like it had been cut with scissors and a bowl. He looked Bolan and Grimaldi up and down, then nodded. "*Sí, sí.*"

It seemed the bartender was used to armed strangers coming into his establishment. He pulled two sweating bottles of beer out of a cooler and poured them into mugs. Bolan turned to Grimaldi and spoke out loud as he lifted his glass. "*Tovarisch.*" It was an old Russian toast that simply meant "comrade."

Grimaldi grinned. His grasp of Russian was extremely limited, and they both knew that Bolan would have to do all the talking. They also knew that Bolan understood more Russian than he spoke. "*Tovarisch.*"

One of the men at the table by the window spoke up in Russian. "Hey! Where did you two come from?"

Bolan shrugged and hoped his vocabulary wouldn't run out too quickly. "Smolensk."

The man frowned in irritation and shook his head. "No. I mean how did you two come to be here?"

Bolan frowned back. "From Mexico City, where do you think?"

The Russian's frown deepened. "Popov told me nothing of this."

Bolan rolled his eyes and took a sip of his beer. "Popov is a rectum."

The man's eyes widened in shock, but a grin split his face.

"This is true, but because I find myself liking you, I will not tell him you said that."

Bolan nodded seriously. "Thank you, Comrade."

The man shrugged and peered at the big Weatherby rifle strapped to Bolan's back. "Sniper?"

"Yes."

The man nodded and looked at Grimaldi. "How about you?"

Grimaldi smiled at the man as Bolan spoke for him. "He's a pilot."

"Ah." The man nodded. "That is good. I hear we lost a helicopter today with all hands on board."

Bolan looked shocked. "Who has done this thing?"

The man shook his head and made a sour face. "Some kind of American policemen or paramilitary agents, I suspect. However, they are on foot, and we have the border sealed. Our men are hunting them down even as we speak." The Russian leered unpleasantly. "By morning, Popov and I will be carving them like lambs."

The Executioner raised an eyebrow. "Really, where?"

"Well, at the ranch house, of course." The man's frown returned. "Didn't you come from there?"

Bolan thought swiftly as he gave a shrug. "No, we drove in."

"Drove in?" The Russian shook his head incredulously. "From where?"

The Executioner consulted his mental map of the border. "Sasabe. We flew in from Mexico City, but then our helicopter was diverted. Some sort of an emergency." Bolan took another sip of his beer. "It must have been your Americans."

The man nodded, but his eyes stayed on Bolan. The Executioner set down his beer. "Where is Popov? It has been a long drive, and we were told to report in upon our arrival."

The Russian shook his head at Bolan again. "He is at the ranch house, of course."

Bolan sighed tiredly. "The road leads there?"

"There is no road. Just the Jeep trail east of town. It is dangerous to drive at night." The Russian looked at Bolan in irritation. "Who briefed you?"

The Executioner looked irritated back. "Popov."

The man scowled. "When?"

"Yesterday."

The Russian blinked. "Yesterday?"

The Mexicans watched the exchange between them with keen interest. They clearly didn't understand the words, but they could tell something wasn't quite right. Bolan knew the situation was deteriorating rapidly.

One of the other Russians stared at Bolan long and hard and spoke quietly. "Their story must be checked, Danilov."

The man named Danilov nodded. "Put your rifle down and have a seat, I am sure we can clear this up with a—"

The Executioner drew his 9 mm Beretta and fired. Danilov sagged backward with a bullet through his forehead. Grimaldi's MAC-10 gave a long whispering hiss, and the Russian's two comrades collapsed as they clawed for their weapons.

Bolan held the Beretta with both hands and his upper body turned like a gun turret as the men at the other table began to rise and draw pistols. The Beretta coughed quietly, and men fell to the floor. Brass shell casings tinkled to the ground as Grimaldi brought his submachine gun on-line. The four men fell before their weapons could clear leather.

Bolan whirled on the bar. Two gunners had yanked pistols from their belts, and the soldier put two rounds into the closer man's chest. The guy fell back against the bar, his .45 booming once into the ceiling as he fell. The other man twisted as Grimaldi put a burst into him, but he didn't get off a shot.

The sound of the single shot rang in their ears for a moment, then all was deathly silent. Outside, several dogs had started to bark in indignation. Bolan and Grimaldi faced the last two men. One sat at the bar, wide-eyed, with his hands in the air.

The bartender kept his palms flat on the bar and was frozen like a statue.

Bolan kept the Beretta pointed between the bartender's eyes. "You speak any English?"

The man swallowed hard. "Yes."

"What's your name?"

"Rojo."

The seated man nodded and looked at Bolan hopefully. "Because of his hair."

Bolan's eyes narrowed slightly. "Who are you?"

The man flinched as he came under the Executioner's direct scrutiny. "Bustavo." He glanced over at Rojo. "I'm his friend."

"Will the shots attract attention?"

Bustavo glanced at Rojo, who gave a tiny shrug. "Perhaps."

Bolan sighed. "You, Rojo. Go outside. Make a little noise. Let anyone who's looking see that you are all right. If anyone talks to you, tell them that the gringos are playing macho games."

Rojo blinked and nodded. "I will go put a case of beer in one of the Jeeps."

"That's a good idea. I think you and your friend Bustavo are going to get out of this alive."

Rojo smiled back feebly and picked up a crate of beer. Grimaldi followed him as he went to the door.

Bustavo's gaze jumped back and forth between Bolan's eyes and the muzzle of the Beretta machine pistol. He didn't seem very comfortable looking into either one. "You are not going to kill us?"

Bolan regarded the man honestly. "That depends on you."

Bustavo mulled over Bolan's statement for several long moments. "I would like to cooperate in any way I can."

"You know the area well?"

"I've lived here all my life."

"Have you been up to the ranch house?"

Bustavo frowned. "Not since the foreigner bought it."

"But you know how to get there?"

"Oh, sure. I did some work up there before the Diegos sold it."

"Good." Bolan lowered his pistol and took a seat at the bar.

There was an old rotary phone beside the cash register, and Bolan pulled it up onto the bar top. He began to dial a number while Bustavo watched him warily. Bolan nodded his head at the bar. "Go ahead and finish your beer." The number began to ring, and the Executioner kept the friendly smile on his face. "Then I want you to tell me what you know about this foreigner."

"WHAT DO YOU MEAN you have not found them yet?" The man in the dark suit wasn't pleased. He could hear the sound of the rotor blades behind Ryuchi Taido's voice as he spoke over the secured link.

"There is no sign of them. I kept the men patrolling the rocks until well after dark, then pulled them back to form a picket line in the open desert. I cannot believe they slipped past us during the day, and even if they had, your men along the border would have seen them. I do not believe they have slipped by us in the night, either. All of my teams have night-vision equipment, and Popov sent me two teams of dogs after night fell. Even if they did slip past us, the helicopters have been sweeping the desert around the clock, and you have even more men sealing the border."

The man in the dark suit frowned. "Could he be trying to go around you?"

"That would take days going through the mountains. It is midsummer, and he cannot have more than a canteen or two of water. Those should already be gone. These mountains are little more than rock and dust. I have talked with the local men. If there is any water in the hills during the summer, they do not know about it.

"You believe he is still hiding in the rocks?"

Taido was silent for a moment. "It is the only logical conclusion, but the longer he waits, the worse his situation becomes. Perhaps he is expecting to be rescued."

The man in the dark suit shook his head. "That is unlikely. Even the local authorities I have not paid are angry about the incursion. They know a helicopter came across the border, and the United States authorities are denying that they authorized pursuit. I do not believe they will risk another incursion."

Taido's voice became grim. "What if the American authorities tell the American government that they suspect our operation is somewhere in this area along with what they suspect we are doing?"

"I do not believe that will be a problem."

Taido's voice turned curious. "How so, if I may ask?"

The man in the dark suit turned and looked with pleasure at Heidi Hochrein as she lay on the bed and smiled up at him. "I have sent certain communications to the United States government."

"What did you tell them?"

"I told them if they tell the Mexican government what they suspect, or try to take any kind of action against us, there will be ten outbreaks of Ebola in ten different states in the Union. I gave them the location of Heidi's second victim, Vernon Richmond, as proof. I also told them I am considering informing their media of the impending biological crisis in the United States."

The man in the dark suit could tell that Taido was smiling. "Did you receive any kind of response?"

"Not directly. It was a one-way communication. However, their police forces have withdrawn from this area of the border. I believe there is a great deal of hand-wringing and argument going on in Washington, D.C. I believe they will sit on their hands for days before they try something."

"What do you wish me to do?" Taido asked.

"Continue the search until morning and kill the Americans

if you can. In the meantime I will evacuate from this base of operations. It is time for us to move. It is dangerous for us if the American authorities have any idea at all where we may be located. We cannot have them getting too desperate and nuking the area in hopes of stopping us.''

"Very well. I will continue the search, and I will report as soon as we make contact. Taido out."

The man in the dark suit looked down at Hochrein again. She smiled back up at him. "Where are we to go now?"

The man in the dark suit smiled, and his expression matched her own. "Among them."

13

The Jeep ground along on the old trail that led to the ranch house. A small searchlight mounted on the edge of the Jeep's hood threw its narrow beam over the rocks and ruts. Across a small sea of darkness Bolan could see the lights of the ranch house ahead. He knew if anyone was watching, they would see the Jeep's lights, as well. He was betting that no one would be expecting an attack from this direction, much less the attackers coming straight to the front gate in plain sight.

Rojo and Bustavo had accompanied Bolan and Grimaldi until the lights of the ranch house had been visible from the top of the rocks. The two men were now taking the long walk back to town and seemed grateful to still be alive. Bolan watched the lights of the house slowly grow closer. He had contacted Barbara Price, and she had been very pleased to know he was still alive. Washington was in confusion. They had a local crisis on the border with the Mexicans, and threats of an Ebola epidemic had been made by provocateurs unknown. For the moment the government was sitting on its hands. There could be no rescue attempt for Bolan and Grimaldi currently, so they would have to stay active. Washington suspected that the enemy was moving out. Bolan's orders were simple.

Search and destroy.

A helicopter flew out to the ranch house from the east and stayed for about fifteen minutes as Bolan and Grimaldi clung to the cliffs and approached on the narrow road. The helicopter took off again and flew south without bothering to look them over as they came ahead.

The Jeep came out of the rocks into flat land again, and they quickly closed the distance to the ranch house. The house was an old Spanish-style white-walled adobe, and nearly all of its lights were on. The dirt had been tamped down where the corral had been, and the wooden fencing removed to make a helicopter pad. A little way down the dirt road was a shack, and two armed men stood beside it with M-16 rifles in their hands. Bolan drove up to them and pulled the Jeep to a halt. One of the men shone a flashlight on the vehicle, and the Executioner spoke in Russian.

"Where is Popov?"

One of the men grimaced in the dim light from the shack and spoke to his partner in what sounded like German or Dutch. He turned again and spoke in a heavy accent. "I do not speak Russian. You have any English?"

Bolan affected his best Russian accent. "A little. Where is Popov?"

The man swung his flashlight behind him. "In the ranch house." He set down his flashlight and raised a small handset. "I will contact him and report your presence."

The Executioner shook his head. "Let me pass. I must speak with him immediately. It is about the Americans. It is urgent."

The man looked hard at Bolan and frowned. "I have not seen you before." He scanned Grimaldi critically, as well. "I have not seen him before, either. You will wait here, understand? Tell me the message about the Americans. I will relay it."

"We're here." The Executioner's hand blurred as he drew the silenced Beretta 93-R and double tapped the trigger.

The man grunted as he took two rounds in the chest, then fell backward into his startled partner. The other man tried to bring up his rifle, and his mouth opened to shout as spent shell casings suddenly began to rain inside the Jeep. A long burst from Grimaldi's silenced MAC-10 killed the shout in the man's throat and left him in a tangled heap on the ground with the other sentry.

Bolan and Grimaldi instinctively swung their weapons on the ranch house. The incident had taken less than two seconds and made no more noise than a man smothering a cough. No one in the ranch house seemed to have taken any notice. Grimaldi pointed up into the northern sky, and Bolan tracked his finger. A light was coming out of the north, and the soldier knew it was another helicopter. It would arrive in moments.

The Executioner jerked his head at the fallen sentries, and he and Grimaldi quickly took their M-16s and bandoliers of spare magazines. The pilot slung his M-16 over his shoulder and retrieved the M-60 from the back of the Jeep. Bolan checked the load of the assault rifle, and the two of them approached the ranch house at a trot. The sound of helicopter blades thrummed the air as they came to the heavy wooden door. Grimaldi adjusted the M-60 machine gun on its sling and draped the trailing ammo belt over his left forearm. "How do you want to play it, Mack?"

"By ear." Bolan tried the door and found it was locked. He pounded the butt of the Beretta against the wooden timbers and shouted as the helicopter swung over the ranch house and began its descent to the helicopter pad in the corral. "Open up! Where is Popov?"

Someone inside shouted something in Russian, and Bolan pounded on the door harder. A moment later the heavy lock turned, and the door began to open. The Executioner drove his boot hard into the door, and it and the man behind it flew backward. Bolan leveled the Beretta as he entered the ranch house.

The man who answered the door fell in a sprawl to the tile floor. Two other men were passing by the entryway, carrying a heavy crate between them. For a moment there was no sound but the beat of the descending rotor blades outside. The three men stared down the muzzle of Bolan's pistol. One or two

eyes strayed as Grimaldi entered the ranch house with the
M-60 slung across his hip.

Bolan stared at the man on the floor. "You speak English?"

The man's eyes narrowed. Bolan jerked his head toward the
corral and the landing helicopter. "What is happening?"

The man only gave Bolan a tight-lipped stare. The Executioner took two strides forward and aimed the muzzle of the
Beretta between his eyes. "I won't ask you again."

The man swallowed and spoke with a Russian accent.
"Evacuation."

Bolan turned his gaze to the lead man carrying the crate.
"What's in the crate?"

The man stared back coolly and spoke with a thick German
accent. "Guns."

A voice suddenly roared from deeper in the house. "Why
are you fools standing around? Move!"

The men continued to stare stoically at the muzzles of the
weapons pointed at them. The voice grew louder as it approached. "Damn you! I said move!"

Bolan dropped the Beretta and yanked the Russian up off
the floor. He spun him and jammed the muzzle of his liberated
M-16 rifle into the Russian's back while he held him by the
collar.

Two men came around the corner and nearly slammed into
the men carrying the crate as they stood frozen. The man in
the lead was six feet tall and nearly as wide. His square face
was florid with anger, and he held a pistol in his hand. The
man behind him carried an M-16 rifle. The big man's voice
cut off in surprise as he took in the scene before him.

The Executioner spoke in English. "Drop your weapons, or
we'll kill you."

The big man stared incredulously for a moment and blinked.
"All right. Don't shoot. I will—"

Bolan's hostage shouted in alarm. "Popov! No!"

Popov moved with a liquid speed that belied his massive
bulk. His pistol whipped up as he grabbed one of the men

carrying the crate by the neck and yanked the guy in front of him as a shield.

The Executioner tried to shove his hostage away from himself as Popov fired, but the Russian's bullets tore through his own man's body mercilessly and struck Bolan's body armor. Grimaldi's M-60 ripped into life, and a long burst sent Popov's rifleman shuddering backward against the wall. Bolan whipped his rifle to his shoulder as Popov fired again. A bullet punched into the Executioner's chest, and Popov raised the muzzle of his weapon for a head shot. Bolan dropped his aim between the German hostage's legs and fired.

Popov's shot went high and wide as the round from the M-16 flew between his shield's legs and smashed his own exposed leg out from under him. Bolan put a burst into Popov's chest as he toppled to the side, and the big Russian fell dead to the floor. Bolan strode forward and the German's eyes flew wide and he screamed in terror. "No! Please!"

The Executioner suddenly raised the butt of the M-16 and smashed it across the man's jaw. The German collapsed as if he had been shot. The other man still held one end of the crate. He looked into Bolan's eyes, then squeezed his own eyes shut and gritted his teeth. The butt of the M-16 cracked into his temple, and the man fell heavily.

Bolan took the lead and the men from Stony Man swept through the house. Luck had been with them. The roar of the landing helicopter had covered the sound of the fight in the foyer. They moved down the hall into a wide kitchen area. Through the window over the sink, Bolan could see the helicopter out on the pad and men loading crates on it. He turned his head at the sound of a muffled scream. At one end of the kitchen a lighted doorway led to a cellar stairway. "Don't let that helicopter take off," he told the pilot.

Grimaldi nodded. "You've got it."

Bolan took the stairs two at a time. The cellar was lit by a single electric bulb, and in its center was a young man strapped to a hospital gurney. He was screaming through a gag and violently struggling against his bonds. A man with a rifle slung across his back was pinning one of the young man's arms against the gurney. The prisoner's shirtsleeve had been rolled up, and a second man was carefully prepping a small hypodermic syringe. Both men were wearing surgical gloves.

The Executioner raised his rifle to his shoulder and fired. The head of the man with the syringe snapped back on his neck as the bullet punched into his forehead. The other man released his captive's arm and tried to bring his rifle into play. He staggered backward as Bolan drilled him with a 3-round burst. The man fell sideways onto his partner.

Bolan moved swiftly to the gurney and drew his knife. The young man's eyes went wide as the soldier cut his gag away and stepped back. The young man swallowed and gasped. "You're a good guy?"

He ignored the question. "Have they given you any other injections?"

The man shook his head. "No. They tied me to this table and left me down here all day."

Bolan looked at the floor. The syringe lay on the concrete. Its glass tube was full of a clear yellow fluid. The Executioner had little doubt that the contents of that one syringe was enough to spread out and kill ninety percent of human life on earth. He turned back to the young man. "Who are you?"

"I'm Peter Vanden." Vanden swallowed again and collected himself. He looked at Bolan and shook his head ruefully. "Some crazy bitch with guns hijacked me and my Jeep this morning and brought me here."

Bolan nodded and cut Vanden's restraints. He grabbed the fallen man's rifle and held it out. "Peter, I want you to stay here. This rifle is ready to go. All you have to do is point it and pull the trigger. Shoot anyone who comes down here who isn't me or a guy in a blue flight suit. Got it?"

Things seemed to be moving very fast for Peter Vanden, but he nodded and took the rifle. "I got it."

Grimaldi's voice shouted from the kitchen above. "Mack!"

Bolan raced up the stairs and into the kitchen. "What have you got?"

"Another helicopter landed, and I think they're both about to leave again."

The soldier glanced out the window. A second helicopter had landed and was mostly shielded from view by the other one. Both were keeping their rotor blades turning. Bolan could see the legs of people conferring between them, and more men were clambering aboard both aircraft. The Executioner slipped a fresh magazine into his M-16 and placed it on the counter. He unslung the big .378 Magnum Weatherby and flicked off the safety. "Take them out."

"You got it."

Grimaldi punched the muzzle of the M-60 through the window glass. He took a second to rest its bipod on the windowsill and raise his aim. Bolan brought the Weatherby to his shoulder and put the crosshairs on the first helicopter's cockpit. The M-60 hammered into life, and sparks began to shriek off the first helicopter's fuselage. The men between the two choppers split and dived through the doors of each aircraft. The engines roared as both pilots strove for takeoff power.

The M-60 clacked open on empty, and Grimaldi released the weapon and spun his stolen M-16 rifle on its sling and brought it to his shoulder. Bolan fired the big .378 Weatherby as fast as he could work the bolt. He could see the copilot slumped forward in his seat. Bolan fired the last round in the Weatherby's magazine and dropped the rifle. Grimaldi sprayed an entire magazine on full-auto into the first helicopter as Bolan brought up his own M-16. The second aircraft suddenly rose into the air from behind the first.

Bolan whipped his sights onto the aircraft's engine housing and let loose in long bursts. Sparks flew off metal as the helicopter continued to rise. Grimaldi's weapon ran dry, and he quickly rammed home a fresh magazine. Bolan hurled open the kitchen door and raised his rifle as the helicopter dipped its nose and began to angle south. The M-16 vibrated against his shoulder on full-auto, and almost instantly the magazine was spent. Grimaldi stood and fired beside him as Bolan reloaded and raised his weapon.

The helicopter thundered off into the night as the two men continued to fire. Their rifles ran dry, and even as they reloaded, the helicopter became no more than a set of swiftly receding lights low in the sky.

Bolan sprinted to the remaining helicopter. The aircraft was a commercial Bell JetRanger. It wasn't an armored military aircraft, and the M-60 had taken a terrible toll on it and its occupants. The Executioner jumped into the cockpit and pulled out the pilot's body. The man was still alive, but his shoulder was smashed. Bolan had no time for mercy. He laid the man in the dirt, then jumped back into the helicopter as Grimaldi glanced unhappily at the instrument panel. Bolan shoved the copilot's corpse out and took his seat. "Will she fly?"

Grimaldi shook his head as red warning lights blinked on the shattered flight console like Christmas lights. "Dammit, Mack! We just got through doing a number on this bird, and now you want me to fly it?"

Bolan was implacable. "I said, will she fly?"

The pilot shoved the throttles forward in answer, and the engine made an unnatural howl as the beleaguered helicopter tried to rise. The airframe shuddered as the skids left the ground, and the aircraft vibrated and skewed sideways. Grimaldi's snarl matched the howling of the engine as he pulled back on the joystick and shoved the throttles all the way forward. The helicopter tilted drunkenly with the additional power and yawed toward the ranch house. He yanked all the way back on the joystick. "No go! She's lost it! Hold on!"

The helicopter lurched as one of its rotor blades smashed into the side of the ranch house and snapped off. The aircraft suddenly lost all lift and fell ten feet to the ground with a bone-jarring crunch. The other rotor blade smashed into the dirt and snapped off with a crack, and the copilot's side of the windshield buckled. The helicopter teetered on one skid, then bellied over on its side in what seemed like slow motion.

Grimaldi shook his head to clear it, then reached forward to cut power to the engine. The engine ground to a clattering halt, and for a moment both Bolan and Grimaldi hung in their harnesses. The Stony Man pilot looked at Bolan guiltily. "Well, dammit, I tried." He braced a boot against the flight console and clicked his harness open.

Bolan grunted and unhooked his own harness. He stood up on the crumpled side door beneath him and braced Grimaldi as he lowered himself out of the pilot's seat. The pilot moved forward into the blood-spattered passenger compartment. "We'd better get out of this thing before it catches fire."

The Executioner stopped, turned back and reached up to take a headset off its hook. He plugged it in and was surprised to hear a burst of static out of the earphones. "Jack."

Grimaldi yanked open the side door over his head and turned. "Yeah?"

Bolan turned the radio's frequency dial. "This bird's pilot was still alive a minute ago. Why don't you go ask him nicely what his flight plan was."

"You got it."

14

Heidi Hochrein gave the man in the dark suit an arch glance. "I told you this American could not be trusted to lie down and die for us."

The man looked back at her sourly. Ryuchi Taido sat in his seat and experimentally stuck his little finger out of one of the many bullet holes riddling the fuselage, and wiggled it in the cold air of the jet stream for a moment. He withdrew his finger and turned to the man in the dark suit. "We should have circled back and killed them. We have a light machine gun and an RPG-7 grenade launcher in the aircraft. The other two helicopters searching the desert had door guns and could have joined us within minutes."

The man in the dark suit turned his gaze on Taido until the little man flinched and looked away. The man wasn't used to having his orders questioned, and he didn't intend to get used to it, either. "That would have been a foolish risk. They had a light machine gun. What if we had been shot down? Remember, our mission is what is paramount. So far, in spite of this annoying American and his friends, it is succeeding brilliantly. The American government knows what we have, and it knows we are serious. It now no longer knows where we are, and we will be free to operate as we will. Loitering about the scene and risking the entire operation so you can take a trophy is the kind of foolishness I do not expect from a man with your reputation, Taido."

The little man flinched again as if he had been struck. Taido

prided himself on his abilities as a field operative. Repri-
manding him for his sense of duty and tactics was worse than
any other punishment the man in the dark suit could have
dealt. Hochrein continued to stare at him. Ever since the
American had knocked her unconscious with the butt of his
rifle in the Libyan desert, she had yearned in her flesh and
bones to see the man dead. He had continually thwarted her
best intentions. Now he had done it again. The dark-suited
man knew his inability to kill the American had made her lose
respect for him. The haughty condemning look in her eyes
spoke it loud and clear.

An irrational part of his mind wanted to lash out and beat
the respect back into her, but the man in the dark suit frowned
and reined in his emotions. She would probably only enjoy
making him lose control, and Heidi Hochrein's disapproval
was symptomatic of the problem. His real anger was for himself. The fact was, he had failed to kill the American. Even
with overwhelming numbers, firepower and having the terrain
on his side, he had still failed. The disapproval of the old man
was much more relevant at the moment. Still, what he had told
Taido was true. The mission, despite the remarkable tenacity
the American commando had shown, was running right on
schedule.

The man in the dark suit glanced at his watch as he thought
about schedules. It was about time to make the United States
government aware of his first demand.

MACK BOLAN SPOKE QUICKLY. "I need as many operatives as
you can find, CIA, DEA, anything you can scrape up and get
to the airport in Chihuahua." Bolan checked his watch. "And
I need them there in less than two hours."

"What do we tell our operatives in Chihuahua they're looking for?" Barbara Price asked.

"At least one helicopter, possibly more. It's a commercial
Bell JetRanger, with a white paint job and blue stripes."

"Anything distinguishing about it?"

Bolan ran his eye around the crumpled airframe surrounding him. "It'll have a lot of bullet holes in it."

The sound of rapid typing was audible over the link. "You're sure Chihuahua is their destination? I don't think they'd keep a base of operations in a big city."

"I agree, but one of their pilots here survived our firefight, and Jack talked him into cooperating. The bad guys here were bugging out when we hit them, and the man says his flight plan was for Chihuahua. After that he doesn't know where they were headed. We have to beat them there, or we're going to lose their trail."

"Most U.S. operatives are either in Mexico City or along the United States border, but I'll scramble every warm body the computer can lay its hands on. What else have you got?"

Bolan glanced out of the shattered windshield. Peter Vanden stood outside looking around dazedly at the carnage and holding the M-16 rifle Bolan had given him as if it were his lifeline to reality. Grimaldi had spread out a number of crates and bags he had pulled from the fallen helicopter. "I've got a wounded South African pilot, two unconscious former members of the East German special forces, a kidnapped U.S. citizen and a syringe full of an unknown yellow fluid they had intended to inject him with before leaving." Bolan paused. "It would be good if you could get some people out here. We need to get the syringe to Dr. Thurman, and we need a biological-containment unit to transport it."

"I'll try. But it might take an hour or two to clear the channels with the Mexican government. The President is leery about showing our hand, particularly when we can't be too sure how deeply some of their officials may be involved. They're pretty angry about your little unauthorized incursion." Price paused for a moment. "What do you intend to do?"

"Well, I can't stick around here, and I doubt trying to sneak back across the border would be too clever at the moment."

"You're going to Chihuahua."

"I don't think the bad guys will expect me to try it. They

probably think they've made Mexico too hot for me. It will take me a little time to get there, but it's where the trail leads.''

"I'll arrange to have somebody for you to contact when you get there.''

"Thanks. I'll contact you on arrival. Striker out.''

Grimaldi looked up from his loot as Bolan clambered out of the wrecked helicopter.

"We've got to get out of here,'' Bolan said.

Grimaldi nodded. ''Chihuahua?''

"Yeah, any ideas?''

The pilot frowned. ''Well, I believe it's at least two hundred miles from here, and we've got the Sierra Madres to cross to get there.''

Bolan nodded. ''And?''

Grimaldi held up an aluminum briefcase with several bullet holes in it. He flicked it open with a grin. The case was full of bundled United States hundred-dollar bills. ''I say we drive to the nearest airstrip and buy ourselves the first thing that flies.''

Chihuahua, Mexico

DEA AGENT ANGELICA DIRAZAR nearly bolted upright. "We've got them!''

"What've you got?'' Her partner, Brayden Foot, raised his night-vision binoculars to his eyes and sighted toward where her finger pointed.

The woman grinned triumphantly. She had been quietly boiling with rage ever since she had been pulled out of her undercover operation half an hour earlier and forced to do stakeout duty at the airport. There had been no warning, and no explanation. Her supervisor was the toughest man Dirazar had ever met, but he seemed visibly shaken by whatever he had been told. He hadn't shared. He had just told her to drop everything and get her butt to the airport as soon as possible. Her partner had been waiting there for her under a camouflage blanket with surveillance equipment and a pair of silenced 9 mm Colt submachine guns. They had been given the description of an inbound aircraft and told to observe and track its occupants. Her current sting operation was now probably blown, and Dirazar was angry enough to spit. But like any good field agent, she loved the hunt, and the hunt had just gotten hot.

"So, what do you make of that?"

Foot's grin matched her own as he watched the helicopter land. "I'd say it's a Bell JetRanger, white with a blue stripe."

Dirazar nodded as she noted the ragged line of black dots along its fuselage. "And someone filled it full of holes." She quickly coupled her night-vision telescope to a Canon F-1 35 mm camera loaded with infrared film. Foot's binoculars stayed glued to the chopper.

"They're getting out."

The woman brought the camera to her eye and adjusted the zoom. The helicopter's image smeared for a moment, then appeared in her viewfinder with crystal clarity. Her eyes narrowed as the door opened, and her camera began to click. "I have an Asian male, bearded, approximately five foot one." The little man scanned the surroundings with his right hand staying near his waist. "He's armed."

Foot whistled. "Check out this action."

"Keep it in your pants." Dirazar's camera clicked and wound as an extremely full-figured woman stepped out of the helicopter. "That's the woman who was on the interdepartmental dispatch we got three days ago! I'm sure of it!"

"You think so?" Foot rummaged through his knapsack and pulled out the dispatch. He glanced back and forth between the file photo and the artist's sketch on the dispatch. "Damn, the hair's different, she seems taller than her description, but I think you're right. That's Heidi Hochrein, wanted fugitive."

They watched two large men clamber out of the helicopter with their hands beneath their coats. Foot smiled. "There's the muscle." Another man in a dark suit got out of the helicopter and slowly scanned the area himself. "We've got a Caucasian male, acting like he owns the place."

Dirazar frowned. "No, I'd peg him as a Latino." Her frown deepened. "Maybe Asian."

"You're sure about that?"

The woman's gaze narrowed as she studied the man in her viewfinder. "No, he's..." She shook her head and looked at him again. "He's...he's so nondescript he's almost weird looking."

Foot grunted. "Here comes another chopper."

The second helicopter landed near the first, and men began to spill out. Most of the eight men were large, and to Dirazar's eye they carried themselves like soldiers. "More muscle, I'd bet anything."

"I agree." He scanned his binoculars toward the terminal. "Check this."

A pair of minivans was driving out from the terminal to meet the arriving party. "They're moving." Dirazar shrugged off the camouflage blanket and scooped up her submachine gun. "We'd better get to the car."

15

Washington, D.C.

Hal Brognola sat in the Oval Office across the desk from the President of the United States. The Man wasn't happy. His gaze went through Brognola without seeing him, as if looking deeply into some terrible middle distance that transcended the walls of the room. The big Fed cleared his throat. "Mr. President?"

The President blinked, and the focus of his eyes changed as he came back into the immediate moment. "Hal, we have a problem."

"Yes, Mr. President, we seem to."

A bleak smile passed over the Man's face. "Well, let me clarify that. To be honest, things have gotten worse."

Brognola took a deep breath. "They've made their demands?"

The President leaned back in his chair. "They've made the first of their demands, anyway."

Brognola waited several long, uncomfortable moments for the President to continue. Suddenly the President leaned forward again and gave the big Fed his undivided attention. "Hal, they've demanded that I order the total withdrawal of all United States military forces from Europe and Asia. It poses an interesting problem. If they had just demanded one or the other, it might have given us some clue as to who we are dealing with. If it had been Europe, my staff and I would have been tempted to believe it was the Russian Communist hardliners. There are some of them who are fanatical enough to try something like this. If it had just been Asia, I'm almost certain we could pin it on the Chinese. As it stands now..." The President let out a long breath. "We know nothing more than we did before."

Brognola shifted in his seat. "What do you intend to do?"

The President glanced at a map of the world on his desk. "If we capitulate, there are certain things we can depend on for certain. First of all, North Korea will take our withdrawal as a blank check to invade South Korea, and without U.S. assistance, they will almost certainly succeed."

"You think the North Koreans are behind this?"

"I wouldn't put it past them, but that is purely speculation." The President sighed heavily. "Almost everything we have is purely speculation." He suddenly smiled grimly. "Almost everything we do know we got from your man Striker."

Brognola nodded and the President continued. "I'll tell you what I'm thinking. I read Striker's report after the British affair. He stated he believed the operation was much larger than the IRA. I agree with him. He has also stated in reports from the field that he believes that incident and the current crisis are related. That is a subject of great debate at the moment among my cabinet."

The President's face hardened. "What we know for sure is this. An unknown enemy of the United States is blackmailing us with an epidemic of flulike Ebola. We know that they have it, and they have used it on us in a surgical fashion to let us know that they mean business. I covertly sent a team of Navy SEALs to the ranch house Striker attacked, accompanied by Dr. Thurman. She has examined the sample Striker captured in the ranch house, and has positively identified it as the Ebola Sese strain stolen from the African research station. There's no doubt in my mind whatsoever. Millions of American lives are at stake, not to mention the rest of the world's population."

The President took a long pause. "We also know that the

leading elements of our enemy have been operating out of Mexico, and at the moment we believe that individuals matching their description have been driven south and fallen back to Chihuahua.''

Brognola's skin began to crawl. "And..."

The President's face was stone. "And I'm considering launching a nuclear strike on Mexican soil. Specifically against the city of Chihuahua itself."

The big Fed stared at the President. Chihuahua was one of Mexico's major cities, and the man across the table was considering nuking it. The President stared back. "Hal, I cannot allow an airborne Ebola virus to be released against the United States. For that matter I cannot allow it to be released in Mexico, either. The stakes are just too high."

Brognola cleared his throat. "Yes, but what if they have kept some of their samples out of Mexico as insurance against capture or destruction? Even with a nuke you can't be sure you got it all."

"I've considered that, and it's my hope that even in that eventuality, the United States's demonstrated willingness to use nuclear weapons will act as a sufficient deterrent."

Brognola considered the ramifications, and they were staggering. The President read his thoughts. "Of course, even if I fully explain my actions, the reactions of the rest of the world will haunt us for decades to come. The United States will almost certainly face economic and political sanctions from the UN. The rest of the world, understandably, simply cannot allow the United States to solve its crises by nuking other countries." The President smiled wearily. "And, needless to say, relations between the United States and Mexico will be somewhat strained. I will most likely be impeached, and I'll personally surrender myself to the United Nations and the Mexican authorities where I will undoubtedly be tried for crimes against humanity."

"I assume that since you are telling me this, Mr. President, you're still considering a nuclear strike as a last resort."

The President nodded. "That is correct. However, as we speak, a B-2 stealth bomber armed with cruise missiles is orbiting in Mexican airspace, and those missiles are armed with tactical nuclear warheads." The President's face grew even grimmer. "Those bombers are also carrying high-yield thermonuclear hydrogen weapons, and if for any reason I am convinced that the Ebola virus has been released into the Mexican population, I will be forced to use multiple high-yield weapons in an attempt to sterilize the entire city and the surrounding area. I also have a pair of C-130 Talons, each loaded with a team of Navy SEALs waiting on standby at the border. They are all volunteers, and have been informed that if the situation changes, I may be forced to launch the nuclear weapons without regard for their safety. However, I consider using them as a second-to-last resort."

Brognola could see where this was leading. "Striker is your first resort."

The President nodded. "In this situation, yes. He is on-site, and has the most chance of doing this quick and clean without devastating repercussions." The President held Brognola's gaze. "However, I can give him only forty-eight hours, and even those are contingent on the situation staying contained. If for any reason it appears that the enemy is escaping, or launching an outbreak, then I will launch, immediately."

Brognola sighed. The situations changed, but it seemed the stakes for Mack Bolan never did. "He could probably use some backup."

The President nodded. "I expect you to use every resource available."

Mexico

MACK BOLAN and Jack Grimaldi touched down at the airport in Chihuahua. They had driven from the ranch house to the nearest town, and the first aircraft they had come across had been an ancient Grumman crop duster. The Stony Man pilot had immediately fallen in love with the battered old biplane, and the plane's equally ancient owner had considered the two gringos insane. However, the fifty thousand dollars they had offered had been real enough, and the old man had been kind enough to fill up the tank for them. Bolan's eyes narrowed as he glanced at his watch. They were at least an hour behind their quarry.

He wasn't surprised to see Gary Manning standing outside the small plane hangar as the old crop duster pulled to a halt on the tarmac. Manning approached as the Executioner and Grimaldi clambered out of the open cockpit.

"What's the situation, Gary?"

Manning shrugged. "We're going to get nuked in about, oh—" the Canadian checked his watch "—forty-five hours."

"I'm surprised they're going to wait that long," Bolan said dryly.

"Well, I guess they just have faith in you."

"Who else is here?"

Manning nodded his head back at the hangar. "Just me and Gadgets. We were the first to be scrounged up. I expect the rest of the guys will be coming as soon as they can be assembled." He folded his arms across his chest. "We did, however, come loaded for bear."

Bolan didn't doubt it. "Where are the bad guys now?"

"They've moved to the outskirts of the city. A pair of DEA agents have tailed them since they arrived at the airport."

"Are they sure?"

Manning shrugged. "They IDed a shot-up Bell JetRanger with a blue stripe, and they claimed a positive ID on Heidi Hochrein disembarking with friends. There were sixteen of them, all told, in two helicopters. The DEA agents seem to think that most of them were muscle, and not local muscle, either."

Bolan nodded. The description fit. "You have some gear for me?"

"Full war load."

"We have a car?"

Manning almost looked hurt.

"All right, Gary, let's go see what the DEA has dug up."

DEA AGENT ANGELICA DIRAZAR leaned back in the passenger's seat of the van. "So when do we get some backup?"

Agent Brayden Foot kept his binoculars on the large, Spanish-style house down the darkened street. The lane was filled with mostly newly made, unfinished upper-middle-income houses. The house they watched was one of only two inhabited homes in the secluded Chihuahuan suburb. "I don't know. The DEA doesn't really have any authority to take any action other than observe in this kind of situation. I'm betting we got pulled because we were all the government really had on-site here in Chihuahua. I think the government is sending in some heavy hitters. Our orders are to sit tight, observe and wait for someone code-named Striker."

Dirazar grinned. She liked the idea of heavy hitters. She did a great deal of her work across the border, and all too often she found her own hands tied in dealing with the scum. "I hope we get to meet this Striker guy."

Brayden grinned back. "Now who needs to keep it in their pants?"

"So, I like heavy-hittin' kind of guys."

"I'm a heavy-hittin' kind of guy."

Dirazar regarded him with a raised eyebrow. Foot shrugged hopefully. "I carry a .45, don't I?"

The woman nodded solemnly. "And that cuts you more slack with me than you'll ever know."

Foot snorted and continued to peer out the window. Dirazar reclined her seat and lay back. She took off her San Francisco 49ers cap and hooked it on top of the head rest. "Wake me up if anything exciting happens."

"How about if some heavy-hittin' Striker-guy comes by with a big gun?"

The woman grinned, her eyes closed. "Make doubly sure to wake me up for that."

"I'll be sure to—"

Dirazar's eyes flicked open as Foot suddenly fell forward and slumped against the dashboard. The driver's-side window had pebbled around a small hole in the glass.

"Brayden!" Something tugged her baseball cap off the headrest and flung it against the passenger's window with a smack of cracking glass. Holes began to appear rapidly in the window and door frames of the van. She dropped to the floor and jerked Foot down beside her. His eyes rolled up in his head without seeing as she shook him, and Dirazar gasped as his head rolled to one side on a neck gone rubbery. A bullet had drilled a bloody hole in his left temple. She hooked her 9 mm Colt submachine gun by its sling and slithered into the back of the van. There was no sound of gunfire, only the metallic chewing noise of silenced bullets tearing through the van's body.

Dirazar had been in three previous firefights, and hard-won instincts worked for her. She could tell that the bullets were all striking the car from the driver's side. That meant the assassins were almost certainly firing from cover across the street. She squirmed between the van's bench seats toward the sliding side door, then paused as she bumped up against it. The van was old and had no back windows. That was good news. The bad guys couldn't see her, but once she opened the sliding door, the overhead light would turn on and they would know she had bailed out.

The woman flinched as a bullet struck close to her head, then yelped as something burned across the top of her thigh. In a moment it wouldn't make any difference what the enemy knew exactly. The next bullet she took would probably be fatal. She pointed her own silenced weapon up at the van's overhead dome light and fired. The little light shattered under the impact of the 9 mm hollowpoint bullet. She reached up a hand and jerked open the sliding door just enough for her to fall out onto the pavement. Bullets continued to smack against the side of the van and whizzed over her head as she hunched as low as she could.

Dirazar craned her head around. There was a mailbox a few feet away up on the sidewalk, and a few feet beyond that, the low adobe garden wall of a house. If she kept the van between herself and—

Her eyes flared as a sizzling, hissing noise like the sound of some giant bottle rocket suddenly interrupted the nearly silent swarm of gunfire. She instinctively curled into a ball, and the world abruptly came to an end.

The van skewed and nearly crushed her against the curb as something smashed into its side. She clutched her weapon as a sound like a thunderclap roared inside the vehicle, and it rose up on its chassis. Orange fire shot out of the van's shattered windows, and bits of burning metal flew in all directions. For a moment the van seemed to hang suspended three feet off the ground. Dirazar shrieked involuntarily as the van came crashing back down on top of her.

An acrid smell filled the air, and bits of glass and metal rained onto the pavement for several moments. Dirazar opened her eyes and was startled to find that she wasn't dead. Viscous fluid was dripping in her face, and something was jabbing painfully into her shoulder. She wriggled her fingers against the van's drive train and realized that the van had been pushed even farther sideways by the explosion. The van had fallen back down with its passenger's-side wheels up on the curb, and that had left just enough space to keep her from being crushed.

Dirazar steeled herself as sudden panic rose. She could smell something burning, but she forced herself to wait. The bad guys would almost certainly admire their work for a moment, if not actually come out and examine the wreckage. Her face twisted, and her hands went white knuckled on her submachine gun as oil continued to pour onto the side of her head. Long seconds went by as the burning smell grew, but she heard no voices or footsteps. She blinked as a stinging wetness suddenly dripped into her eyes, and her throat nearly closed with choking fumes.

Gasoline was dripping into her face and hair, and she quickly came to a decision. Being shot was infinitely preferable to burning to death.

Dirazar flicked the Colt submachine gun's selector to full-auto and began to wriggle violently toward the van's bumper and the open street beyond.

THE MAN IN THE DARK SUIT checked his watch. "They are dead?"

Ryuchi Taido nodded as he entered the room with the big South African, Renko. "Indeed. I took one of them with a direct head shot, and then Renko destroyed the van with an RPG-7. It was a direct hit. The American agents are currently smoldering down the street."

The man in the dark suit regarded them dryly. "Don't you think using an RPG-7 was somewhat rash?"

Taido shrugged. "Our only neighbors on the street were more than happy to spend the evening in town at our expense, and the police have been paid not to respond to any calls in this neighborhood. The van is burned out from the inside. No fire will spread, and no one in the surrounding neighborhoods will see anything to call the fire department about. I stand by Renko's action. Once we attacked, it was important to prevent them from using their radio. The RPG-7 ensured that. Besides, we are leaving in a few minutes anyway."

The man in the dark suit nodded. Taido's tactics were usually sound in these matters. He glanced at his phone as it rang almost as if on cue. His face creased with momentary irritation.

Taido cocked his head. "Bad news?"

The man shook his head. "Our pilots do not consider the first helicopter airworthy for an extended trip. I myself am not pleased with the idea of flying anywhere during daylight in a helicopter full of bullet holes."

"What do you wish to do?"

The man glanced toward the roof. "Standard procedure. We shall split the team. I will take half of the men and matériel as soon as the first helicopter arrives. A second helicopter is being procured and should arrive close upon its heels."

He turned to Renko. "You will stay here until the second helicopter arrives, and then follow. If we encounter any problems, we will radio back to you, and you will go to the alternate site. Understood?"

Renko nodded. "I understand perfectly. It will be as you say."

"Good." The man glanced at his watch again. "See that everything is readied. The first helicopter will be arriving in minutes."

16

The Executioner peered around the low adobe wall and took in the shattered, smoldering hulk of the van down the street. His nose twitched as he smelled the acrid odor of burned high explosives and rocket propellant, and his face turned to stone as he detected the all too familiar odor of burned human flesh. The Executioner's voice was iron.

"We're late."

Manning looked grim as he cradled his silenced 9 mm Heckler & Koch submachine gun and took in the wreckage. "I'd say they got taken out with an RPG-7."

Bolan nodded. They had seen a helicopter fly over the area on their way out of Chihuahua, but there had been no way of knowing its final destination. If it had already landed and taken on its passengers and cargo, the game was lost. Bolan looked at Gadgets Schwarz. "Get on the horn, Gadgets. Tell them the bad guys might have already fled the scene in a helicopter."

Schwarz's voice was subdued. They all knew that more than one million lives might have just been saved from a nuclear strike, but possibly billions still were on the line from the worst plague in human history. "You got it."

Bolan scanned up and down the street, and his gaze fixed on one of the few finished houses on the block. Its lights were still on. That in itself proved nothing, but it was the only card left to play.

Grimaldi spoke up from the rear of their four-man line. "I think I hear a helicopter."

"Sit tight, I'm moving to the van."

The Executioner crept around the corner and slid through the shadows in a fast crouch, picking his way through bits of twisted metal and shards of glass. The stench of burned flesh quickly grew overpowering. The shattered van had been partially blown up onto the sidewalk. Its sliding side door hung almost off its track, and he scanned the interior through his night-vision goggles. A burned and broken body lay twisted and contracted inside, and it was barely recognizable as a human male. Bolan consulted his mental notes, then examined the ground around him.

A trail of dark smears like motor oil led away from the van, and several partial footprints were visible near the wall. Bolan followed them and found a bloody handprint on the top of the adobe. He leaned close to the wall and spoke in a clear low voice.

"Agent Dirazar, this is Striker."

There was a short intake of breath from the other side of the wall, and Bolan heard the metallic click of a safety being pushed off. A woman's tired voice spoke. "The heavy-hittin' guy."

The Executioner considered that. "Well, I guess that would be me." He waited for a moment. "I'm coming over the wall."

"Do it slow."

Bolan slid over the wall and found a short, dark-haired woman seated against the wall and pointing a silenced Colt submachine gun at him. He looked at her critically. She was covered with what looked like oil, and blood ran down her leg from under a bandanna she had used as a field dressing. "Are you all right?"

Dirazar coughed and spit. "They shot me, then they blew me up."

"I'm sorry, but your partner is dead."

"I know."

Bolan cocked his head as the sound of the approaching helicopter grew louder. "Can you walk?"

She considered the notion. "I think so."

"Want some payback?"

Dirazar seemed to almost magically inflate with strength. "Always."

The lights of the helicopter were visible now as it flew across the city and into the suburbs. It was making a beeline for the house across the street. "I think that chopper is coming for our friends."

The DEA agent pushed against the wall and levered herself to her feet. "A chopper already came here about five minutes ago. It landed across the street in the backyard and then took off again."

"I was afraid of that."

Dirazar shook her head. "No. They're still there. There were about sixteen suspects we observed at the airport. The first helicopter that came here wasn't that big. I think there's still got to be some bad guys left in the house."

Manning's voice spoke in Bolan's earpiece. "That chopper is almost here, Striker. What have you got?"

"I've got one DEA agent dead, one wounded. We were right. That helicopter we saw earlier came and made a pickup, but not all of the birds have left the nest."

"How do you want to play it?"

Bolan watched the helicopter sweep over the neighborhood. "We let the helicopter land. Its noise will cover our initial attack. Under no circumstances is it to be allowed to take off again, and I want as many of the enemy captured alive as possible. We need information more than we need bodies. Gary, you're with me through the front door. Gadgets and Jack will flank the house on the right side and make sure the helicopter stays put."

"Roger that, Striker. Gadgets and Jack moving out now."

Bolan turned to agent Dirazar. "Let's go." He gave her his hand, and the two of them slid back across the wall where

Manning was waiting for them. A pair of shadows had detached themselves from the wall down the street as Schwarz and Grimaldi flanked the house. "Front door?" Manning asked.

"Why not."

The trio moved quickly across the street and kept out of the line of sight of the lighted house's gate. They crept down along the adobe wall as the helicopter seemed to blast into existence over the house and began to descend into the backyard.

Schwarz's voice spoke over the radio. "Helicopter has touched down. It's empty except for the pilot, and he's not shutting down the engine. I believe he's making a pickup."

"Roger that. Can you see anyone in front from your vantage?"

Bolan could hear Gadgets shift on his perch up on the side wall. "You've got one man with an AK-47 and a radio standing in the front yard."

"Roger that." Bolan moved along the wall until he came to the gate. "Making entry now." The Executioner swung around to face the wrought-iron gate. A man with a slung rifle gaped and tried to bring up his weapon. Bolan's silenced 9 mm Colt vibrated, and the man tumbled backward as a 3-round burst walked up his chest. Bolan swung the muzzle down and put another burst into the gate's lockbox. Sparks flew, and the double gate swung open under Bolan's boot.

The front yard was unfinished and little more than dirt and half-seeded lawn. It would have been a killing zone against intruders if anyone had been watching, but no one had. Bolan could see people moving in the windows, and they seemed too busy to look outside. Bolan, Manning and Dirazar moved to the front door unchallenged.

Schwarz's voice spoke in Bolan's ear. "They're loading the helicopter with men and matériel."

"Engage them. We're going in now."

"Roger."

Bolan waited several seconds. Schwarz's and Grimaldi's weapons were silenced, and the noise of the helicopter's rotors would have covered most noise anyway. But he was waiting for a noise from inside the house, the one that would tell him no one would be facing the front door.

Suddenly there was shouting inside the house.

The Executioner put a burst into the heavy oak door's knob and put his boot into it. The door swung back on its hinges, and he swept into the house with Manning and Dirazar behind him.

Two men with rifles stood in the foyer, and they swung about as the door smashed inward. Bolan squeezed the trigger of the M-203 grenade launcher clipped under his Colt's barrel, and pale flame roared out of the 40 mm muzzle. The personal defensive round sent a hailstorm of buckshot through the foyer, and the two guards were caught in the middle of its twenty-seven-pellet pattern. Bolan came on even as the two men twisted and fell.

The soldier moved into a spacious living room with a vaulted ceiling. Four men with rifles had dropped a pair of crates and had been moving toward the firefight in the back-yard when Bolan had fired his weapon in the foyer. He jerked back into the hallway as two of them fired their weapons, drew a flash-stun grenade from his bandolier and hurled it high around the corner.

A thunderclap rolled out of the living room in the wake of a blinding strobe of white light. As Bolan came around the corner, two men were on their knees shaking their heads. The other two reeled on their feet and discharged their rifles blindly toward the hallway. Bolan put a burst into each standing man, then shouted above his own ringing ears as they fell. "Dirazar! Take the two still alive and sit on them! I want prisoners!"

The DEA agent nodded and pulled a pair of handcuffs out of her jacket. She strode up to one of the kneeling men, kicked him in the face, then grabbed his arm as he toppled and cranked the cuff around his wrist. The other man had started to crawl away, and she quickly jumped up and butt-stroked him with her submachine gun in the back of the neck. The man sprawled senseless, and she cuffed him to his fallen comrade.

She gave Bolan and Manning the thumbs-up signal as they moved deeper into the house. They reached the kitchen. Out the window they could see the flickering orange flame of gunfire. Two men were down on the back lawn, and two more were firing from behind a large brick barbecue. On the other side of the kitchen, a cellar door hung open, and Bolan remembered the unpleasantness he had found in the last open cellar he had been in.

"Gary, take out the two outside, and then you and I will sweep the rest of the house."

Manning nodded and moved to the kitchen door as Bolan crouched and ejected his nearly spent magazine. He whirled as the wooden cellar stairs creaked. A big blond man's face grimaced as the creaking stair gave him away. He held what looked like a silver cigarette case in one hand, and the other raised a pistol. Bolan flung aside his empty weapon and lunged up out of his crouch. His hand clawed for the big Desert Eagle pistol on his hip as he dived into his opponent.

The man flinched from the spinning submachine gun and leveled his pistol as Bolan leaped forward. The pistol barked twice, and the soldier felt the twin blows of bullets punching into his armored vest. He hit the man with his full weight, and the two of them toppled backward down the cellar stairs. Both were big men, too big for the narrow stairwell, and their backward fall stalled into a cramped, slow-motion tangle of limbs. White-hot pain shot up Bolan's arm as it was pinned for a split second between his opponent's weight and the edge of a stair, and the Desert Eagle slipped from his suddenly nerveless fingers. The two men continued to tumble until the dirt floor of the cellar seemed to rise up and meet them with a crunch. Bolan rolled out on top.

The Executioner ignored the pain in his right wrist and

drove his good left hand into the side of the man's head and felt flesh break under his knuckles. The blond man snarled and seized his adversary by the throat with both hands. Bolan brought his knee up between them and broke away. He staggered back and tried to draw his Beretta from its shoulder holster with his left hand, but the draw was too awkward and there was no time. The blonde lunged to his feet and drove into him. Bolan hooked his right elbow under the man's throat as he was lifted up and driven back into the wall. His body armor softened the blow, and he slammed his left elbow viciously into the back of the man's neck. His opponent grunted with pain and suddenly twisted with all of his strength. Both men crashed to the dirt floor.

Bolan heaved, wedging his right knee between them, and his left hand groped for the snub-nosed 9 mm revolver in his ankle holster. The blond man's left hand held the soldier by the throat, and Bolan jammed his damaged forearm into his opponent's throat, as well. The man didn't resist, and he realized the man was reaching for something with his right hand.

As the Executioner's hand slipped around the Smith & Wesson's grips, his opponent's right hand came up and around in a stabbing motion. In the glare of the single, bare bulb illuminating the cellar, Bolan saw the gleaming needle of a syringe. He jerked his head, and the needle stabbed down and caught in the woven Kevlar collar of his armored vest. The needle plunged in and broke as the man twisted it. The Smith & Wesson came free with a ripping of Velcro, and Bolan jammed the weapon into the man's ribs and fired.

The man's eyes were pinholes of hatred as he withdrew the broken needle. Bolan fired again, and the man tensed and coughed blood. His adversary's thumb pushed down, and yellow fluid sprayed from the tip of the broken needle. Bolan's blood ran cold as it splashed into his eyes. The man went limp, and the Executioner shoved the corpse off him and rose to his feet. Manning stood at the top of the stairwell.

"Mack! Are you—?"

"Stay where you are! Close the door!"

Manning's boot creaked on the top landing. "What's—"

Bolan's voice rose to a parade-ground roar. "Do it!"

The door slammed shut. Bolan wiped his eyes and put his earpiece back in place. He spoke calmly into his throat mike. "Gary, the virus is loose down here in the cellar. I've been exposed. What's the situation up there?"

Manning was silent for a moment and Bolan repeated himself. "What's the situation up there?"

"We've got six dead in the house and Dirazar is sitting on two prisoners. Four enemy are dead outside. We've got the chopper. Their pilot surrendered."

"Any sign of Hochrein or the two men Dirazar described?"

"That's a negative. I think they got out on the first chopper."

Manning cleared his throat. "Jesus, Mack. Are you sure?"

Bolan crouched and looked at the broken needle in the dirt. A few feet away a small silver case lay open with a twin syringe still held in place by foam. Bolan let out a long breath. "Yeah. I'm pretty sure."

There was a long moment of silence before Manning spoke again. "What are your orders?"

Bolan glanced up the narrow wooden staircase. "Seal the cellar door. Use the double-sided waterproof tape we brought along for placing explosives. Then seal the rest of the house if you can."

"You've got it."

The Executioner looked around the bare cellar. In one corner a stainless-steel container the size of a small suitcase gleamed dully. He walked over to it and read the biohazard warnings on its side. His frown deepened as he examined the dirt around it. Almost right next to the case was a square imprint in the dirt that matched the remaining case's dimensions like a fingerprint.

"Tell Washington that we have captured the hatbox, and that I believe there's a second one that went out with the first

helicopter. The threat is still alive, and it has fled the scene."
Bolan let out a long breath. "Tell them to call off the nuclear
strike. We were too late."

Manning's voice was grim. "What about our present...
situation?"

"I'm sure they'll get back to you on that. Just make sure
you seal up the house as best you can."

The big Canadian could no longer prevent himself from
asking the question. "What about you, Mack?"

Bolan considered the question. The usual way humans got
the flu was that they unknowingly touched something with
infected material on it, then at some point wiped their eyes.
The eyes were the number-one contact point for most viruses
to successfully enter and infect the human body. Bolan grimaced. He had every reason to believe he had taken a full
syringe of Ebola Sese virus right in the eyes.

"Gary, we have a strain of Ebola that is transmitted like
the flu. There's no cure. It's airborne, and it's out of medical
containment in this cellar. That door can't be opened unless
this whole house is put under a decontamination tent and
nuked with formaldehyde gas. That's probably going to have
a bad effect on me, as well as on the virus, and unless the
government is going to tell the Mexicans what has happened
and what the situation is, I don't think they're going to fly the
men and material necessary to come down here, put me in a
mobile containment unit and fly me out. It's just too risky,
medically and politically. If I had to bet, they're just going to
try and keep this house contained and then slowly sneak people in here to clear out the virus."

Manning's tone didn't change. "What about you, Mack?"

They both knew the answer to that question. "Gary, I'm
expendable. Everyone at the Farm is. We knew that when we
signed up."

"We can get Dr. Thurman and some space suits and get
you out of there."

"I don't think that Washington is going to authorize that."

Manning's voice went hard. "Screw Washington. We've got a chopper and we've got guns. We can grab Thurman and be back here in a matter of hours."

Bolan smiled at his friend's loyalty, but his own voice hardened, as well. "Gary, I'll shoot anyone who opens that door. You read me?"

The line was silent for a moment. "I read you. I'll contact Washington, and then I'll let you know what the situation is."

"Thanks." Bolan went and sat down next to the gleaming biological-containment unit and leaned against the wall. "One thing you can do for me, Gary."

"What's that, Mack?"

Bolan glanced at the body of the dead man lying in the middle of the cellar. "Shut these bastards down for me."

17

The man in the dark suit watched the men refuel the helicopter. They seemed to be moving at a snail's pace, but he didn't let his nervousness show on his face. Heidi Hochrein sat in her seat and was a study in silent outrage and scorn. The second helicopter had sent a message that they were under attack, then the transmission had been abruptly cut off. The helicopter hadn't radioed back. Neither had Renko or any of the men back at the house in Chihuahua. The men outside pulled back the fuel hose, and the helicopter's rotors increased their speed for takeoff.

Ryuchi Taido glanced about at the desert scrub that surrounded the fueling station. There was nothing to see other than a rusty old pickup truck with drums of fuel on its bed. The truck had been staged here in the middle of the desert so that they could avoid landing in towns or cities. The truck sat in the middle of a dirt road that seemed to lead to nowhere in both directions. Taido cleared his throat. "I believe the house in Chihuahua has fallen. I believe the American commando somehow managed to follow us."

The man in the dark suit peered at Taido from behind his dark glasses, and his voice was thin with irritation. "Your powers of deduction are astounding."

Taido blinked at the sarcasm. His mouth opened, then he shut it again without saying anything. The petulant remark had been totally uncharacteristic of the man, and it told Taido that something was profoundly wrong. The little man's eyes narrowed behind his own mirrored sunglasses. If Taido hadn't known better, he would actually believe that the man was afraid. He crushed down that idea and its implications. "I do not believe it is an insurmountable loss. As I see it, it does not truly affect our mission one way or the other."

The dark-suited man's face remained impassive as he gazed at Taido like a stone Buddha. For a moment Taido believed the man could sense the doubts he had felt for his commander, and he wondered if the man would kill him. The man turned his gaze toward the desert, then spoke. "I believe you are correct. All we have really lost are gunmen, which are easily replaceable. The only real setback is the loss of half of our samples of the Ebola virus. However, that is also easily replaceable. Once we are safely at our base of operations, it should be easy enough to replenish it."

Taido suppressed a grimace. Replenishing their supply of the virus would mean kidnapping someone and infecting him with it. Once the virus went on its rampage of reproduction within the host's body, their supply of living viral material would be for all intents and purposes nearly unlimited. The thought tasted bitter in Taido's mouth. He believed in their mission and what it would accomplish, but the method left his spine crawling. It made the American act of using atomic weapons against his own country during World War II seem like a sideshow.

The men outside jumped into the back of the helicopter, and the aircraft rose up into the morning sky. Taido peered ahead into the horizon.

He suspected they would be across the border within the hour.

MACK BOLAN WAS getting thirsty. He sat cross-legged against the bare wall of the cellar and sucked a pebble he had dug out of the floor. The old Indian trick stimulated saliva and fooled his mouth, but he was all too aware of the effects of dehydration through long experience. Bolan had been sitting in the cellar for twenty-four hours, and the symptoms of thirst were beginning to manifest themselves. Bolan grimaced. It was waiting for the other symptoms to start that was preying upon his mind.

The radio earpiece crackled on his web gear, and he put it in his ear. "This is Striker."

Gary Manning's voice spoke. "How are you doing down there?"

Bolan was silent for a moment, and he could almost hear Manning's sudden embarrassment. It was a very stupid question, and very human.

The soldier relented. "The best I can, Gary. How is the situation topside?"

"Well, the government has bought the house you're in and the two on either side of you. They also bought about forty acres of hillside behind you, so you're effectively quarantined, and we've managed to keep the situation under our hats. We've snuck in some SEALs and some more DEA agents, and they're making sure no one wanders into the situation accidentally." Manning was silent for a moment as he tried to find easier ways to say what he had to. There weren't any. "Mack, we're arranging for a fumigation tent. Once it's installed over the house, the guys in the space suits are going to come in and chemically nuke the place."

Bolan nodded. "I'm surprised it's taken them this long as it is."

Manning swallowed and tried to lighten his voice. "You probably have a day or two. The government is doing everything to keep a lid on this, so they're dribbling in the men and equipment slowly."

Bolan considered that. He figured two more days without water, and a big deep breath of formaldehyde gas would probably be a blessing. "How's Agent Dirazar doing?"

"She's fine. The wound across her thigh will leave her a scar to show her grandkids, but she's walking fine. Dr. Thurman is here with me."

"Put her on."

Eliza Thurman was obviously struggling to keep her voice smooth and professional as she spoke over the radio. "What symptoms do you have, Striker?"

"None, other than thirst and fatigue. I don't think they're currently related to the virus."

"I agree." Her voice broke a little. "I'd get you some food and water if there was any way I..." Her voice trailed off.

Bolan sighed heavily. "It would only prolong the inevitable, Eliza. It's probably better this way." Bolan was silent for a moment as he looked steadily at the .44 Magnum Desert Eagle pistol where it rested by his knee. "Don't worry about my suffering. I have a way out of this if it gets too bad."

Thurman was silent for long moments, and Bolan could tell that she was crying. When her voice came back, it had steeled to a professional tone. "What can you tell me about the hatbox?"

Bolan looked at the portable biological-containment unit beside him. "It's about the size of a small suitcase and made out of stainless steel. It has triple locks, and a small display panel in the left-hand corner. The markings on it are in English, but there's no serial number or makers marks. I'd bet it was a custom job, and built by our friends with this job in mind. I haven't attempted to open it. I figured you'd want it left like I found it when you and your men get down here after the sterilization."

There was another pause, and the unthinkable was pondered again. Bolan filled the uncomfortable silence. "There was also a much smaller case, just big enough to hold two syringes. The case is double lidded and double gasketed, and has a small sliding panel with warning lights. One of the syringes was used on me. It's on the ground and the needle is broken. The other syringe is still intact and in its slot in the case. I haven't moved them. I'm going to leave them where they fell."

"Any other observations?"

Bolan looked at the corpse of the big blond man and smiled

bleakly. "My roommate here is starting to get a little fragrant.
I checked him over. He had a wad of hundred-dollar bills,
some keys, a handgun and a radio on him. No identification.
On his left bicep there is a tattoo of some kind of big cat, and
underneath it is some Cyrillic writing underneath it. I can't
read it, but I'm betting he's Russian and ex-military."

"Right." Bolan could hear her scribbling notes. "I'm putting your friend back on."

Manning spoke. "We don't have much to go on. The first
helicopter got away clean."

Bolan frowned. "What about the pilot we captured from the
second chopper?"

"He didn't know what his next flight plan was, or anything
about what was going on, apparently. He was just a free-lance
pilot who had been contracted at the Chihuahua airport. That's
probably why he surrendered so quickly. Once he took his
helicopter to the house, some guy named Renko was going to
tell him where to go after that. According to the prisoners that
Agent Dirazar took, the man down in the basement was
Renko. One of them was going to kill the pilot after he had
taken them where they were going. The two prisoners we took
are both Russians. They don't know where their final destination was, either. Apparently this Renko character was in
charge of the second team and had all the information. Unfortunately you capped him."

Bolan eyed the Russian on the floor and the broken syringe
lying by the dead man's hand. "Sorry about that. Things got
a little out of hand between us."

"I can understand that." Manning's voice trailed off into
another uncomfortable pause. "Gadgets has managed to patch
our personal radios into the satellite link. Do you want to talk
to Barbara or Hal?"

Bolan thought about it for several seconds. He was a dead
man, and he knew it, but he wasn't yet prepared to make any
goodbye speeches. He wasn't sure if he would be. He had
cheated death so many times that he had run up a debt with

statistics, and that debt had caught up with him in a cellar in Chihuahua. His attacker was implacable, unstoppable and unmerciful.

He was finished.

"No, not yet. I'll let you know when I make a decision." Bolan took a deep breath. "How is Barbara doing?"

"Not well. She knows the situation, but…" Manning sighed. "She's not doing well, but she's tough. I think it's your circumstances that are killing her. If we just brought you home all shot up in a bag she could grieve, but the way things are…"

"I understand. Tell her…" Bolan looked again at the .44 Magnum pistol by his knee. "Tell her I'll talk to her before this is over. Striker out."

THE MAN IN THE DARK SUIT was pleased with himself. He could tell over the satellite link that the old man was pleased, as well.

"You are sure you were not followed?"

"Positive." The younger man looked out the window at the rolling hillsides. Except for some scrubby pines they were brown with summer.

"You have begun to acquire more of the virus?"

The younger man almost smiled. "Yes. We found a subject and will soon infect her with the virus. We will be able to get all of the virus we need from her once she is infected."

"A kidnapping?"

"Yes."

"You are sure she will not be missed?"

The younger man was almost irritated by the line of questioning, but he kept his voice neutral. "Taido is clever about these things. The subject is a prostitute and a runaway. No one will come looking for her."

The old man grunted over the line. "What is the situation in Mexico?"

The man in the dark suit almost smiled again. "Intriguing.

Our agents tell us that the houses on either side of the property we were renting in Chihuahua have suddenly been bought, as well as the land behind it.''

"The Americans have instituted a quarantine."

"Exactly. This indicates to me that something happened during the firefight."

The old man paused. "Perhaps they are simply taking no chances with the hatbox."

"I do not believe so," the younger man replied. "I believe if it was just the hatbox they would have taken it and spirited it back to the United States. I believe the virus was loosed in the fight in the house."

"Oh?"

"Indeed. They have men patrolling the grounds, and a van that I believe is full of communications equipment has been parked across the street for many hours. Yet our spys tell us that no one is entering. I believe that the virus is loose in the house, and, the way they are behaving, that they have people inside who have been exposed."

"Excellent."

"Indeed. With any luck, it will be our American commando friend. I would bet a great deal that it was he who led the attack."

"I would not count on that. That one has the luck of the Devil."

The younger man actually smiled. "A man can dream, can't he?"

The older man guffawed. "Yes. I will pray that it is so." He paused a moment and collected his thoughts. "So, the plan still moves ahead according to schedule."

"Yes, the operation will go as planned. What are the Americans doing?"

The old man sounded pleased. "They are engaging in 'strategic movements' in Europe. Nothing has been withdrawn yet, but they are moving men and matériel to staging points. There has been no movement in Asia yet."

The younger man stood straighter. "You believe they will withdraw from Europe and Asia?"

"I do. My contacts say they are scared. They are all too aware of what this virus can do to them. They have no cure, and they know we have it." There was a smug pause. "They have no choice."

The younger man leaned back in his chair. "I will await your go-ahead before infecting the girl."

The old man sighed contentedly. "Is she pretty?"

The man in the dark suit smiled. He was aware of the old man's predilection for blond women. "Indeed. She is just your type."

The old man grunted. "A shame. What are your plans for disposing of her after she is infected and the supply of virus replenished?"

The younger man stared down at the sweltering city below. "She is young, attractive and a prostitute. Once we have gotten what we need from her, I will release her into the general population and let her begin our work for us."

"Execellent. I will keep you advised." The line went dead with a click, and the man in the dark suit kept his gaze on the sprawling city below. Los Angeles would be as good a place to start the plague as any.

18

Thirst burned through every cell in Mack Bolan's body. He had been a little over a day and a half without water, but that seemed like the least of his problems.

Ebola Sese had attacked his body with even greater speed than Dr. Thurman had predicted. Bolan stared down at his hand. His symptoms were getting worse. Star-shaped blood bruises bloomed under his skin as the Ebola virus attacked the sheath of connective tissues between skin and muscle. His eyes felt like rocks in his head, and he knew that if he looked in a mirror the whites would be a bright crimson from hemorrhaging blood. Behind his eyes, a headache like turning screws was nearly blinding him. The Ebola Sese virus had only begun its onslaught, and his body was already swiftly succumbing.

Bolan found his center and put his mind there, where he could remain lucid like the calm inside the mounting hurricane of pain and panic. He knew he couldn't remain lucid for very much longer. It was beyond a question of controlling the pain. The Ebola virus attacked and thrived on the connective tissues of the body, but its favorite targets were the internal organs. The blinding headache behind Bolan's eyes told him that the virus was attacking his brain. The Executioner took his remaining moments of mental competence and put his mind into the eye of the Ebola virus's assault.

The Executioner contemplated his fate.

The saying in the medical community was that Ebola did in ten days what AIDS did in ten years, and Ebola Sese seemed to be even more deadly than her sister strains. Still, there was a predicted five to ten percent chance he could survive the viral war inside his body. If he was within that tiny percentage, his body would take the full round of symptoms, then slowly shrug them off as his immune system got back off its knees and fought back. That, of course, assumed that he was in a hospital receiving fresh units of blood and IV units of nutrients and fluids to keep him alive while his body became a viral war zone.

Bolan grimaced.

He was by himself, in the bottom of a cellar, and he was quarantined. No help would arrive until after he was dead. His one consolation was that he would never break down and crash out under the Ebola virus's final assault like Robert E. Lee Leland had. Thirst would kill him before that. However, what he did have to look forward to was terrible pain, massive internal bleeding and the loss of his mental faculties before his parched body curled up and died of dehydration. An average-sized man could go three to four days without water, and that assumed he was in decent health. He had been without water for over thirty-six hours and he had already started to bleed internally. Of course, there was always the possibility that at any time the government would send in the decontamination unit and fumigate him with formaldehyde gas.

Bolan stared for the hundredth time at the .44 Magnum pistol resting by his knee.

He had some time left, and the ability to take his fate into his own hands. Bolan stared over at Renko's body, and he felt a pang of almost amused envy. Renko didn't have any worries, or at least any terrestrial ones. Bolan had made the man's decision for him. The Executioner squinted as the pain behind his eyeballs seemed to turn up a notch, but his mind ran the situation over again for the thousandth time.

He ran his eyes over Renko's body, then the broken needle on the floor. He gazed again at the small syringe case and the gleaming stainless steel of the hatbox. There was a piece miss-

ing. Of that he was sure. The enemy acted like a small cell of
terrorists, but their network seemed to operate on a worldwide
scale and have almost unlimited resources to draw upon. They
had weathered every attack and always had redundant fallback
positions. Using the Ebola virus as a weapon seemed incredibly crude and dangerous, but their methods and their operation had gone ahead with smooth sophistication. Heidi Hochrein was involved, just as she had been on the attack on
Buckingham Palace in England. There again, the enemy's attack had been crude and terrorists used, but the infrastructure
had been sophisticated and the attacks themselves had been
brilliant.

There was a bigger picture. Bolan knew it in his bones. The
question was, who was involved?

The Executioner stared at the hatbox. The virus itself had
to be the key. Ebola Sese was ninety percent lethal. There was
no cure, and it was transmittable like the flu. It was a doomsday weapon if ever there was one. That in itself was the puz-
zle. Who would dare to use it?

The attacks the enemy had made with it already had been
surgical, in remote areas against single individuals. But even
with all the precautions they had taken, there was still a small
chance of there being an outbreak. Once an outbreak occurred,
there would probably be no stopping the virus. Nearly every
point on Earth was within a twenty-four-hour plane ride from
any other. Once the virus broke out of containment, it would
burn across the globe like wildfire. Hardly any political ob-
jective could be worth that risk. Only fanatics or madmen
would attempt it.

Bolan didn't believe his opponents were either fanatics or
madmen.

Which left the question, how could anyone dare such an
attack? Bolan crushed a thought down in his mind. It was too
much like the mad desperate hope of a dying mind. He knew
that the virus was attacking his brain, and even without that,
he knew that he wasn't immune to the hopelessness of his

situation. The Executioner steeled himself, then considered the alien thought again. After long moments of reflection, a grim smile crossed his face. It actually made sense. It made total sense. In fact short of the enemy being madmen who didn't care if they killed ninety percent of the human race, including themselves, it was the only scenario that made any sense at all.

The enemy had to have a cure.

Again, Bolan crushed down wild hope and kept his mind steely. The question was, now, who would benefit? The enemy had demanded the withdrawal of American military forces from Europe and Asia. The United States had begun the motions of compliance. What would that accomplish?

Europe and Asia would be open. The Russians could reestablish themselves among their former satellites, and possibly take over Western Europe. Except the Russians already had enough problems, and a great deal of their armed forces had been divided up among the breakaway states. Bolan doubted they were eager to reform the former Soviet Union and engage in a war in Europe. The Chinese could take Asia and the Pacific, but they would undoubtedly run straight into India, who would have something to say about China owning all of Asia. Bolan frowned. Even with her forces withdrawn, the United States would feel compelled to act if such wars were taking place.

The Executioner's gaze narrowed. The enemy didn't want a war. Their adversaries had tried to destroy the English government by attacking the Royal Family, and the Stony Man data indicated they had been aiming at the capitals of France and Germany, as well. It seemed the enemy wanted Western Europe destabilized, and in the meantime a plague in the United States, a plague for which they alone had a cure.

What was the goal? Bolan put himself in the attackers' frame of mind. If the United States withdrew its military forces from Europe and Asia, they wouldn't be immediately reassigned. They would be brought back to the United States. Bolan grimaced. That would be the time to start the attack. If the isolated incidents of Ebola within the United States increased, America would be forced to quarantine itself. The borders would be closed, and no air traffic would come in or out. Once the United States was quarantined, the real attack would begin.

Ebola Sese would be released into the general population.

Millions of Americans would die, and the rest of the world would shun the stricken country. As the death toll mounted, America would become increasingly desperate. The enemy wouldn't have to let the disease run its course. As a matter of fact, killing ninety percent of the American population would probably be against the enemy's best interests.

One out of four would be plenty. The death of one out of every four Americans would be more than enough to cripple her political structure, her military, her economy and her technological base.

Those who possessed a cure would be able to ask anything they wanted. They wouldn't even have to ask. They could offer it altruistically, already ostensibly an ally of the United States and wanting to help, and unsuspected in the attack. Such an unsuspected enemy could move in with financial and technological support and help lead America out of chaos and, at the same time, take control of her wealth and industry. Such an enemy would have the greatest nation in the world crippled and indebted. The enemy would become the de facto head of the most powerful nation on Earth, and the United States would be pathetically grateful for it.

The final question was who, and the answer was already forming in Bolan's mind. The enemy had a cure, but it wouldn't want to risk millions of its own people dying before it could be distributed. Once the plague broke out, the enemy would ideally want to be able to remain isolated.

An island nation would be ideal. Who would have the technological, financial and strategic resources to come in and assist a crippled United States, particularly if the first part of the plan had gone ahead and the governments of Western Europe were destabilized? Who also would have had the biological technology to have come up with a cure for the Ebola Sese virus and develop portable equipment for its use as a weapon? Bolan leaned back against the wall of the cellar. There was only one real answer that addressed all these questions.

Japan.

The Executioner took a deep breath. He didn't believe the Japanese government would do such a thing. But there were Japanese consortiums who held long-standing grudges against the United States, whose almost openly stated goals were the ascendance of Japan as a world power. Many of the consortiums were run by old men, veterans of World War II who had neither forgiven or forgotten.

A plan that would bring the United States to its knees and make Japan its de facto ruler would appeal to such men, and they would have the power and the resources to implement it. The Japanese government would never have to know. They would simply act in Japan's own self-interest, and the plan would fall into place by itself. As a matter of fact, it would be the consortium's duty to keep its action from the Japanese government. The Japanese understood duty. If the plan was discovered by the West, the consortium would offer itself and its holdings up for justice. Bolan suspected that its leaders might indeed actually commit ritual suicide in atonement, and to prevent an actual war with the United States.

The idea was so far-fetched that even Bolan might believe that he was starting to lose his mind. But it was also the only scenario that made sense. He had fought the Japanese Yakuza, and he had fought Japanese business consortiums before. He had experienced their utter ruthlessness. There were individuals in these consortiums who had the will and the power to execute the operation that was under way against the United States.

Bolan stared across the floor at the broken syringe he had been infected with, and another thought suddenly occurred to him. He sat up straighter and tried to control a surge of hope.

The enemy was using Ebola, and he suspected they had a cure. It made sense that if their agents were handling the disease, they would take precautions. They were probably already immunized against it, but...

Bolan looked over at the small, portable syringe case.

Why two needles?

Bolan frowned. Redundancy was safety in both biological and military matters. He was desperate and grasping at straws. Then again, other than waiting around to go insane and die of thirst, he really didn't have anything better to do.

The Executioner rose to his feet and put a hand against the wall as his vision swam. Shooting pains ran through his insides and down his limbs in white-hot streams. He steadied himself and walked across the cellar floor to the broken syringe. He bent over awkwardly and picked it up and examined it. The needle was broken off an inch from the base from where it had snapped against his armored vest. A tiny amount of yellow residue stained the inside of the syringe itself. Other than the metric-capacity lines along its length, there were no markings. Bolan turned the syringe over in his hand and blearily looked at the plunger.

The flat disk for the thumb was marked with an indelible scarlet dot.

Bolan dropped the syringe and went over to the syringe case by Renko's body. He squatted on his heels and sat for a moment to catch his breath. He grimaced at the pain in his skull, then removed the second syringe from its slot. Yellow fluid filled the tube and it was an exact twin to its broken mate on the floor. Bolan turned the needle over and looked at the base of its plunger.

A bright green dot sat in its center like a bull's-eye.

Red for danger and green for safety were fairly universal signs in the modern world, but that in itself proved nothing. Bolan pulled off the needle's safety cap and tapped out the air bubble in the top of the tube.

A tiny amount of fluid gushed out, and he stared at the shining needle under the light of the cellar's single naked bulb.

It was a gamble. He could easily be injecting himself with another 40 cc's of hot virus, but he realized that really didn't matter. He could already feel his face becoming numb as the fascia under the flesh came under attack.

In for a nickel, in for a dime, and he was literally up to his eyeballs in Ebola anyway.

Bolan steadied himself as his vision wavered again, then pressed his bicep against his side until the veins stood out in his forearm. He took a breath, then slid the needle into his arm just above his inner elbow. The yellow fluid expressed as he shoved the plunger down, and it disappeared from the needle into his bloodstream. He removed the needle, then dropped it to the floor. Bolan kept his finger against the injection site and awkwardly put his earpiece back in. He fought a sudden wave of nausea and cleared his throat as he spoke into his throat mike.

"This is Striker."

Thurman's voice replied. "How are you?"

"Not good, but I might be getting better."

There was a stunned silence on the other end. Bolan grinned again as Thurman seemed to struggle for something to say. "Listen, I think I'm going to pass out in a minute, so listen carefully."

Thurman sounded extremely wary. "I'm listening."

"I've had a couple of ideas...."

19

The man in the dark suit was almost insufferably pleased with himself. Heidi Hochrein lay on the king-size bed that dominated the small room and grinned up at him lasciviously as he adjusted his tie. "Now, tell me."

The man stood in the exquisitely appointed private room and looked at himself in the mirror. He ran an appreciative eye over Hochrein's recumbent form, and the warm glow he felt inside himself grew. Victory was sweet. He indulged himself and gave in to the woman's wheedling for information. She had earned it. "Our agents tell me a fumigation service came to call on the house in Chihuahua. They put it under a tent."

Her eyes narrowed slightly. "And?"

"And afterward men came in a helicopter. Our agents could not see exactly what they did from their vantage point in the hills, but we do know that several of them entered the house. They were wearing Racal environmental suits. They stayed for several hours, and then the helicopter was observed flying away."

Hochrein arched an eyebrow at him. "And?"

The man shrugged. "And then they left."

"They left?"

"Indeed." The man allowed himself a smile. "Our agents also inform me that the house in Chihuahua, as well as the two neighboring houses and the hillside acreage behind them were suddenly sold at a loss by their mysterious buyer, all within an hour of the helicopter's departure." The man waited for the woman's impatience to build a little. "Our agents also report that the house in Chihuahua has mysteriously caught fire and burned to the ground."

The woman arched her back and regarded the man. "Tell me what I want to know."

The man shrugged. "Oh, well, our electronics team did intercept a transmission."

Hochrein sat upright on the bed. "That is suspicious. I do not believe the Americans would be foolish enough to openly transmit anything that wasn't encoded."

The man in the dark suit nodded in agreement. The woman's instincts in these matters were excellent. "Indeed, I agree. However, our experts determined that the transmission they intercepted was from a tactical-band radio. It was a local transmission that was then encoded and patched into a satellite link."

Hochrein frowned as she absorbed this. The man in the dark suit smiled. "Someone in the house used a tactical radio to communicate with a satellite link outside the house. The satellite transmission was encoded. The radio transmission was not. I believe the men in the house were in communication with the van that had been parked across the street for the last twenty-four hours. Then the van sent the information on to the United States."

"What did the intercepted transmission say?"

The man spoke from memory. "'Quarantine successful. Results of decontamination, successful. No trace of virus found in environment. Hatbox is secure, samples within appear viable. Setting incendiary charges and returning to base.'"

Hochrein smiled. "So. They decided not to let the Mexican government in on their little incident and have destroyed all traces."

"Apparently so. Revealing what happened, particularly since they have failed to stop us, would be politically embarrassing, if not a disaster."

Hochrein frowned again. "They still have one of our hatboxes."

The man shrugged. "Yes, they do. One of them. However, they were designed with the idea that they might fall into the hands of the United States authorities. Its construction will tell them nothing."

The woman stretched back again leisurely. The man in the dark suit couldn't restrain a grin. Hochrein raised an eyebrow. She wasn't used to the man smiling, or showing any emotion for that matter. "And what is it you are grinning about?"

"There was something else in the transmission I forgot to mention."

"Oh? And what is that?"

The man folded his arms across his chest as he quoted again from memory. "'Striker is dead. Repeat, Striker is dead. Gary taking command.'"

Heidi Hochrein licked her teeth. "What do you think it means?"

The man in the dark suit smiled craftily. "One cannot be sure. However, logic tells us that this 'Gary' individual is now in command. He was not in command before. 'Striker' is dead, and 'Gary' is taking his place."

Hochrein's eyes sparkled. "Just say it."

"I believe that Striker was the American commando, and he and his confederates attacked the house in Chihuahua. I believe in the struggle the virus was somehow released in the house." The man grinned from ear to ear. "We know that the Americans quarantined the house. We also know that they were in communication with someone in the house while the fumigation rig was being set up. There was not enough time for whoever was trapped inside to die of the virus itself."

"They killed their own man in decontamination."

The man nodded. "There is no known living thing on this planet that can withstand formaldehyde gas. So either he died with every other living insect and microbe in the house, or…"

"Or what?"

The man shrugged in false indifference. "Or he took his own life."

Hochrein flung herself backward on the bed, and the man in the dark suit watched with some amazement as one of the most lethal killers he had ever met scissored her feet in the air like a giddy teenager. She sat up again and raised a petulant eyebrow. "He should have suffered more."

The man in the dark suit snorted. "I believe he suffered a great deal, both mentally and physically, before he died."

"And now?"

The man in the dark suit turned and examined himself in the mirror again. "It gets even better. Our agents tell us that large numbers of troop ships are deploying from both the east and west coasts of the United States. Our agents also inform us that large numbers of commercial transports are being chartered by the United States government."

"They are complying with your demands."

"They have no choice. It is that, or death on a scale even beyond their nuclear strategic planners can comprehend."

"And that death will come to them anyway."

"Indeed. The plan goes ahead as scheduled." The man in the dark suit walked to the single door of the room that led back into the complex. He smiled with great satisfaction, then turned as his hand rested on the knob. "The United States will fall, and there is no one who can stop us."

Atlanta, Georgia

MACK BOLAN OPENED his eyes.

The glare of the single, bare bulb of the cellar had been replaced by the even lighting of a stark white overhead fixture. He found himself on a wide mechanical bed, which was surrounded by a plastic isolation tent. The tent itself was inside a plastic dome. The dome took up most of the space in a gray-walled room with a wide observation window in one side. Bolan relaxed back into the bed.

He was inside a level-four containment area, and he was very sure he was no longer in Mexico.

Bolan glanced around at the forbidding gray walls and the single steel door without a knob. It wasn't a particularly friendly-looking environment, but even this claustrophobic cell of gray concrete and steel was definitely a step up from the cellar in Chihuahua. An IV dripped into his right arm, and while his mouth was dry, the burning thirst had disappeared. A voice that was slightly distorted by an electronic speaker spoke from slightly behind his bed.

"How's our patient feeling today?"

Bolan turned his head, and Dr. Eliza Thurman grinned at him from behind the faceplate of a Racal space suit.

Bolan cleared his throat. "Hungry and thirsty."

Thurman's grin spread from ear to ear. "Excellent. I'll have some food sent in here immediately."

Bolan scanned the room again. "What's the situation?"

"Well, the fact that you're the only man Western medicine knows of to cure himself of Ebola kind of made you a priority. We couldn't risk letting you die of thirst or go taking deep whiffs of formaldehyde."

Bolan accepted that and nodded gratefully as she poured him a glass of water from a beaker on a small medical table. He swallowed half of it in large gulps, then savored the rest of it slowly. After his ordeal in the cellar, the simple act of drinking water took on great signifigance.

It was good to be alive.

"So what's my situation, currently?"

Bolan finished the water and handed her back the glass.

Thurman nodded her head at the room. "Well, you're in Atlanta, Goergia, and you're in quarantine, but that's mostly a formality. You've been unconscious and under observation for about the past twenty-four hours. We've been monitoring you around the clock, and your last blood test showed no living Ebola Sese virus in your body. As far as we can tell, you're clean. It seems someone has really developed a cure for the Ebola virus.''

Bolan flexed the muscles in his legs and arms and experimentally arched his back. He still felt stiffness and pain, and he felt much weaker than he wanted to admit. "How soon until I can be returned to active duty?"

The soldier had seen the sudden disapproving scowl on Thurman's face mirrored by dozens of doctors. "Listen, you're recovering from Ebola. On top of that, you were in an advanced state of dehydration when we pulled you out of that cellar. You've lost about ten pounds of lean body mass, and the virus did attack and damage a wide spectrum of your bodily tissues from just under the skin to your internal organs. I'm expecting you to make a complete recovery, but you and I both know that's not going to happen overnight. Now, why don't you lay back and relax before I have you put in restraints."

Bolan grunted and lay back. He couldn't be totally sure if she was joking or not. He knew he made a poor patient, but he'd been sick and wounded in enough ways not to kid himself that he could jump out of bed the minute his eyes opened. Regardless, being bedridden still rankled, and rankled deep. He looked at the IV unit dripping into his arm. "How about some real food, then?"

Thurman folded her arms across her chest. "That I can arrange." Her grin broke out again. "I suppose you want a sixteen ounce steak and half a dozen eggs."

"For starters." He looked at a chart hanging on a hook near his head. "So tell me. Do we have an antidote?"

Thurman's smile faded. "No."

Bolan was puzzled. "If I've beaten the virus, shouldn't we be able to take antibodies from my blood?"

"You would think so." She sighed wearily, and Bolan became aware of the dark circles under her eyes. While he had been recuperating, she had probably been working around the clock. She nodded toward the chart. "The antidote was literally that. An antidote, not an inoculation or a booster shot to your immune system. Whatever you injected yourself with down in the cellar went through your system like a broom. We're still not sure how it worked, but it seems like whatever it was broke into the Ebola Sese virus like a genetic safe-cracker and made it self-destruct from the inside. If that theory is true, then it was one incredible feat of biochemical engineering.''

She shook her head at the chart and spoke almost to herself. ''Almost no side effects on the human subject, either. Remarkable.''

Bolan leaned back into his pillow again. ''So you're saying it's not recoverable?''

''We're doing the best we can, but it looks like a lost cause. Whatever the serum is, it seems to have a very short shelf life in the body. It killed the virus and was then almost immediately broken down and absorbed by your body. The traces left in the needle didn't stay viable once the seal of the syringe was broken. We're working with those traces now, but they're highly degraded. I can't really promise any kind of results.'' She blew at a stray lock of hair that had crept out from under her skull cap inside the helmet. ''To answer your question, we still don't have any kind of viable defense against this virus. If the bad guys release this stuff anytime soon, we're toast.''

Bolan nodded. ''I need to make a phone call.''

Thurman folded her arms again. ''You bet you do. A lot of people have been wanting to talk to you.''

''Anyone special?''

''Most of them informed me I didn't have high-enough security clearance to ask.'' She shrugged and smiled again. ''The President, on the other hand, was nice enough to identify himself over the phone.''

''Are they on hold now?''

''No, but I told them I'd inform them as soon as you woke up.'' Thurman rolled a small communications console to the bed. "Why don't you relax for a little bit while I set up your conference call?"

Bolan leaned back into the bed to rest for a moment. He wasn't aware of closing his eyes.

THE OLD MAN sat at the head of a massive teak wood table and faced the board. The room was soundproofed, shielded and swept for electronic bugs on a daily basis. Five men nearly as old as himself sat ramrod straight in their ornate chairs with faces of graven stone. This day the destiny of the modern world would be decided.

The old man ignored formality and went straight to the point. "Despite minor setbacks the operation goes exactly as we have planned. The government of the United States is very much afraid. We have demonstrated our threat and proved that it is viable. They have no idea who we are, and they are acutely aware of the fact that they have no defense against us whatsoever. As a nation they are facing biological Armageddon."

He glanced around the room. All of the men in the room looked resolute, and he doubted any of them had changed his mind. But a vote had been agreed upon at the outset. "Already their troops in Europe and Asia are being moved toward staging areas. At the moment they are doing this under the guise of strategic exercises. The movement of large numbers of military troop carriers on the sea and the large reassignment of planes back to the United States—those they are having a harder time explaining." The thin smile creased across the old man's mouth. "Nonetheless, they are withdrawing troops and planes from Europe and Asia with great speed. They are acceding to our demands."

A man with a face like a hatchet spoke gruffly. "This is known to us."

"Indeed." The old man nodded. "However, there is a question of the timetable. It will take several months for them to totally withdraw all men and matériel. However, removing the majority of their troops is simply a matter of putting men on planes. This will take very little time."

The thin-faced man nodded. "What is it you are suggesting?"

The old man put his hands flat on the table. "I am suggesting we move up our timetable."

The men around the table grunted and shifted in their chairs. Most of them didn't seemed pleased with the idea. The thin-faced man's expression remained intense but neutral. "Why?"

The old man shrugged. "It is simple. For us, time is vulnerability. The enemy does not know who we are. Not yet. They have no defense against us currently. The longer we wait to strike, the more of a chance there is of something going wrong. Our scientists discovered a cure for Ebola. We must assume their doctors and scientists are working feverishly to come up with one, as well. Every man in this room knows the folly of underestimating the Americans. During this operation itself, we have been constantly surprised by their tenacity and their cleverness. We have held all the cards, and we have prevailed despite setbacks and failures. I suggest we do not give the Americans time or opportunity to give us any more unpleasant surprises."

The thin-faced man seemed to have assumed the role of spokesman for the rest of the board. "What exactly do you suggest?"

"I suggest we wait as little as possible. When the majority of the United States military is back on United States soil, I say we strike. It does not matter if the Americans still have thousands of tanks or artillery pieces overseas if their crews are already back at home and decimated by the virus. The logistic and transport troops who will still be overseas supervising the equipment are trivial." The old man leaned back in his chair and looked each man around the table in the eye. His gaze finally returned to the thin-faced man. "I suggest we cut the timetable. If the troop withdrawal numbers are right, I say we strike in two weeks."

The rest of the men around the table regarded one another. Each man slowly nodded. The thin-faced man took in each man's nod, then nodded himself. "It is agreed, then. We strike in two weeks."

20

The Executioner opened his eyes as someone wiggled his toe. Eliza Thurman stood at the foot of the hospital bed with an amused look on her face. "Paging Mr. Striker, your conference call is ready."

Bolan smiled. "Who's on the line?"

"I believe it's the President, and two guys named Hal and Bear."

"Put them on."

Thurman punched two buttons on the console, and there was a click as the speakers came on. Hal Brognola's voice came crystal clear across the speaker in the communications console. "You there?"

"I'm here."

The President's voice spoke. "I want you to know I appreciate the sacrifice you were prepared to make. I also appreciate the fact that you've been under quite an ordeal, and Dr. Thurman has stressed the fact that you aren't fully recovered. But I feel we need to talk, just the four of us, urgently."

Bolan looked at the speaker. "Dr. Thurman has been taking good care of me, Mr. President. She thinks I'm going to make a full recovery, and I can certainly answer questions."

The President sounded relieved. "Good. Your intuition about the enemy having a cure for the Ebola Sese virus seems to have paid off. Hal tells me your hunches have a habit of doing that. I'm very interested in discussing your idea about who our enemy really is in this situation."

"Sir, I believe the enemy is Japanese. I suspect they are a high-level branch, if not multiple branches, of a corporate conglomerate."

Bolan could hear the President shift in his chair over the link. "Can you back that up?"

"No, sir. I can't prove it." Bolan glanced around the gray walls of the level-four containment room. "At least not from here. But it's the scenario that seems to fit the situation best. Not a whole lot else makes any sense."

"Why do you say that?"

"Well, for one thing, the organization. They act like a small group of terrorists, but their network and resources seem to be on a global scale. Then there's the weapon they're using. You'd have to be insane to use Ebola as a weapon. The chance of it killing your own people is too great. That, of course, made it look even more like it had to be the work of a group of terrorist fanatics. The only other viable notion is that the enemy had a cure for the virus, which they did. Dr. Thurman told me that the cure they have developed is a marvel of chemical and biological engineering. That narrows down our suspects immensely. The majority of the nations on this planet don't have adequately equipped level-four containment areas for hot viruses. You can't work with this stuff in a garage. Their hatbox seems to be of even higher quality than the ones used by the CDC and the United States military. The United States has lots of enemies, so almost anyone could have the motive, but who has the money, who has the technology and who has the facilities? Those are the real questions."

"That's still all pretty circumstantial, Striker. My strategic advisers tell me that this operation still could have been run by the Russians, the Chinese or, for that matter, any one of several European powers."

Bolan frowned slightly. "That's true. But there are other factors. Japan is an island nation. Once the virus is released into the United States, it would be much easier for them to close their borders and isolate themselves than any continental power. They also have the technological and economic resources to come to our rescue once the United States is on its knees. The same can't be said of the other powers you've mentioned.''

The President sounded unhappy. ''That's still circumstantial.''

Bolan took a slow breath. ''I know, sir. But I feel it.''

The President sighed. ''I'm informed that you believe they intend to use the virus on a large scale, rather than just as a leverage to blackmail us.''

''That's correct.''

''What exactly do you envision?''

Bolan had been giving that a great deal of thought. ''I believe the isolated outbreaks of Ebola will escalate. They'll be engineered so that they can be contained, like the ones before. But their number and their intensity will increase until you're forced to close the borders of the United States. This will most likely coincide with the return of our military forces from Europe and Asia. Initially I believe the military withdrawal was a kind of feint to throw us off the trail, but I think they also want our military pared down and crippled along with the rest of the population. Once the borders of the United States are closed, you can expect a full outbreak, and I mean full. They're going to release the virus into the general population, most likely from a large number of sites all at once. I believe they're willing to let millions of Americans die before they come forward with a cure. I suspect their acceptable death toll to be anywhere from one-quarter to one-half of the United States's population.''

The President was silent for a long time. ''I can accept everything you say, but my problem is that this is still all conjecture. I can't declare war on Japan on a theory, and from the way you've put it, the majority of the Japanese government probably has no idea that this is even going on.''

''That's true. They've covered their tracks extremely efficiently''

Aaron Kurtzman spoke up. "Mr. President, I'd like to make a suggestion."

"Go ahead."

Bolan could almost hear Kurtzman warm to the subject. "Assuming Striker is correct, we still have some options. Declaring war on Japan probably isn't one of them. Even if we did it, the enemy's response would simply be to release the virus. We have to hit the enemy in a preemptive strike."

The President sighed. "But we still don't know for sure who the real enemy is."

"Granted, but I like Striker's logic. Also, in the mission that led us to an attack on the Royal Family, we found that disk in Libya. We still haven't completely broken its coding, and everyone from our people at the Farm to the NSA have all been working on it. Like the technology to work with the virus, that kind of computer encryption can't be done by just anyone. I'm willing to bet it came from a Japanese resource. I'll admit it makes me uncomfortable without further confirmation, but I suggest we assume our enemies are of Japanese corporate extraction."

The President cleared his throat. "Assuming we do that, what course of action are you recommending?"

Kurtzman went into high gear. "We run a sweep of all Japanese resources in the United States. We know that when the enemy fled the house in Chihuahua they were flying north, in small helicopters. They most likely have a base in the United States. I'm thinking it's in property already held by whichever Japanese conglomerate is responsible. The base would have to have a fully equipped laboratory, capable of level-four virus-containment procedures. Probably some kind of pharmaceutical or biological research group. It wouldn't surprise me if the lab they are using in the United States is the same one that came up with the cure in the first place. They'll only want their own people on this, and that would include scientists, security and staff. I doubt they'll have any American employees. That will help narrow the search down.

They would also probably be located in or near a big city. One that is a nexus for a lot of domestic travel, some place like Los Angles or New York. I suggest we narrow down that list, and then we find them and hit them.''

The President saw where this was going. "Using the personnel of Stony Man Farm?"

Hal Brognola spoke. "Well, sir, we are deniable. If you send in the Navy SEALs or Delta Force, and we're wrong, there's going to be one hell of an international incident. Striker and his teams are deniable, and while I hate to say it, they are expendable. If they're caught, they can just as easily be mercenaries from a rival business concern, hired to wipe out the competition.''

The President sighed. "This is one hell of a gamble, gentlemen, and none of this can be substantiated.''

Bolan spoke. "Once we have our potential sites narrowed down, surveillance may help us to be sure. But in my opinion we have to act fast. We're probably only going to get one shot at this, and the enemy has to be operating under the assumption that we're actively trying to find out who and where they are. They're not going to wait around for us to do that. We're on their timetable, and I'm betting time is short. I don't think we have much choice.''

The President's voice grew cold with decision. "Very well. Use whatever resources you need. Run with it.''

21

Los Angeles, California

The southern California night was a sweltering eighty-five degrees. Up on the hillside it was cooler, and a slight breeze ruffled the sea of waist-high, midsummer golden brown grass. Below, the lights of Los Angeles sprawled out like a vast lake of stars, and the clouds and smog caught the city's light and gave the night a humid, roseate glow. Just to the west, the Pacific Ocean rolled in with the evening tide. Up on the hillside a patch of the grass moved imperceptibly, and, unseen, a man brought a pair of laser range-finding night-vision binoculars to his eyes.

Mack Bolan scrutinized the Nishiki-Tetsuo biotech facility where it perched farther around the hill.

Nishiki-Tetsuo was an up-and-comer in the world of biotechnology. Its stock had an extremely high buying-price-to-earning ratio, even though it had very few actual products on the market. It was most known for its innovative research techniques, and its annual report said that many wonder drugs were awaiting U.S. government approval. Investors were anxious to buy shares of their stock. The latest Nishiki-Tetsuo annual report hadn't included any mention of a cure for Ebola, or even having ever worked with the virus. However, developing antiviral drugs was one of its strong points.

Bolan grimaced as he scanned the compound. Those factors alone proved nothing, and this facility was one of fifteen possible targets in the Los Angeles area. But, Kurtzman had a feeling about Nishiki-Tetsuo and had red-flagged it as the number-one target. Bolan had long ago learned to trust Kurtzman's instincts. He had also learned to trust his own, and the corners of his mouth turned up slightly as he continued to scrutinize the compound.

For such a small facility, it certainly seemed to have extremely heavy security.

Bolan ran his binoculars around the compound's perimeter. The facility was surrounded by a twelve-foot-high chain-link fence. The fence split into a Y shape at its top, and coils of razor wire glinted wickedly in the fence's crotch. Every eighth fence post had a surveillance camera mounted on a swiveling post, and the compound itself had a series of powerful floodlights that would light up the night for hundreds of feet when they were turned on. Bolan swept the fence again with his binoculars. The tall grass had been mown to lawn height in a five-yard swath all around the fence. He examined the small dark shape of a coyote that lay a foot away from the fence. The little body was folded up like a cricket.

Gary Manning's voice spoke in Bolan's earpiece. "What do you think?"

"I think that fence is electrified."

Manning's voice filled with mock indignation. "I don't believe these boys have posted any warning signs."

"No, they haven't."

"Well, now, that's downright illegal in this state."

Bolan gazed at the fence. He very much doubted it was fully charged all the time. Probably just enough current ran through it to tell their security operators if something or someone was breaching the fence or climbing it. Bolan had no doubt whatsoever the security operator could surge the fence voltage to lethal levels anytime he chose.

He began to creep forward along the side of the hill toward the fence. "Cover me. I'm going to try a little experiment."

Manning lay in a hide thirty yards back up on the hill. Like

Bolan, he wore a night camouflage suit that held in his body heat against infrared viewers, and its outer layer of fibers had been woven in a disruptive pattern to fool light-enhancing night-vision devices. On top of this, tufts of grass and straw had been woven into their camouflage suits until the two of them looked like scarecrows that had been turned inside out. In daylight, one would almost have to literally step on them to know that they were there. In the night, they were less than shadows. Manning flipped the safety off his suppressed .308-caliber Steyr rifle. "You've got it."

Bolan pulled his night vision goggles over his eyes and moved forward at a snail's pace around the hillside. The grass around him hardly moved with his passage, and the breeze blew over him, favorably covering his movements. Ten minutes later he was holding his silenced Beretta 93-R and peering into the cleared area in front of the fence. He looked at the coyote. Its legs were pulled up against its body, and it was as stiff as a board. Bolan had seen more than enough human bodies in the same condition to recognize a death by electrocution.

Bolan spoke into his throat mike. "How close is the nearest camera?"

Manning's voice came back. "About ten yards to your left."

"Which way is it pointing?"

"It's swiveling away from your direction now."

Bolan unhooked a thin coil of rope from his web gear. "Keep me advised."

"You've got it."

The soldier clicked out one of the grappling hook's tines and uncoiled ten feet of rope. He took a moment to aim, then flicked the aluminum grapple out and over the coyote's body.

Manning suddenly spoke. "Camera's coming your way again. Whatever you're doing, do it fast."

"Roger." Bolan gently pulled the rope back until the grapple's tine pulled to a rest against the animal, then he rapidly reeled in the small body. Every muscle in the coyote's body was locked from the current that had run through it.

Bolan recoiled the rope and grapnel. "Gary, I'm going to move fifty yards uphill. It'll take me a few minutes."

"You're covered."

The Executioner began to move up the hill on his knees and elbows with his stiffened prize lying across his forearms. Fatigue began to burn in his limbs, and he grudgingly admitted to himself that he still wasn't one hundred percent recovered from his illness. He ignored the sweat dripping down his face and the burning of fatigue and continued on. He neared the crest and peered out of the grass at the fence again. It seemed to be as good a spot as any to play doorbell-ditch-it. "Gary, I'm in position, let's see if anybody's home."

"You have cameras twenty-five yards to either side."

Bolan kept his eyes on the patch of fence in front of him. "Give me my window."

"Roger."

Bolan glanced at the stiffened coyote in silent empathy. The poor creature was about to be fried a second time.

Manning suddenly spoke. "You've got five seconds."

The soldier did a push-up off the ground with one arm and hurled the small body against the fence.

A bright blue arc of electricity flared in Bolan's night-vision goggles as the coyote bounced off the fence and fell smoking to the cropped grass. Bolan pulled off his goggles as the entire compound blazed with the sudden white glare of the floodlights. He ignored the light and began to creep backward in slow motion through the grass. He spoke into his mike as he moved. "What have we got?"

"We've got lights, but you probably noticed that. The cameras have swiveled your way." Manning paused. "They keep panning back and forth. I'm thinking either they're on automatic or else they're at the wrong angle to see your little friend."

Bolan kept moving backward an inch at a time into the shelter of the darkened hillside. "What else?"

Manning's voice suddenly dropped. "You've got company."

"What kind."

"You've got a Jeep coming out of the compound, coming your way."

"How many men?"

"I count four. They're armed." Bolan could almost hear Manning thinking. "Striker, you'd better freeze now or move fast."

Bolan felt his left foot slide slightly downward. He crept backward another three feet and found himself in a narrow fold in the hillside. "I'm sticking, keep me covered."

"Roger."

The soldier could hear the Jeep's engine as it rapidly bounced along the hillside, and he hunched lower into the fold as searchlights swept the top of the grass over his head. He pushed his body deeper into the depression as the Jeep suddenly ground to a halt close by. Manning spoke into Bolan's ear. "I've got four males, Asians, armed with what looks like M-16s. I see no activity outside the fence."

Bolan lay motionless and listened intently. He could hear voices over the idling engine of the Jeep. The glare of the searchlight swept down the hillside and the smaller beams of flashlights stabbed out across the grass. Bolan's grasp of Japanese wasn't extensive, but he recognized the language over the Jeep's noise. There was a sudden expletive, and the other men laughed.

The coyote had been found.

Manning's voice went urgent. "Freeze, Mack! Don't move a muscle!"

Bolan waited for several long seconds. There was the sound of another laugh, then the Jeep ground into gear. A single flashlight beam played out over the top of the grass again before the vehicle's tires ground into the dirt and the engine sound began to move off. "What was it, Gary?"

Manning sounded relieved. "The driver pulled out a rifle. A big one, with a really big scope. He swept the grass with it. I'm betting it was a night-vision device. They've piled back into the Jeep and are pulling out."

"So are we. Meet me on the other side of the dark side of the hill in fifteen minutes."

"Roger." Manning's voice went conspiratorial. "I think we've got a live one here, Mack."

"We've got something, anyway."

THE MAN IN THE DARK SUIT strode into the security suite. Ryuchi Taido stood with his powerful arms folded across his chest, and the disgusted look seemed to have been etched in stone across his bearded face. Two men sat at the security console with guilty looks on their faces. The man looked to Taido. "What has happened?"

Taido ran a caustic eye on the man at the left-hand seat. "Mas has managed to electrocute a coyote."

The man in the dark suit turned his gaze on Mas, and the man kept his own gaze firmly on his shoes. Mas was nearly as short as Taido and twice as thickly built. His bullet-shaped head was shaved and at the moment beet red. Mas had made sergeant in the Tokyo police before he had been lured into more-lucrative fields. He was a second-degree black belt in judo, and, in the man's mind, had proved himself reasonably competent.

The man in the dark suit frowned. That was the problem with static security. It fostered boredom, and long hours of boredom fostered poor attention and mistakes. He much preferred to take the offensive in these matters. But the current situation couldn't be helped, and such foolishness couldn't be tolerated. "You are sure it was just a coyote?"

Taido shrugged. "I sent Harada out with a team. They found an electrocuted coyote by the fence. He ran an infrared scope over the area, and there were no heat signatures in the grass within range.''

The man frowned. This was the second incident in the same day. He didn't like coincidences, and vague suspicion crawled up and down his spine. ''At first light I want the area around the contact site searched thoroughly.''

Taido nodded. ''Yes, sir.''

The man folded his arms. ''I also want a helicopter brought to the site. I want it armed and a team standing by to man it.''

Taido thought that odd, but kept his opinion to himself. ''I will see to it immediately.''

''Good.'' The man in the dark suit turned to leave, then suddenly spun on his heel. His arm whipped around nearly 360 degrees, and his stiffened palm cracked against Mas's face like a gunshot. The blow sprawled Mas out of his chair and onto the floor. He writhed for a moment in agony and clutched at his face for several seconds. Then, with an immense effort of will, he forced himself to his feet and held himself at attention. The entire left side of his face was swelling with vicious purple bruising that undoubtedly went right down to the bone. Tears of pain rolled down his cheeks, and blood spilled down from his lips, but he held himself rigid.

The man in the dark suit was somewhat impressed. Mas had an admirable level of self-control. When the man spoke, there was no anger in his voice. ''Do not ever surge a contact until you have a visual. If it had been some stupid kids you had fried, the cost to our operation could be enormous. Next time I will kill you.''

Mas fired off a low bow from the waist. *''Hai!''*

The man in the dark suit turned again on his heel. ''I want that helicopter tonight.''

22

"I've got a good feeling about Nishiki-Tetsuo. I think we're on target."

The rest of the people around the table looked at Bolan. Hal Brognola nodded thoughtfully. The President of the United States spoke from the speaker of a secure satellite link. "How much of a good feeling?"

Bolan shrugged. "I didn't see Heidi Hochrein sunbathing naked on the roof, but they've got an overabundance of security."

Manning leaned back in his chair. "I agree. They've got the place buttoned up tight, and they're armed to the teeth. Even if they aren't our boys, it sure smells like something is going on in there, and I doubt if it's legal. The Bear says they are the most likely target in the area, and L.A. itself is a prime target. I say he's right. Let's hit them and hit them hard."

Kurtzman spoke over his own link. "There's been another development, as well. Satellite reconnaissance shows that a helicopter flew to the complex almost immediately after Striker ran his probe."

The President's heavy sigh was audible over the link. "One more suspicious behavior that doesn't prove anything. Hal, I'm just not sure if I can have your men level the place on suspicions and circumstantial evidence. This is United States soil, and Nishiki-Tetsuo is a legitimate business."

Bolan sat up. "I agree. We can't just go in and pull a scorched-earth routine on them."

Brognola looked at Bolan. "What are you thinking?"

"We have to go in and confirm one way or the other whether these are our same friends with the virus. I say we go in airborne, and we go in soft. We insert a small team by parachute and have a backup team waiting outside the perimeter. If we're on the money, the cavalry comes in. We capture or destroy the virus and take the people inside the facility. If we come up short, then the inside team will try to bug out without hitting any friendlies. If we can't, or we get cornered, we'll just surrender. We keep our mouths shut, make bail, then disappear."

Brognola nodded and steepled his fingers. "How small a team are you thinking?"

Bolan looked at the satellite map of the Nishiki-Tetsuo facility. "As small as possible. Their security seems tight and sophisticated. I'll need Gadgets for countermeasures."

Brognola raised an eyebrow. "That's it?"

"No. I need one more person. Once I get inside, I won't know what to look for, and neither will Gadgets. If we were looking for bombs or guns, it would be one thing, but when we get in, we'll need someone who knows the way around a lab and knows what to look for." Bolan turned his gaze on Eliza Thurman. "I've been in a firefight with Dr. Thurman before. I trust her, and she's already deeply a part of this mission. I want her, if she'll come."

Thurman's eyes flew wide. There was a moment's pause, then the President's voice came over the speaker. "Dr. Thurman, you're an officer in the United States Army, but I want you to know I can't order you to do this if you don't want to."

The woman looked back and forth between the faces around the table, then glanced hesitantly at the President's speaker. "Well, sir, I'm not exactly Special Forces material..."

Bolan folded his arms across his chest. "You did all right in Uganda, and you have technical expertise we're going to desperately need. On top of that, you're here now, and I say we go in tonight." Bolan raised an eyebrow. "Have you ever made any jumps?"

Thurman smiled nervously. "I've been bungee jumping."

"It's almost the same thing."

She looked around the room again, then nodded slowly. "Well, I want something bigger than a .22 target pistol this time."

Bolan nodded. "That can be arranged."

THE AC-130U HERCULES gunship rumbled down the runway of China Lake Air Force Base and rose up into the night sky. Jack Grimaldi's voice spoke almost immediately over the intercom. "ETA forty-five minutes, Striker."

"Roger." Bolan sat back and relaxed. They were jumping from thirty thousand feet with clear skies, and their target was a flat and well-lit roof. The only technical problem was that Bolan would have to jump in a tandem rig with Dr. Thurman, and both of their gear loads, as well. Bolan glanced over at the woman. She looked a little nervous, but she seemed to be holding up well. She had qualified in the Army with both the M-16 rifle and the .45 Colt automatic. The silenced 9 mm Colt submachine gun she held across her knees worked almost exactly the same way. A .45 automatic in a shoulder holster was lashed over an armored vest they had scrounged for her from LAPD stores.

Gadgets Schwarz appeared to be asleep. His black bag of tricks lay between his feet, and a silenced 9 mm Heckler & Koch MP-5 SD submachine gun sat at his side. Bolan himself wore a full war load. Like Thurman, he carried a silenced 9 mm Colt subgun, but his weapon had a customized 40 mm M-203 grenade launcher clipped under the barrel. Off to the west, elements of Able Team and Phoenix Force were already shadows in the tall grass surrounding the Nishiki-Tetsuo facility. If the flag went up, they would come through the wire and storm the facility.

The plane Bolan flew in was their safety valve. The AC-

130 was the latest version of the special operations Spectre gunship. The four-engined Hercules carried a lethal load of cannons. The AC-130 could bring to bear an L-60 40 mm Bofors antiaircraft gun, a GAU-12 25 mm automatic cannon, and the heavyweight punch of an M-102 105 mm howitzer. A sophisticated suite of infrared sensors and radars allowed the Spectre to find concealed targets. The AC-130U had been designed to rule the night, and once the gunship dropped Bolan and company out the back, it would ensure that nothing escaped the Nishiki-Tetsuo compound intact. A team of Air Force operators sat by the weapons and sensors with their oxygen masks ready. They watched their display screens as the radars examined the terrain far below.

Grimaldi spoke again over the intercom. "ETA is ten minutes, Striker. We've got a tailwind and we're making good time. Will advise ground."

"Roger." Bolan stood and motioned to Thurman. "Let's hook up."

She got up and looked about the plane again. Her diminutive form was festooned with weapons and armor. Bolan smiled at her. "It's very simple. Just like I told you. When we bail out, arch your body hard. When we get close to the roof, lift your legs when I tell you to. Other than that, just relax and enjoy the ride."

The woman swallowed and nodded uncertainly as she turned around. Bolan began buckling her harness to his own. Their weapons and gear made it awkward, but they were quickly locked together to fall as a unit. Schwarz rose and gave their straps a few experimental tugs.

"Looks shipshape."

Bolan pulled on Schwarz's rig and nodded to him as a red light came on in the cabin. Grimaldi's voice spoke again from the cockpit. "We're at thirty thousand. ETA five minutes. Begin your oxygen. I'm depressurizing the cabin."

The soldier pulled his oxygen mask over his face and twisted the valve on his bailout bottle. He made sure Thurman's mask was on securely and checked her airflow. Schwarz gave him a thumbs-up, and Bolan spoke into the intercom. "We're ready back here."

The plane rumbled on through the high atmosphere over Los Angeles. Grimaldi's voice spoke again. "Opening rear door."

The interior lights dimmed, and the Hercules's airframe vibrated. A blast of cold wind rushed through the cabin as the cargo-bay door began to open with a hydraulic whine. Outside the plane all was icy blackness. Bolan, Eliza and Schwarz moved toward the ramp. The dim form of the Hercules's massive tail loomed above them, and below there was nothing but empty space. The jump light went from red to green, and Grimaldi gave them their final warning.

"You have a green light, Striker! We'll be over the target in thirty seconds!"

Bolan and Thurman shuffle-stepped together onto the ramp door, and Schwarz came up behind. Since Bolan would be flying for two, Schwarz was the jump master. He shouted above the roar of the icy wind. "Ready?"

Bolan and Thurman nodded. Schwarz grinned. "Go!"

The Executioner stepped out into space. Thurman gave a little shriek, but she immediately arched against him and spread her arms and legs the way she had been shown. They tumbled through the blackness for a moment as the roaring wind buffeted them, then Bolan managed to stabilize their fall. Below them the lights of southern California were like puddles and strings of tiny stars on a field of black velvet.

The doctor let out a whoop of pure exhilaration that was barely muffled by her mask.

Bolan spoke into his throat mike. "So how are you doing?"

Thurman almost lost the power of speech as she experienced free fall from thirty thousand feet. "Wow! Wow! Wow!"

Bolan smiled. Falling through space was the easy part. On the ground things were probably going to get interesting real fast. "Where are you, Gadgets?"

Schwarz's voice came back. "Somewhere a little above you, Striker. Don't have you on visual."

Bolan checked the altimeter on his wrist, then looked down as the darkness rushed up at them. They had just passed twenty thousand feet, and Grimaldi's aim was as accurate as ever. From Bolan's plunging perspective, the city itself was slightly to the east and they were falling directly toward a darker patch that indicated the rural Los Angeles hills and Topanga Canyon. Past the hills the vast dark expanse of the Pacific Ocean.

Schwarz spoke again. "I just hit ten thousand."

"Roger." Bolan scanned the darkness below. There were scattered lights in the hillsides, and he locked on a set of them that seemed to hold the geometry of a building complex. He spoke into his throat mike to Thurman. "All right, quit your whooping. We don't want to wake up the neighborhood."

Schwarz's voice came again through their personal radios. "Five thousand."

Bolan could make out the dimmer, tiny circle of red lights that had to be the helicopter pad.

"Two thousand."

Bolan's hand closed around the rip cord.

"One thousand! Pull!"

Bolan pulled the rip cord, and a second later Thurman yelped as their harnesses suddenly took the massive yank of the main chute's drag.

"I see your canopy, Striker."

"Roger." Bolan took the steering toggles in his hands, then leaned into Thurman's ear. "You all right?"

The back of her head nodded vigorously. "Let's do it again!"

Bolan pulled his oxygen mask and his jump goggles down around his neck, then lowered his night-vision goggles over his eyes and switched them on. The blackness below lit up into an eerie landscape of oddly flat-looking green-and-gray hills. He could see a few scattered ranch houses off in some of the canyons, and almost directly below him were the Nishiki-Tetsuo buildings. Bolan noted the ghostly light that now seemed to form a web with the complex itself, sitting in the middle like a giant spider. Nishiki-Tetsuo had turned on its infrared lasers. To the naked eye they would have been invisible, and anything that broke their net of light inside the perimeter would set off alarms. Fortunately the roof seemed to be devoid of such security measures, and Bolan took their descent into a slow spiral. A helicopter sat in the middle of the landing pad, and he chose a flat space of roof off to one side of it.

He leaned into Thurman's ear again. "Get ready to lift your legs."

She nodded again. "Yup."

Schwarz spoke in Bolan's ear. "I'm right behind you, Striker. Go ahead and make your approach."

"Roger." Suddenly the roof seemed to be flying up to meet them, and Bolan began to pull back on his toggles. He adjusted their angle slightly as they swung toward the parked helicopter. "Pull up your legs!"

Thurman pulled up her legs, and Bolan yanked the big tandem chute into a full stall. For a split second they seemed to hang suspended five feet over the roof. It was higher than Bolan had wanted. As they hit, he took the doctor's full weight and they landed with what seemed like an earthshaking thud.

For a moment they both froze. There was no sound except for a light breeze that rustled their chute. The roof floodlights didn't come on, and sirens didn't split the night. Bolan quickly stood and began to unclip their harnesses. The roof could have pressure sensors, and even now the alarm could be wailing in the Nishiki-Tetsuo security room. The Executioner glanced up at a rustling noise, and Schwarz descended to the roof in a textbook landing. He flicked his harness toggles and stepped out of his jump harness.

Bolan spoke quietly into his radio. "We're on the roof. No visible enemy reaction."

Gary Manning's voice came back in Bolan's earpiece. "Roger. We saw you come in. Ground team is in position, and the gunship is orbiting your position. There are no patrols evident outside of the building. You are a go for entry."

Bolan unclipped his silenced Colt submachine gun. "We're going in."

The Executioner flipped off the safety. The M-203 grenade launcher below its barrel held an antipersonnel buckshot in the breech. Bolan ran his gaze over the roof. Opposite the helicopter was a concrete shack with a steel door. It was obviously the door to the stairwell.

Bolan and Schwarz had a hurried conference. "You think anyone heard us?"

The Able Team electronics expert frowned. "No. This is a biological-pharmaceutical building. It's climate controlled. All the windows are sealed, and I bet the building is heavily insulated. The space below us is probably where they have all of their cooling and heating systems. If they had pressure sensors on the roof, I think we would have heard about it by now."

"You think they have any kind of alarm system linked to that door over there?"

"Now, that's another matter entirely."

The two of them moved to the door and examined it critically. Schwarz scratched his chin. "I think we might be in luck. This is a basic industrial building, and I believe it was constructed before any illegal activities began. A lot of their security will be recent add-on stuff, and I'm doubting whether the security designers were anticipating an airborne assault."

"What are you thinking?"

Schwarz reached into his black bag and produced a long thin strip of metal. "I'm thinking there's probably an electrical circuit that breaks when the door is opened. Probably spring loaded." He knelt and worked the metal strip into the seam between the door and the jamb. He slowly moved the shim up the seam, then suddenly stopped when it reached waist height. "I think I've found it. Go ahead and blow the lock."

Bolan reached into a pouch in his web gear and pulled out a short roll of thick triangular wire. He cut a six-inch length with his combat knife and pulled off the protective strip of the wire. Adhesive coated one side of the wire, and it was filled with flexible shaped-charge explosive. He pressed the adhesive against the door in a circle around the doorknob and pushed a detonator pin through the plastic coating and into the explosive.

Schwarz kept the shim in place with one hand and held his padded black bag up in front of his face. "Do it."

Bolan stepped back and pulled a small black box from his gear. He flipped the safety shield up from the detonator's button and rested his thumb on it. "Detonating now!"

He pressed the button, and a circle of orange fire made a hissing crack around the doorknob. Bolan stepped forward and grabbed the knob before it could fall. The shaped charge had cut a perfect circle through the steel door, and the white glare of overhead lighting spilled out through the hole. He set the knob on the roof and took the second shim that Schwarz handed him.

Schwarz jerked his head toward the door. "Go ahead and go in. Cut a piece of shim and tape it over the plunger in the door."

Bolan opened the door and moved inside. There was a narrow concrete landing, then a stairwell wound downward to another door. The air was smoky and reeked of burned explosive.

He turned to Thurman. "Come in and cover the stairs."

The doctor walked forward and crouched at the top of the stairs with her weapon trained on the landing below. Bolan quickly cut a piece of shim and pushed it down over the little metal plunger in the doorjamb. "I'm on top of it."

"Roger." Schwarz's shim snaked back through the crack in the door, and a moment later he came onto the landing with his weapon ready. Bolan taped down the piece of shim, then turned to Thurman. "Well, what do you think?"

The woman frowned. "Well, at the CDC we do our level-four viral work on the upper floors, but this is a commercial facility. I'd bet they have their level-four containment area in the bottom of the building."

Bolan nodded. "Down we go."

He took the lead as they went down the stairs. They came to another steel door, but rather than a knob its handle was a push-in bar that crossed it at waist level. Bolan and Schwarz glanced at each other. Then the Able Team commando knelt and plugged a thin wire with a bead on one end into his earpiece. He gently worked the bead beneath the door and listened intently for several moments before he spoke. "I don't hear anything."

Bolan nodded. "Eliza, cover the stairwell. Gadgets, cover me."

He pushed the door open just enough to admit his body and slid through the doorway. He put his back against the wall and looked in both directions. The interior was a plushly carpeted hallway with a series of expensive oak doors running along both sides.

Schwarz trained his gun out the doorway. "Looks like office suites."

Bolan nodded. At one end of the hallway were the sliding steel doors of an elevator. At the other end was a massive set of oaken double doors.

"Command and control?" Schwarz guessed.

"The head honcho's office, anyway." Bolan spoke into his throat mike. "Eliza, stay on the landing with the door cracked. Don't come forward until I give you the go-ahead."

"Gotcha."

Bolan moved down the hall toward the double oak doors. He knelt in front of them and listened. They were thick, and they mated with the floor almost seamlessly. There were no keyholes in the door. On the left door there was a metal slot for an electronic card-key swipe. He motioned Schwarz forward. Bolan stood and covered the hall behind them as his teammate eased his audio wire under the door. He put a finger to his earpiece and listened intently for several long moments. "I've got some kind of electrical or mechanical hum. Maybe a computer with its disk drive running. But no typing sounds, no voices, no sound of movement."

Bolan kept his eyes on the hallway. "Pick it."

"If this is the boss's office, there's bound to be better security on the door. This could take a minute."

"I trust you. Pick it."

Schwarz began to pull various electronic implements out of his black bag. He took out a plastic blank the size of a credit card and attached a pair of wires to it. He plugged the wires into a small back box with a keypad and nodded to himself. A moment later he was making his technological assault on the door.

Bolan glanced at his watch. Thurman's voice suddenly spoke in an urgent hiss in his ear.

"I hear something!"

"Where?"

"Two doors down from me, on the left."

Bolan whipped his weapon to his shoulder as the door Thurman indicated opened. A pair of Asian males stepped out of the office, and they were laughing and speaking Japanese. One of the men turned to close the door behind him and froze with his hand hovering over the knob. The other man turned, and his eyes widened as he stared down the twin muzzles of Bolan's weapon.

The Executioner's voice was deadly calm. "Don't move. Be quiet."

The men locked eyes for a moment, but neither one moved. Bolan spoke softly into his throat mike. "Gary, we have contact."

Manning's voice spoke from somewhere out on the hillside. "Acknowledged. You want the cavalry?"

"Don't know yet. No positive ID. Will keep you advised."

"Roger. Standing by."

Bolan raised a finger off the Colt submachine gun and beckoned the two men to come forward. Their eyes met again, but they didn't move. The Executioner was almost deafened as Thurman shouted over the radio. "Look out!"

The door to the stairwell flew open, and Thurman burst out with her weapon at her shoulder. She aimed the silenced 9 mm Colt submachine gun diagonally across the hallway at the open door the Japanese stood in front of. The weapon hissed in her hands as she squeezed off a long burst. Returning gunfire cracked deafeningly as someone inside the room fired several rapid pistol shots. The doctor continued to fire and was suddenly knocked off her feet as something smashed into her chest.

The two men in the hallway dived to the floor and clawed under their jackets.

Bolan tracked the man on the left and put a 3-round burst into him as his pistol came out from under his jacket. The soldier swung his weapon onto the man on the right. The guy had drawn his weapon, but he twisted and his shot went high and wide as bullets struck him. Schwarz knelt before the door, his Beretta automatic in one hand and the door scrambler in the other.

The Executioner sprinted forward and whipped his weapon around the left-hand door and fired a burst. There was no reply, and he swung into the doorway. Two men lay dead on the floor of the office. One had a pistol in his hand, and an Uzi submachine gun lay next to the other. Bolan turned and knelt by Thurman. Her eyes were wide, and her breath came in labored wheezes. He dug his fingers into the twin holes in her armored vest, and his fingers felt the base of two big bullets.

Thurman had taken two .45 rounds in the chest, but her armor had held. Bolan helped her to her feet and pulled her arm over his shoulder. "Come on!"

Manning came over the radio. "What's your situation, Striker?"

"We've got problems. Hold your position."

Schwarz pulled his door scrambler and dumped it into his bag as he stood. "The hell with this." He holstered the Beretta and picked up his Heckler & Koch MP-5. He lifted his knee to kick the door.

The double doors suddenly flew outward and smashed him backward to the floor. Bolan shoved Thurman down and fell on top of her as a weapon snarled on full-auto. Bullets cracked over the soldier's head as he raised his own weapon.

A man in a dark suit snarled as the gaping 40 mm muzzle of Bolan's M-203 grenade launcher tracked onto him. Over the man's shoulder, the face of Heidi Hochrein was a mask of rage.

Bolan squeezed the M-203's trigger as the man and Hochrein hurled themselves backward. The grenade launcher roared and shot out a blast of pale yellow flame. The personal defensive munition sent out a storm of buckshot that rapidly expanded to fill the hallway with lead. The double oak doors shuddered as the hail of buckshot struck them and the rest of the load flew into the office.

Schwarz levered himself into a half sit-up and began to fire bursts through the doorway. Bolan grimaced as the heavy double doors began to close by themselves. Schwarz rolled to one side as a burst raked the wall above him. The doors swung shut with a locking click.

Bolan racked open the smoking breech of the M-203 and drew a 40 mm armor-piercing round from his bandolier. At the other end of the hall the elevator gave an electronic chime. The Executioner swung his weapon around and fired, the M-203 recoiling against him. The armor-piercing round slammed into the metal elevator doors, and its shaped-charge warhead detonated. He roared at Schwarz. "Drop a grenade down the stairs!"

Schwarz rose from the floor with a fragmentation grenade

in his hands. Bolan strode up to the nearest office door and kicked it in. He entered firing short bursts from his Colt. The office was lit, but apparently empty.

Outside there was an echoing crack as the frag grenade detonated in the stairwell. A moment later Schwarz came through the office door with Thurman in tow. Her eyes had cleared of their shock, and she held her weapon ready. Bolan shut the door, and he and Schwarz shoved the heavy office desk in front of it.

Bolan spoke into his mike. "We have positive ID. Hochrein in building. Unknown man in surveillance photos in building. We have engaged. Move in!"

Manning's voice came back. "Acknowledged! Moving in!"

The Executioner slipped a fresh magazine into the Colt. "We have to secure the virus. We have no idea what their contingency plan is."

Schwarz nodded. "I agree, but they're going to have men up here any second."

The soldier pushed a fresh grenade into the breech of the M-203. "Let's not be here when they arrive."

"I've got rope. We can smash the window and rappel out of here."

Bolan shook his head. "There's about to be a firefight inside the perimeter, and we'd be sitting ducks. Besides, I'm not ready to leave the building yet." He glanced at the pack on his teammate's back. "How much C-4 do you have?"

"Twenty pounds."

He nodded and glanced at the carpeted floor. Outside he could hear men yelling. "Five pounds should do."

23

Heidi Hochrein's face was ugly with rage, and she turned that
rage onto the man in the dark suit. "Here! The American
commando is here!"

Yonekawa Shirata slapped a fresh magazine into his Uzi
and silenced her with a look. He punched the intercom button
on his desk and was pleased to find it still functioned after the
storm of lead had torn through his office. "Security! We are
under attack! Prepare to defend the perimeter and send men
to the fourth floor."

Mas's voice came back. "Taido is already on his way! We
are breaking out the heavy weapons! Do you wish to initiate
evacuation procedures?"

Shirata grinned. The situation had become a worst-case scenario. He had failed in his mission. Now survival and vengeance were their only hopes. "Yes. Prepare for full evacuation. Get those men up here to me, now!"

"They are on their way!"

Shirata pulled on a headset and clipped its receiver and
power pack to his belt. He stuffed his pockets with 25-round
Uzi magazines, then turned toward the double doors. He could
hear men yelling out in the hallway, then the ripping noise of
automatic rifles firing. A fist pounded on the door.

"Commander! Are you all right?"

Shirata strode to the door and flung it open. Ryuchi Taido
stood before him with an M-16 rifle in his hands. Out in the
hallway security men in blue coveralls were taking turns firing

bursts through one of the office doors. Shirata nodded. "The commando and his friends—they are in that room?"

Taido nodded. "Yes, they are trapped. There is no way out except the window. I already have men on the first level who will cut them to pieces if they try to rappel out the window or jump."

Two of the security men jumped back as an answering burst came tearing back through the office door and stitched the walls. Shirata looked at his watch and scowled. "I do not want the commando to sit back and relax behind his barricade while his friends come to rescue him. I want them to find him dead."

Taido smiled broadly. "Yes, I anticipated as much." He knifed his hand through the air at a security man as he came out of the stairwell. "Toshiro! As we planned! The door!"

"*Hai!*" Toshiro reached into a bulging knapsack at his side and pulled out an olive drab sphere the size of a large cantaloupe. The sphere had a nozzle on one end, and he clicked it onto a bracket mounted underneath the barrel of his M-16. He marched close to the door of the office where the Americans hid and waited for a burst from within to end. Instantly he turned and disappeared through the doorway across the hall from the Americans.

Shirata frowned. "What is he doing?"

"When the alarm went out, I told Mas to break out heavy weapons. He is armed with a RAW. It is a rifleman's assault weapon developed for the United States Marines for urban combat. It was designed to breach barricades and kill those behind them. He will need a little space for the rocket motor to ignite."

Toshiro shouted out from within the office. "Ready!"

Taido waved the rest of the men away. "Get behind cover!" Both he and Shirata moved back toward Shirata's office.

The security team fired a few farewell bursts, then retreated into empty offices up and down the hall. Taido's grin went from ear to ear. His mouth opened, then froze in midcommand. There was a thunderclap from within the office the Americans inhabited. The bullet-riddled door shuddered on its hinges, and the floor vibrated beneath their feet. Taido recovered and roared at the top of his lungs. "Now, Toshiro! Fire!"

A hissing crack came from within the office where Toshiro hid, and a second later the 140 mm RAW sphere seemed to fly out of the door and across the hallway in slow motion. It spun lazily as it flew, then hit the beleaguered door protecting the Americans. The RAW detonated, and the world seemed to almost come to an end. Taido and Shirata both staggered backward into the office as the shock wave filled the hallway with orange fire. The floor shuddered beneath them and the heat of the shaped-charge weapon rolled over them in a wave that singed their eyebrows. Shirata blinked away pulsing spots of color from his eyes, and he and Taido came out of the office with their weapons ready.

Down the hall the target door had disappeared. Most of the doorjamb and a good portion of the wall surrounding it had disappeared, as well, and smoke filled the air.

Taido yawned to clear his ringing ears. Shirata found himself grinning. There was no way anyone in the office could have survived. Taido shouted out, "Now! Take the room! Move! Move!"

The security men burst out from the other offices and swarmed to either side of the charred doorway. Two guards jumped into the shattered threshold and filled the smoky room with bursts of automatic fire. One of the men turned with an incredulous look on his face. "Commander!"

Shirata ran forward with Taido right behind him. Shirata shoved the guard aside and swung up his Uzi to cover the room as he glanced about. The heat and blast of the RAW had devastated the room. The concussion had blown out the windows, and the heavy teak desk and filing cabinets had been overturned. Flame and superheated gas had expanded into the room, and the fireproof walls were blackened and charred. The carpet was smoldering. Shirata was dumbfounded as he looked at the carpet more closely.

A ragged, round, four-foot hole had been blown through the middle of the floor.

"Quickly! I want—"

Shirata and Taido staggered back as flame and smoke shot up out of the hole in the floor and a third explosion rocked the building. Shirata grimaced as smoke choked him, and the stench of burned high explosive became almost overpowering. He stepped forward and emptied his Uzi down the smoking hole in the floor. His weapon clacked open on empty, and he quickly shot a glance down the hole. Below, a second hole had been blown in the floor directly below the first one.

The Americans had leapfrogged their way down from the fourth floor to the second.

Shirata snarled into his headset. "Security! Converge on the second floor! Now!" He slipped a fresh magazine into his weapon and wheeled about. Heidi Hochrein was gone as he stormed into his office. The light above the door of the head office's private elevator showed the car descending. He punched the button for the second floor as he spoke into his microphone. "Mas! Patch me in to the lab."

MACK BOLAN STEPPED BACK as a long spray of bullets rained down out of the smoking hole over his head and tore into the carpeting near his feet. He forced his jaws wide to make his ears pop. They had used the heavy office desks as screens against the blast, and the floor-breaching charges had been packed to blast downward, but that didn't change the fact that you didn't want to be in the same room when five pounds of C-4 plastic explosive went off.

The Executioner quickly went over their alternatives. They had to secure the virus at all costs. "The elevator. If the grenade I fired disabled it, we can go down the shaft."

The three of them raced down the hall. Without speaking, Schwarz cut a six-inch piece of flexible charge and stuck it in the seam of the elevator door. He pushed in a detonator pin, and the three of them stepped away. He depressed the button on one of his small black boxes, and the charge detonated with a hissing crack. Bolan stepped forward and yanked the doors open. He stuck his head in and looked up. The bottom of the elevator was two floors above him. The shaft down was clear to the bottom floor.

"Gadgets, stay here and keep our friends diverted until I can get the door open down there. Eliza, you're with me." Bolan stepped out into the elevator shaft, grabbed the cables and quickly descended hand over hand. The cable was greasy, but Bolan clamped the lugs of his boots against it to control his descent.

Schwarz's voice spoke in his ear. "They're coming."

Bolan's boots came to rest on one of the cross braces of the shaft floor. "I'm down. Send Eliza, and then keep them busy."

The cable jerked as it took Thurman's weight, and Schwarz's voice came back. "Roger."

There was a set of heavy steel doors three feet up from the shaft floor. Bolan pulled out his coil of flexible charge and used the elevator cable to pull himself up to the lip of the doors. He pulled the adhesive strip from the bottom of the shaped charge with his teeth and began to press it down the length of the doors' seam.

The crack of a grenade going off echoed down the shaft, and it was almost immediately followed by another blast. A second later Thurman thumped down beside him. Bolan pushed a detonator pin into his flexible charge. "Cover your face."

Thurman complied as Bolan pulled the detonator from his webbing. He brought his forearm before his eyes and thumbed the red button. A snake of orange fire hissed down the elevator doors as the shaped charge blasted inward and warped the doors apart. Instantly bullets began to fly into the elevator shaft and shriek off the wall. Bolan crouched under the lip of the elevator and shoved the muzzle of the Colt submachine gun and its grenade launcher through the two-foot twisted crack in the doors. He squeezed the M-203's trigger, and the weapon recoiled with a boom.

A second later the rifle grenade detonated with a crack. The Executioner pulled a frag grenade from his bandolier and pulled the pin. He mentally counted down the numbers, then tossed the grenade through the doors. He crouched as the grenade went off, and some of its steel fragments flew back into the elevator shaft. Bolan racked a buckshot round into the M-203's breech and rammed a shoulder against one of the twisted doors. It grated in protest and slid back a foot. He rolled to the floor and came up with his weapon ready.

The soldier was in a long room with a row of lockers along one wall. Shrapnel from the two grenades had scored the walls, and two of the blue-clad security men lay bloody and moaning on the floor while a third lay motionless. At the end of the long room was a steel door with a biohazard sign over it.

Schwarz spoke with mild urgency. "It's getting hot up here." Bolan could hear the ping of a hand grenade cotter pin over the line. "I'm coming down."

"Roger. Doors are breached. We're waiting for you."

A second later the twin cracks of grenades going off echoed down the shaft. Schwarz came sliding down the elevator cable and quickly scrambled into the room. "They'll be right behind me."

Bolan nodded. He pulled a CS tear gas grenade from his bandolier and removed the pin. Schwarz did likewise, and they tossed the gas grenades into the elevator shaft. The two men dragged back the twisted steel doors as best they could as the grenades began to hiss and release their gas. The warped doors jammed and refused to close completely. Schwarz frowned. "A lot of the gas should expand upward, but this room is still going to fill up fast."

Grayish white gas began to leak into the room around their boots almost as the words were spoken. The odor of pepper began to fill the air. Bolan looked down the room. There was nowhere to go but forward. He turned to Thurman. "What's the setup going to be?"

Thurman looked around the narrow room. "Those lockers are probably for coats and personal effects. The next room is probably for suiting up into biohazard protective gear. The room after that will most likely be the decontamination room. After that, will be the lab."

Bolan knelt and examined the dead guard. A plastic key-card hung around his neck. The Executioner snapped it off of its strap and went to the steel door. He swiped it through the lock, and a green light came on in the ceiling. The door slid open almost soundlessly except for a slight hiss of air. The three of them went through the door. The next room was almost identical to the first, except rather than lockers, Racal suits hung on racks. The door slid shut behind them, and Bolan turned to Schwarz. "Can you jam the lock?"

"I can disable it, but that won't stop them for long. We know they have explosives."

Thurman suddenly grabbed Bolan's shoulder. "They don't have gas masks, though!"

Schwarz frowned. "Neither do we."

"Yes, we do."

Bolan grinned as he got it. He looked at the Racal suits where they hung on their racks. "Yeah, we do. How much more CS do you have?"

Schwarz pulled a pair of banded canisters from his bandolier. "Two skip chasers."

"I've got one. It should be enough. Let's suit up fast." Bolan stripped off his web gear as he went to the rack and found an extralarge suit. He unzipped the Racal and stepped into the bright orange coverall. Thurman zipped and sealed him, then adjusted the helmet. Schwarz stepped into a similar suit as Thurman adjusted Bolan's helmet and started his air supply. She went over and sealed the Able Team commando's suit as Bolan pulled his web gear over the suit. It was a tight fit, but the soldier found he had enough leeway to move and fight. He turned as there was a thump on the steel door behind them. "We've got to hurry."

Thurman nodded as she got into a suit several times too large for her diminutive frame. She pulled her helmet on, and Schwarz sealed her suit for her. She gave Bolan the thumbs-up sign, and they moved on to the next door. Schwarz and Thurman moved to either side as Bolan ran the key-card through the electronic lock. The door hissed open to reveal a much smaller room, which was bare except for ultraviolet-light fixtures and shower heads in the ceiling. There was a steel door on the opposite side of the room.

Bolan moved in and swiped the card. The door made a beeping noise but refused to slide open.

Schwarz frowned. "They've overridden the code. Someone's locked it from the inside."

The Executioner pulled out the last of his flexible shaped charge and Schwarz pulled out a slightly shorter length. Bolan eyed the faceless steel door. "We'll use it all. I want the whole door down all at once. We hit them with flash-stuns, and then watch where you shoot. I don't want to smash the place up and take a chance on releasing the virus."

Schwarz nodded, and they stuck the flexible charge around the inside of the door frame. The charge ran out before they could wind it around the top. Bolan frowned. It would have to be enough. "Do it."

Schwarz stuck in the detonator pin and stood to one side. Bolan nodded, and the electronics whiz pushed the button. Orange flame streaked around the bottom half of the door frame. Bolan took a step forward and put his boot into the door with all of his strength. He felt the blow run up the bones of his leg, but the door sagged in the top of its frame. He drove his foot forward again, then stepped aside as it fell out of its frame with a clang.

Bullets streaked through the doorway and tore into the decontamination room. Schwarz pulled the pin on his flash-stun grenade and hurled it around the door frame. Bolan threw in a second one and squeezed his eyes shut. A moment later white light strobed in a blinding pulse from the lab, and a thunderclap shook the walls. He stepped around the corner, then jumped back as tracers reached out toward him.

The brief glance was enough. The lab was full of armed men, and they had barricaded themselves behind worktables. The flash-stun grenades hadn't taken them out. Bolan pulled out his gas grenade and pulled the pin. Schwarz took out his two and handed one to Thurman. "Throw it high and wide. We want maximum dispersal."

She pulled the pin and Bolan nodded. "Now!"

All three of them hurled their grenades around the corner. The gas grenades arced through the air, and with a popping noise, tiny charges separated each grenade into three disk-shaped dischargers. The disks fell to the ground and skittered across the floor like hockey pucks as the gas squirted out of them in high-pressure jets. Bolan pulled his last flash-stun grenade and hurled it in to add to the confusion. The grenade detonated, and again thunder and light exploded through the lab.

Bolan dropped to the floor and rolled into the doorway.

Three armed men charged forward through the gas. They coughed and tears streamed down their faces, but they came forward with their M-16s blazing. Bolan squeezed the M-203's trigger. His weapon recoiled against his shoulder, and the 40 mm buckshot round bloomed out of the launch tube in a fountain of yellow flame. The charging men twisted and fell as they were caught point-blank by the massive buckshot pattern.

Through the expanding gas Bolan could see that the walls of the lab were lined with banks of computers and medical equipment. The center of the room was a mass of overturned tables and filing cabinets from which armed men had risen and were firing their weapons almost blindly in Bolan's direction. The Executioner dived into the lab, then rolled to his left. One skip-chaser grenade would have been enough to saturate the lab with gas. Three together filled the room like a dense fog. Bolan continued to roll, then rose in the corner and saw that Schwarz had gone in the opposite way.

The soldier spotted a man at one of the computers along the wall desperately hitting keys. Bolan drilled him with a burst that punched him to the floor. Men began to collapse as their eyes swelled shut and their lungs burned in agony. The CS gas wouldn't be lethal, but it was so highly concentrated its temporary effects were terrible.

Schwarz swore as he leaped up and ran toward the computer. "He's deleting data!"

Bolan covered his teammate as he ran. A man rose from behind the barricade and shook his head violently, trying to clear his vision as he began to aim his rifle. The soldier aimed his front sight on the guard and put him down with a 3-round burst. Bolan moved through the fog of tear gas and flanked the barricade. He jacked another buckshot round into the breech of the M-203 and crouched as he came around the pile of chairs and tables. Men in blue coveralls lay coughing and retching on the floor. One man held a handkerchief over his nose and mouth and whipped a pistol around as he saw Bolan. A 3-round burst from the silenced Colt submachine gun toppled him backward on top of one of his choking comrades. Bolan paused as the gas around him suddenly seemed to pulse and shift.

There was a draft in the room.

As the gas shifted again, he could see the dark shape of a door on the far side of the lab and people rushing through it. One of the figures fell as Schwarz fired a burst. Bullets shrieked off of the wall beside Bolan as one of them aimed a rifle. Two of the enemy gunners were carrying something between them.

Bolan fired the M-203.

The 40 mm buckshot round erupted outward, and the shot pattern spread as it flew across the lab. The two men carrying the load jerked and fell. Schwarz fired burst after burst at the open door, and Bolan flicked his selector switch to full-auto as he ran forward. A short, bearded man tracked the soldier as he sprinted forward and fired an M-16. Bolan felt a punch against his armor and fired a burst of his own. The short man staggered backward through the doorway. A gunner stood in the darkness behind him and fired a long burst from an automatic weapon. Bolan held down his trigger and the figure dropped backward into the darkness. The Executioner's burst sparked off steel as the door slid shut between them.

Bolan skidded to a stop and trained his weapon on the fallen enemy by the door. One man lay dead, his entire upper body riddled with buckshot. The soldier took a step forward. Heidi Hochrein lay on the floor weeping and swearing. Her face was swollen and tear streaked from the gas, and she had taken bullets through both of her thighs. Beside her lay a larger version of the hatbox they had found in Mexico. Its gleaming stainless-steel outer casing was dinged but seemed to be intact. Bolan kicked aside an M-16 rifle as she groped for it. Three other men in security uniforms lay dead on the floor.

He grabbed the woman roughly and dragged her back several yards from the heavy steel door. Bolan turned and saw Thurman enter the lab. He stabbed a finger at Hochrein. "Get her back! Cover her!"

Thurman hurried forward and dragged Hochrein back none too gently by the hair. Bolan pulled an armor-piercing 40 mm round from his bandolier and loaded the M-203. He aimed at the middle of the door and fired. The grenade smashed against the door and detonated in a blast of orange fire. He opened the launcher's smoking breech and loaded a second armor-piercing round and fired. The second round detonated beside the first, and molten metal slagged down the front of the heavy steel door. Bolan reached down into his bandolier, but there were no armor-piercing rounds left. All he had was a white-phosphorous grenade and a frag.

There was no more flexible charge left, and they had used all of their plastic explosives in their descent through the floors. Two dinner-plate-sized holes smoked in the heavy steel door. Bolan kept himself out of the firing angle from the holes and approached the door. He swiped the key-card through the lock. The door beeped, but nothing happened.

Bolan swore under his breath.

He pulled the frag grenade from his belt and loaded it into the M-203. He stepped to the door at an angle, jammed the M-203's muzzle against one of the holes in the door and fired. The weapon recoiled, and a second later the grenade detonated behind the door.

Bolan turned to Schwarz. "What have you got?"

The man didn't turn as his fingers flew across the keys. "They hit the delete on their computer files. I don't know how much we can retrieve. But—" Schwarz suddenly hurled himself to the floor. "Down!"

Bolan instinctively threw himself to the floor. Computer screens along the wall blew outward in jets of fire, and glass flew across the room. Schwarz stayed down for a moment, then got back to his feet. He raised his orange-gloved hands helplessly. "I don't think we're going to be able to retrieve much of anything."

The soldier turned and cautiously peered through one of the holes burned through the door. The smoke inside was clearing. Through the darkness he could see dim orange lights that faded in the distance.

The Executioner roared into his throat mike. "Gary! They have a tunnel!" Bolan ripped open the Racal suit over his wrist and exposed his diving watch. He turned his arm and watched the compass dial spin. If the tunnel stayed straight, it would go due west.

"The enemy is heading west. Tell the gunship to sweep the area west of here." Bolan's face was like a tombstone. "Scratch that. Tell them to go for the coast."

EPILOGUE

Shirata dragged Taido along the dark corridor. Taido had two bullets in him, and he was losing blood rapidly. The little man stumbled frequently, and several times told his superior to leave him.

Shirata refused, as his sense of duty was very strong. The mission was an utter failure. The facility had been captured; their supply of the Ebola virus had been captured; Heidi Hochrein had been captured. Even if he managed to escape, it was very likely that Shirata himself would be ordered to commit suicide for his monumental failure. Still, he was determined to salvage something from the operation. Even if that something was only Ryuchi Taido's worthless hide.

He flung the protesting little man across his shoulders in a fireman's carry and began to run down the dimly lit corridor. The land Nishiki-Tetsuo had bought had originally been a small chemical plant that had done research on chemicals for the American aerospace industry in the 1960s. That facility had usually dumped its waste products into the Pacific Ocean. Environmental reform had ended that practice but the pipeline to the ocean was still intact.

Nishiki-Tetsuo was nothing if not a frugal organization. It had steam-cleaned the pipe and strung emergency lights down its length. Shirata gulped air as he ran on. Taido barely cracked five feet tall, but he was solid muscle, and the tear gas Shirata had breathed in sapped his lung capacity and still burned in his chest. The pipeline itself was just over a mile long. He opened up his stride despite the pain, and his footfalls rang through the narrow corridor. He almost ran into the dull gray steel door before he saw it. Shirata skidded to a halt and slid his key-card into the lock. Bolts mounted into concrete clicked back, and the circular hatch hissed open. Shirata blinked out into the darkness. The night was overcast, but the smell of the sea came to him on the evening breeze and he could hear the waves breaking on the shore.

He waited several moments for his eyes to adjust, then made his way down the narrow cliff to the strip of beach below. He set Taido onto the sand and pulled the camouflage netting off a small Zodiac assault boat. Three more boats lay under the netting, but none of their intended occupants had made it. Shirata hauled Taido into the boat, then dug his heels into the sand as he painfully began to drag the boat toward the water.

He cast his eyes skyward. The enemy had a gunship in the area. He had seen the Jeep full of men torn to pieces by automatic cannon fire. Out in the boat they would be sitting ducks. Time was crucial now. Water slopped around Shirata's ankles, and the boat suddenly seemed much lighter. He continued to drag the boat out into the water until it was around his waist, then he pulled himself up over the Kevlar pontoon.

The motor started on the first try, and Shirata took the wheel and headed out toward the open ocean. He glanced up into the sky again. He was about to be saved or kill himself, but he had little choice. Shirata flicked a switch, and a bright strobe began to flash on the prow of the boat. Almost immediately the radio crackled. "We see you. Continue on for another two hundred meters."

Shirata kept his course straight and soon, ahead of him, he could see a dark bulk in the water. A bright light pulsed at him, and he cut the strobe as he came in. He could make out two men standing on the bridge of the small submarine. Shirata brought the boat alongside. "I have an injured man, and there is a gunship in the area."

The captain glared at Shirata. "A gunship?"

"Yes. Hurry."

He handed Taido up, then clambered onto the submarine. The captain and the mate had already handed Taido down and were descending into the boat. The captain's voice was a snarl. "Emergency dive! Dive! Dive! Dive!"

A crewman crawled up the ladder and pulled the hatch shut. The hull of the submarine vibrated as the engines throbbed for an emergency dive. Two other crewmen carried Taido toward the sick bay. The captain stared long and hard at Shirata. He wasn't pleased that his boat had been exposed with a gunship in the area. He bowed, but the gesture was shallow and stiff necked. "We shall be incommunicado for two weeks until we are deep into the Pacific. When we are in safe waters, we will surface and communicate with the secure satellite." The captain's eyes were steely. "I suspect the old man will wish to have words with you."

Shirata returned the bow even more shallowly. He was still the commander of the operation. As the captain turned to his duties, Shirata let out a weary sigh. He would wait until he spoke with the old man before he blew his brains out.

Stony Man Farm, Virginia

MACK BOLAN SAT in front of the fireplace at Stony Man Farm. Barbara Price poured him another cup of coffee, and they stared into the flames. "We won, and you're alive. You don't have to look so grim."

Bolan smiled. "Sorry."

"What's going to happen next?"

The soldier gazed into the fire. "We stopped them, but that's all. The fact is, a Japanese business consortium tried to politically destabilize Western Europe and now they've attempted to kill one-half to one-quarters of the United States's population. We can't just let that slide. If we do, they're more than likely to get it into their heads to try something else."

"What do you think the President will do, Mack?" Price

asked. "I mean, he can't really declare war on Japan, and there hasn't been anything in the news about anything happening at Nishiki-Tetsuo in L.A."

Bolan sipped his coffee. "Officially nothing is happening. Neither side wants this to get out. So they're pretending nothing has happened."

Price looked at Bolan's face in the firelight. "But it's not going to rest."

"No." Bolan shook his head. "Robert E. Lee Leland, Dr. Eugene Penn and Vernon Richmond all died horribly. Elements of Nishiki-Tetsuo are responsible. Something will have to be done about that."

Price felt she knew the answer, but she asked anyway. "What?"

"We have to find the people responsible within Nishiki-Tetsuo and hit them on their own turf. We have to send a message and take heads. We're going to have to stick our necks way out, and the people involved will have to be deniable in case of any mishap. There's going to be a small war in the Far East, and it isn't going to make the news."

Silence filled the room except for the crackle of the fire. The two of them watched the flames and waited for the phone to ring.

* * * * *

*Don't miss the exciting conclusion of
the Power Trilogy.
Look for The Executioner #236,
Vengeance Rising, in August.*

James Axler

OUTLANDERS™

DOOMSTAR RELIC

Kane and his companions find themselves pitted against an ambitious rebel named Barch, who finds a way to activate a long-silent computer security network and use it to assassinate the local baron. Barch plans to use the security system to take over the ville, but he doesn't realize he is starting a Doomsday program that could destroy the world.

Kane and friends must stop Barch, the virtual assassin and the Doomsday program to preserve the future....

One man's quest for power unleashes a cataclysm in America's wastelands.

Sinanju software?

THE Destroyer™

#112 Brain Storm
The Fatherland Files Book 1

Created by
WARREN MURPHY
and RICHARD SAPIR

Ordinary bank robbery turns into larceny of the highest order as the very secrets of CURE (and the minds of its members) are stolen and laid bare on a computer disk. It's up to Remo and Chiun to find a way to restore CURE's abilities while there's still time.

The first in The Fatherland Files, a miniseries based on a secret fascist organization's attempts to regain the glory of the Third Reich.

Look for it in August 1998 wherever Gold Eagle books are sold.